CRIM

CRIME OF PASSION

ROY GLENN

URBAN SOUL
URBAN BOOKS
www.urbanbooks.net

URBAN SOUL is published by

Urban Books
10 Brennan Pl.
Deer Park, NY 11729

ISBN 1-59983-005-1

First Printing: October 2006
10 9 8 7 6 5 4 3 2 1

Printed in the United States of America

CLOSING ARGUMENTS

"Mr. Douglas, are you ready to proceed?"

Marcus stood up and glanced at the jury. "Yes, Your Honor," he said, and walked slowly over to the jury box. "Good morning, Ladies and Gentlemen." Marcus paused briefly as his eyes scanned the jurors. "Well, here we are. It's been a long road we've traveled together."

Throughout the trial, Marcus had worked hard to develop a relationship with the jury. During his opening arguments, he promised to act as their advocate. He assured them that he would ask the questions they wanted answers to. Whenever Marcus questioned a witness, he always stood in front of the jury box. When a prosecution witness said something he felt was damaging to his client, he would casually glance at the jury. Sometimes he would smile; other times he would just shake his head. This tactic proved most effective. So effective that when certain members of the jury heard something they thought was questionable, they would look in Marcus's direction, seemingly seeking his approval as to whether they should believe it or not.

"When we first met, I told you that the prosecution would present you with a strong argument for finding Roland Ferguson guilty of the murder of his wife, Desireé Taylor Ferguson, and Rasheed Damali. The prosecution promised that they would present to you, Ladies and Gentlemen, the facts in this case. And that once presented with those facts, you will find Roland Ferguson guilty of these two brutal murders. However, I also made you a promise. I promised each of you that their presentation would consist of not only the facts of this case, but it would be mixed with theory. A theory of how and why those events took place in order to lead you, Ladies and Gentlemen, to believe that Roland Ferguson had the motive and the opportunity to commit this horrible crime. A theory that will be presented in such a manner that the facts of this case will support the prosecution's assertions. However, it is a theory all the same. The American Heritage dictionary defines theory as an organized set of *assumptions* devised to explain a particular event or phenomenon. So let's talk about the facts in this case, and then we'll talk about theory. Okay?" he said, and each member of the jury acknowledged him. He had them and he knew it.

"It is a fact that on Friday, December second, at six-thirty P.M., Mr. Damali checked into a cabin at Laurel Mountain Cabins in Hiawassee, Georgia. This fact is supported by records provided by Laurel Mountain Cabins. We know that Mrs. Ferguson arrived at the cabin occupied by Mr. Damali at approximately eight P.M. This fact is supported by testimony provided by William Anderson, who occupied the cabin next to the one occupied by Mr. Damali. He testified that he arrived at his cabin around seven-thirty and that there was a black Corvette, belonging to Mr. Damali, parked outside the cabin. However, at eight-fifteen when Anderson returned to the car to get something he'd left, he saw the gold Mercedes-Benz belonging to Mrs. Ferguson was now parked next to the Corvette. These are facts. The coroner has established the time of death to have occurred somewhere between one-fifteen and one-forty-five that following morning. Now this is where the theory begins. It is the contention of the prosecution that Roland Ferguson entered the cabin and attacked Mr. Damali."

Marcus walked to the evidence table and picked up the murder weapon. "Hitting him repeatedly about the head and shoulders with this golf club," he said as he walked slowly back toward the jury, swinging the golf club in a chopping motion. "Nineteen times, until he was dead. After which he turned to his wife, who was in the Jacuzzi, and hit her fifteen times with this club. Theory! An assumption devised to fit the facts," Marcus said quickly.

"The body of Mr. Damali was found on the floor approximately eight feet from the door. Mrs. Ferguson's body was indeed found beaten to death in the Jacuzzi. At the heart of the theory is Roland Ferguson's motive for these murders. According to this set of assumptions that the prosecution would like you, Ladies and gentlemen, to believe is that Roland Ferguson found out that his wife was having an affair with Mr. Damali. And once this was discovered, he came to the cabin with this club in his hands and murdered the two of them. Adultery!" Marcus said loudly with one finger raised in the air to accentuate his point. Then he gave the jury an easy smile and said softly, "A pretty compelling motive for murder. But let's look at the motive as it relates to the facts, shall we?" Once again the jury acknowledged him, giving their consent for him to proceed.

"You have heard testimony that on the night preceding the murders, Roland Ferguson attended a reception hosted by the Atlanta business community. He arrived sometime around nine P.M., and he remained there until sometime after eleven P.M. He was seen by and spoke with countless people, most notably the mayor. Witnesses have stated, both in testimony offered in these proceedings and in sworn affidavits, that Roland Ferguson was in good spirits throughout the evening. That he didn't appear to be distressed or anguished or apprehensive. When asked where Mrs. Ferguson was that evening, he replied on more than one occasion that Desireé was out with a business associate of theirs, a Rasheed Damali. So it is a fact that Roland Ferguson knew of his wife's association with Mr. Damali but did not appear to be distressed by that knowledge.

"Now, after Roland Ferguson left the reception, he stopped for gas. Information from the store and his credit card company supports that Roland Ferguson paid for his purchase at eleven-twenty-two P.M. Mr. Ferguson said in his statement to the police at their first interview, which in fact, he volunteered to participate in without the benefit of counsel, that he arrived home at eleven-forty P.M. When the detectives asked him how he could be sure of the time, he responded that he was certain of the time because he noted that he was home before midnight, which was rare after attending a function such as the one he'd attended that night. After which he had a brandy and went to his study to call his assistant, Connie Talbert's voice mail. This voice mail was set up with a longer recording capacity that allowed Mr. Ferguson to make some observation about the evening and to make recommendations as to several courses of action based on those observances. The tape of that conversation and the transcript has been entered into evidence and was heard by this panel. Telephone records support the fact that the call was placed at eleven-fifty-four P.M. and concluded at twelve-twenty-one A.M. After which he went to bed. Now, according to the prosecution's *theory*, at some time immediately following this point, Roland Ferguson got in his car and made the one-hundred-twenty-seven-mile drive from his home to the cabin in Hiawassee to commit this crime of passion.

"Ladies and Gentlemen, there are two questions that we must ask ourselves. One, how did he find out where they were? Did Mrs. Ferguson call and say, 'Hi, honey, I'm at Laurel Mountain Cabins in Hiawassee, Georgia, with Rasheed Damali'? Telephone records that have been entered into evidence prove that no calls, incoming or outgoing, were made or received at the Ferguson residence or the cabin. Cell phone, maybe? Maybe someone called his cell phone? But the phone records don't support that either. Maybe he checked his messages at home and one of those messages delivered the information about their whereabouts? No. The police confiscated, in their search of the premises, the answering machine tape and found nothing to support that. But, the theory asks you to accept that he knew where they were and drove one-hundred-twenty-seven miles to the cabin to commit murder. To make it to the cabin at the time the murders were committed, Mr. Ferguson would have had to drive at speeds in excess of one hundred miles an hour. You heard the testimony of Officer Dunn of the Towns County Sheriff Office that he was on duty, parked on Georgia State Highway 76, the only road leading to the cabin. He offered, in his colorful testimony, that if any car came through there speeding, he would have given them a ticket. Which he didn't. So the second question is, once Mr. Ferguson had that knowledge, how did he get there so quickly? The logical answer is, he didn't."

Marcus returned to the defense table to give the jury an opportunity to think about the questions he posed and the solution he offered. He poured a glass of water and drank half before returning to the jury box.

"Let's go to the murder scene. Mr. Damali and Mrs. Ferguson were in the cabin. Mrs. Ferguson was in the Jacuzzi, and Mr. Damali had at some point prior to the murder removed his clothes. He was naked! It is the assertion of the prosecution that Roland Ferguson entered the cabin, killed Mr. Damali and then his wife. How did he get in? There was no sign of forced entry. Did he have a key? No sign that a struggle occurred at the door. So how did he get in? Did Mr. Damali let him in? Now ask yourselves this question: If you're in a cabin in the mountains with somebody's spouse, regardless of how well you may know him, are you going to let him in? I know that I wouldn't. And even if I was going to let him in, I would think that I would put some clothes on before opening the door. But since the facts show no indication of forced entry, that's exactly what the prosecution would have you believe. That a naked Mr. Damali let Mr. Ferguson into the cabin while Mrs. Ferguson was naked in the hot tub. The police report states that the body of Mr. Damali was found eight feet from the door and in clear view of the Jacuzzi. So based on that fact, it is safe to assume that Mr. Damali unlocked the door, let Roland Ferguson in, and took three or four steps before he was attacked."

Once again Marcus picked up the murder weapon and walked back to the jury box. "While the attack is going on, Mrs. Ferguson is watching while her husband hits Mr. Damali nineteen times." Marcus began to wildly and repeatedly swing the golf club.

The assistant district attorney, Izella Hawkins, watched Marcus in horror as he swung again and again. She looked at the jury's reaction, then sprang to her feet. "Objection, Your Honor!"

"Sustained. Mr. Douglas, there is no room in this court for that type of theatrics."

"My apologies, Your Honor." Marcus looked at the jury and smiled. He had accomplished his point. "And my apologies to you, Ladies and Gentlemen. However, it was necessary to demonstrate how long it would take to beat somebody nineteen times. It took a little less than thirty seconds. And that is only if Mr. Damali's attacker didn't stop. Now, Mrs. Ferguson was watching this and was too petrified by what she was seeing to move. The attacker moves toward her and fifteen hits later, she is dead too. The attacker then drops the murder weapon and leaves the murder scene. The bodies were discovered that same morning about eleven A.M. by housekeeping, who testified that the door was locked when she entered, after knocking of course, with her key.

"Now, after Roland Ferguson committed this crime of passion, he is careful to lock the door on his way out, goes home, and gets in bed. End of theory, blended with fact. The murder weapon was left at the scene. Police inventory of the golf clubs found both in Roland Ferguson's home and at the country club where he is a member indicates that the murder weapon was not a part of either of those sets." Marcus started to walk away from the jury but turned around quickly. "By the way, in case you were wondering, the police checked with the club staff and no one reported a missing nine iron."

Marcus turned away from the jury and was handed a piece of paper by Tiffanie Powers, one of the lawyers at his firm. He stood before the prosecution's table. For the first time he addressed the jury from a different spot. He wanted the jury to be looking at the prosecution before he continued.

"Once the murder is discovered, Roland Ferguson is informed by police at seven o'clock that evening that his wife had been murdered. Why the delay in notifying her next of kin? The detectives don't go into any detail about the crime. They don't tell him that she was found brutally murdered in a cabin with another man. Detective Benjamin testified that upon receiving the news of his wife's death, Roland Ferguson began to cry, and, I quote from detective Benjamin's testimony, 'He got weak in the knees and became somewhat hysterical.' Roland Ferguson comes into the morgue to identify his wife's body and is asked to speak with the detectives assigned to the case. The murder occurred in the city of Hiawassee, in Towns County. Why were the City of Atlanta police assigned to the case?

"You see, the prosecution had spoken with officials of Towns County and just that quick, had the case transferred to their jurisdiction. Before the investigation was complete, the prosecution had already found their man. Roland Ferguson was their only suspect. Roland Ferguson is the owner of Atlanta Life Insurance Company, among other things. He is a wealthy, well-known, and high-profile member of the Atlanta business community. The press, after hearing of Roland Ferguson's arrest, had a field day. What a feather in their cap to bring down a man of his caliber. States attorney general, Justice Department, maybe even attorney general of the United States. This city has a long history of unwarranted prosecution of high-profile individuals like Roland Ferguson. This was a rush to judgment of the highest order. I submit to you, Ladies and Gentlemen, that the prosecution looked no further than Roland Ferguson and created an organized set of assumptions devised to convict him of the murder of his wife, Desireé Taylor Ferguson, and Rasheed Damali. Ladies and Gentlemen, Roland Ferguson didn't commit these murders; he couldn't have. And the prosecution has not presented you with any evidence to support their theory of how this crime took place. I only ask that in your deliberations you consider the facts of this case. That you then separate the facts from the organized set of assumptions. Once you do, I am confident that you will return a verdict of not guilty. I thank you, Ladies and Gentlemen, for your attention."

THE VERDICT

The courtroom was packed with spectators and members of the press, all anxiously awaiting the jury's verdict. It had been two days since Judge Wynn gave the jurors their instructions and sent them to their task.

"Have you reached a verdict?" Judge Wynn said.

"Yes, Your Honor, we have," the jury forewoman said as she stood and handed their verdict to the bailiff, who in turn handed it to the judge. The judge looked it over carefully and then looked briefly in the direction of the prosecutors. "Will the defendant please rise?" Roland Ferguson stood up, and Marcus stood with him. "On the first count of the indictment, murder in the first degree, how do you find?"

"We find the defendant not guilty."

The courtroom erupted, and the judge banged his gavel. "On the second count of the indictment, murder in the first degree, how do you find?"

"We find the defendant not guilty."

Roland Ferguson looked at Marcus and shook his hand.

"Thank you, Marcus. You did a fine job, an excellent job. I am forever in your debt."

Ferguson was immediately surrounded by supporters and reporters. As the crowd began to sweep him out of the courtroom, he turned back to Marcus and said, "I'm having a little get-together tonight. Drop by around nine and we'll talk then."

"I'll see you then," Marcus replied as he gathered his materials together. Izella Hawkins walked over to him with her hand extended.

"Congratulations, Marcus," Izella said.

"Thank you, Izella."

"You shot holes in our whole case. Excuse me, what am I saying. Our theory, designed to fit the facts."

"Izella, you know that all I did was add reasonable doubt."

"No, Marcus, it's not that simple. You controlled the jury from the word *go*. Had them eating out of your hand. Their advocate, huh?" Izella rolled her eyes. "I'll have to use that one on my next case. Well, enjoy the moment. You deserve it. You worked hard for it," Izella said as she walked out of the courtroom. "Call me sometime; we'll do lunch. And, Marcus."

"Yes, Izella."

"You have fun talking to the reporters. You seem to have a flair for it." Izella faked a smile. She hated talking to reporters, and losing would only make it worse.

"You first," Marcus said as he motioned toward the door.

At nine-thirty that evening, Marcus arrived at Ferguson's house. As soon as he entered the room, it exploded in applause. As he made his way around the room, people rushed at Marcus to shake his hand. "Congratulations!" Others patted him on the back. "Nicely done!"

Once the crowd of well-wishers faded, he made his way to the bar and ordered a drink. "Congratulations, Mr. Douglas," the bartender said. "What will you have?"

"Hennessy neat," he replied, and looked around for Ferguson. *I do not want to be here,* Marcus thought. But he knew why he was there. He had just won his first high-profile media case. And here before him was a room full of potential clients. So he knew it wouldn't be his last. Still, Marcus had other things on his mind. It had been a little more than a year since he and Randa had separated and he embarked on his adventure with Yvonne Haggler. His divorce had proved to be a long process and had turned downright ugly at times. The sticking point was money. His winning this trial would only add fuel to Randa's already burning desire for more money. And now she wanted to talk. Until that day, Randa had resisted all his attempts to talk. But when got home, he was met by her voice when he checked his voice mail.

"Marcus, this is Randa. I know you're surprised to hear my voice. But I just wanted to say congratulations on winning your case. You probably won't believe this, but I'm proud of you. And I . . . Now, I don't know what to say. Funny, huh? The way we used to be able to talk about anything. Now look at me. Well, I've been thinking . . . you know, about the way I've been acting. And I think maybe you and I just need to sit down and work this whole thing out together. If you want to talk, you can reach me at 678-555-7931. I hope you call me, Marcus."

"Excuse me, Mr. Douglas," Connie Talbert, Ferguson's assistant, said, bringing Marcus out of his trance.

"Hello, Connie."

"Mr. Ferguson would like to see you in his study, when you get a chance. And by the way"—Connie extended her hand—"congratulations. We're all very pleased with the work you've done for us."

"Thank you, Connie. I appreciate that," Marcus said as he finished his drink. "Where can I find his study?"

"It's right over there," Connie said, and pointed to a door on the other side of the room. "I'll take you to him." Connie extended her arm.

"Well, thank you, madam. It would be an honor to be escorted by a beautiful lady," Marcus said as he locked his arm in hers. They weaved through the crowd, stopping several times to make small talk with the other guests. Once they reached the study, Connie knocked twice, opened the door, and showed Marcus in, closing the door behind her. Roland was on the phone but waved Marcus in and gestured for him to have a seat.

"You were saying, Ms. Dent," Roland said, smiling a very satisfied smile as he continued his conversation.

Marcus sat down thinking, *Listen to him. His wife is dead and he's moved on with his life.* He wondered why he couldn't do the same. Move on with his life. Maybe once the divorce was over, it would be easier. But now, with almost daily reminders, with their lawyers going back and forth, the pain of his separation still ate at him like a fresh wound.

He thought about Randa and how they were together. They did just about everything together. People called them the poster children for the perfect relationship. Randa was a wonderful woman. She was beautiful, intelligent, and had so much energy. She was always doing something to help somebody and even volunteered at a retirement home a couple days a week, besides mentoring a teenaged girl. She and Marcus had been very happy together. Marcus considered Randa to be his best friend. They had so much in common and would spend hours together just talking. That was the hardest part of dealing with it. Sure he loved her, but they were so close that Marcus felt like he had lost the best part of himself. He saw so much in her, but he only saw what he wanted to see. Marcus had put her on a very high pedestal. So high that she was bound to fall off.

The day started out like any other. The alarm went off, and they made love to each other, just like they did every morning. They showered together and then Randa cooked breakfast while Marcus got ready to go to the office. Randa mentioned that she might go shopping with her girlfriend. They ate breakfast and he left for the office, just like they did every morning. Marcus had been working at home the night before, getting ready for a meeting with a client that he had that afternoon, and he had left the papers at home. He called Randa to see if she could bring him the papers and suggested they have lunch together. But there was no answer. Marcus needed those papers, so he went home to get them. When he got home, her Benz was in the driveway, so Marcus simply figured that her girlfriend came and picked her up and they had gone shopping. He went inside and called her name a few times, but she didn't answer. He went into the den to get his papers. After searching for a few minutes, he decided just to reprint the documents. Once they had all printed, he picked them up and had just begun to review them when he thought he heard a noise. Marcus stood still for a second but didn't hear anything else. He turned off the computer and headed for the door. He was out of the house and was just about to close the door when he heard the noise again. He turned around and walked up the stairs straight to the bedroom and slowly cracked the door. There she was, in bed with another man. Marcus stood there, watching. He couldn't move. After a full minute of standing there in complete shock, he walked outside and sat down on the steps. He wasn't sure how long he'd been sitting there when he heard the door open and close and open again. When he looked up, Randa was standing in front of him.

She asked him if he had been in the house, but Marcus just looked at her, unable to speak. Once Randa got frustrated with his staring at her but not saying anything, she went back in the house. Minutes later, she and her lover came out of the house, got in the Benz he'd paid for, and left.

While Randa was gone, Marcus thought about all the things he would say to her.

How could you?

Who is he?

How long has this been going on?

But when she came back, he still couldn't say anything. She knew she had been caught and tried to explain that this was the first time. Through gasps, sobs, and large tears, she told him how sorry she was and promised that if he forgave her, it would never happen again. Still, he couldn't say a word. He had thought of a hundred things to say, but he was so mad, the words just wouldn't come out. After an hour of listening to her beg and apologize, he could take no more and just got up and left.

"Well, Paula, we'll just have to see that you get one of those." Roland laughed. "I have to go now; my lawyer is here. . . . No, no, there's no trouble, Paula. Just some things we need to go over. . . . We'll get together soon, Ms. Dent." Roland hung up the phone and turned his attention to Marcus. "Sorry, Marcus," Roland said, coming around the desk to shake his hand.

"No need to apologize, Mr. Ferguson."

"Roland, please, call me Roland. I thought it best to maintain a certain level of professionalism during the trial. You understand. No need to be so formal now." Ferguson started walking toward the bar in the corner of his study. "Drink?"

"Hennessy neat."

"I thought we might have a glass of champagne together," he said as Marcus followed him to the bar.

"That'll be fine, sir."

Roland uncorked the bottle, filled two glasses, and handed one to Marcus. "Here's to you, Marcus. Congratulations on a job well done."

"Thank you. And congratulations to you."

"Me? I didn't do anything. I just sat there and tried to look innocent. You did all the work. I like the way you handle things. It made me mad at first, though. I thought about firing you a number of times. But I see now that you knew what you were doing. I might be interested in your firm doing more work for me."

"Thank you," Marcus said, somewhat surprised. He knew that Roland had a team of lawyers working for him. "I'm sure my staff can handle any of your needs."

"If they have the same dedication that you do, I'm sure they can. You know that was one of the first things that impressed me about you, Marcus."

"What's that?"

"That you own your law firm and you still practice law. I know many people who own law firms, and none of them have cracked a law book in years," Roland said, draining his glass. "But we'll talk about all that some other time. Right now, there's a party going on and you're the guest of honor. So enjoy the party."

Marcus finished his champagne and followed Roland out of the study to rejoin his guests. Once again the room erupted in applause.

For the next two hours, Marcus made his way around the room. He heard the word *congratulations* so many times he felt like slapping the next person who said it. But that would be bad for business. So, he talked about the high points of the case and his law firm. There were even a few ladies who inquired about his marital status. A conversation he had little interest in having. The first chance he got, Marcus headed for the door.

HOME

Carmen Taylor parked her rental car in the driveway and turned off the lights. This would be the first time she had been home since Desireé's funeral. She missed her sister, missed her more than she ever let on. It had been more than a year since the murder. Carmen had been shooting a layout in Tokyo when she got her father's call. She knew something was wrong when she hadn't heard from Desireé in two days. The news of her sister's death was devastating to her. She spent the better part of the next two days traveling, from Tokyo to Hawaii to San Francisco to Chicago to Atlanta and arrived the night before the funeral. After the funeral, Carmen went back to Tokyo and back to work. She didn't want to give herself any time to dwell on Desireé's death. So Carmen did what she always did when things became stressful. She worked print ads, shows, commercials, anything to keep busy.

From the moment her father, Carlton, snapped that first picture, everybody knew Carmen Taylor was going to be a model. Her mother, Dominique, had planned it all out for her. Her every waking moment was dedicated to accomplishing that goal. As young girls, Carmen and Desireé were taught to walk a certain way, talk a certain way. Dominique saw to it that they even looked a certain way. Dominique controlled everything. Dominique always had control of everything.

She sat quietly outside of the house she grew up in and thought. Thought about what she was about to do. First she had to decide if she was going to do it at all. Was she going to walk up to that door and ring the bell? If she did, Carmen knew that her mother would answer the door and she would have to talk to her. And she didn't want to. Carmen got out of the car and walked toward the door. She rang the bell, and as she expected, her mother answered. "Hello, Mother. Can I come in?"

"Carmen?" Dominique said, not believing her eyes or ears as she stood blocking the door. "What are you doing here?"

"Can I come in?" Carmen asked again, staring impatiently at her mother. Dominique stared back, only her look was not one of impatience; it was more shock than anything else. It had been four years since she'd seen her daughter, and these were the first words they'd exchanged in seven. Finally, Dominique stepped aside, but just enough for Carmen to pass.

"Thank you, Mother. How are you?" Carmen asked as she walked through the foyer into the living room.

"I'm fine, Carmen."

For Carmen it was like stepping into a time machine. Nothing had changed in all the years since she'd last set foot in the place she'd called home for nineteen years. She could almost see herself and Desireé as kids running around the room, playing in front of the Christmas tree. She'd been around the world, lived and worked in New York, Los Angeles,

London, Paris, Madrid, and Tokyo, but there was no feeling like this in the world. In her mind's eye, this was still home to her. She took a deep breath and could smell the scent of her father's cigar in the air. "Where's Daddy?" she asked as she continued to wander around the living room.

"He's downstairs." Carmen started to walk away, heading for the basement door, but Dominique grabbed Carmen by the arm. "You still haven't answered my question, Carmen. What are you doing here?"

Carmen jerked her arm back. "I came to see Daddy . . . and you."

"You couldn't come to pay your respects to your sister, but you can show up now? You've got some nerve."

"What are you taking about? I was at Desireé's funeral."

Dominique looked at her daughter. She hadn't seen her at the funeral and would have sworn she wasn't there. "You were there? You were there and you couldn't come and say something to me and your father?"

"I talked to Daddy."

"When?"

"At the funeral, Mother."

"I didn't see you there."

"I saw you," Carmen said, apparently frustrated by Dominique's questions. She slid into her father's chair. "My sister had died, Mother. I knew that I couldn't stay for long, and I didn't want to spend that time arguing with you."

"We wouldn't have argued, Carmen."

"Of course we would've. That's all we ever do."

"We're not arguing now." Dominique sat down on the couch.

"No, not yet. But we will before I leave this room. I know it. I know you. You can't help yourself."

"What is that supposed to mean?"

"Nevermind," Carmen said as she stood up and once

again headed for the basement door. "You know exactly what I'm talkin' about because we've had that argument too. And my answering that question will just lead us into that same argument and I'm really not with it, Mother, not tonight. So, if it's all right with you, I'm going to go downstairs and say hi to Daddy."

"That's it? Just like that? You walk in here after all these years, and this is all you have to say to me, Carmen? I'm your mother, and this is all you have to say?"

"What do you want from me?"

"A conversation, maybe? Yes, that's it, a conversation."

"Okay, a conversation. It's always got to be your way. All right, then. Hi, Mommy," Carmen said, posting a fake smile. "How are you?"

"Go. If that's the best you can do, then go," Dominique said as a tear rolled down her cheek.

Carmen rolled her eyes at the sight of that single tear and started once again for the basement door. Then she stopped and looked back at her mother. "I'm sorry." Carmen walked back into the living room and faced Dominique. "Look, Mother, I'm tired. I flew into New York from London, and then I caught a flight here. I promised Daddy that I would come and say hi to him, and then I wanna get some rest."

"I really think we need to talk, Carmen."

"I promise we'll talk tomorrow."

"You know I love you, Carmen," Dominique said tearfully, reaching out for her daughter's hand. "You're all I have now."

"Mother, please." Once again Carmen started for the basement door, knowing that Dominique was right. They were all each other had, and they did need to talk. "We'll talk tomorrow." There was a lot that she needed to get off her chest. She had carried the burden around with her long enough.

"You're welcome to stay here. Please stay."

"I've got a suite at the Marriott; I'll be fine."

"I know you'll be fine, Carmen. That's not the point. This is your home. I know, why don't I get your old room—"

"Mother, please. I just wanna say hi to Daddy and get to my suite so I can get some rest. I have a big day tomorrow," Carmen said, finally turning the knob and closing the door behind her before Dominique could say anything else.

Carmen stood motionless at the top of the basement steps as her eyes filled with tears. Her ears were flooded with the sounds of jazz music. It was her father's passion. She walked slowly down the steps, and once again her thoughts turned to Desireé. She thought about the many hours she and Desireé had spent in that basement with their father. Sitting and listening to the likes of Thelonious Monk, Charlie Parker, and John Coltrane. But her father's favorite was Miles. "Picked up another Miles Davis CD, huh?"

"Carmen." Carlton Taylor could hardly believe his ears. He jumped out of his chair. "Come here, girl. Don't just stand there; show your daddy some love."

Carmen walked across the room, looking at the pictures on the walls. Once again she began to cry, looking at the pictures of her and Desireé. Looking at those walls was like looking at a pictorial biography of their life. This was actually the first time that she allowed herself to feel. The tears came harder and she rushed to her father's embrace.

"Let it out, baby girl," he said softly.

She held on to Carlton tightly for several seconds before finding her voice again. "I'm all right, Daddy. Seeing these pictures. . . . I just never thought that—"

"It's okay, Carmen. You don't have to say anything. Just let it out." Carlton stood quietly, holding his daughter while she cried.

After a while, Carmen asked if they could go outside. "I just can't stay in here looking at those pictures."

"Sure, Carmen, we can sit out by the pool and talk."

The change in location did little to change her mood. Carmen couldn't stop herself from thinking about Desireé. She and Carlton sat outside for hours, reminiscing about the good times they'd spent together. A few times, Carmen began to cry. Carlton could see that maybe it was time to change the subject.

"Where are you staying, Carmen?"

"I've got a suite reserved at the Marriott," she replied.

"Which one?"

"By the airport."

"You know that you're welcome to stay here. You know we'd love to have you."

"Mother already invited me."

"And?" Carlton lifted an eyebrow.

"And I said no. I have to get up early and go see Roland's lawyer. It would just be easier if I stayed in the suite."

"Easier on who?"

"Daddy . . ."

"Okay, Carmen, but you can't blame a man for trying. Or a woman, for that matter. Did you talk to your mother when you came in?"

"I spoke. It would have been hard not to, Daddy; she answered the door."

"You know that's not what I meant." Carlton moved his chair closer to his daughter. He put his arm around her and said, "Nobody knows better than I do how your mother is. And I know she was hard on you girls, but we all suffered a great loss. Don't you think it's time you put your differences aside and make peace with your mother?"

"I know I should, Daddy; she's trying to reach out to me. She said I was all she had left."

"I'll try not to take that personally. But raisin' you girls was her life."

"I told her that we would talk. And before I leave, I promise, Daddy, I will. It's just hard for me to let it go. But I will."

"How long are you going to be in town this time?"

"I guess that depends on the lawyer."

"What you goin' to see Roland's lawyer about?"

"His office contacted me some time ago about testifying at his trial. They said that since I talked to Dez every day I may be able to testify about her state of mind. I told them that I wasn't opposed to it. I have an appointment to see him tomorrow at two to give my deposition."

"Nobody told you?"

"Told me what?"

"Jury found Roland not guilty this morning."

"What?"

"They're having a party at his house right now. Celebrating. Trial took less time than they thought it would. He had a good lawyer. Douglas had the jury eating out of his hand."

"So what happens now?"

"The police say the case will be reopened."

"Are there any other suspects?"

"I don't know, Carmen. Detective Benjamin at the police station said I could come down and talk to him about it, but I don't hold out much hope."

"Why not?"

"They had their man, and the jury let him walk. Police aren't gonna do too much now; it would be like admitting that they had the wrong man."

"Do you think he did it, Daddy?"

"He could have. You talked to Desireé all the time. What do you think?"

"If there were any problems between her and Roland, she didn't tell me. He was an asshole, but Roland never did seem like the type to beat somebody to death."

"I was sure that he did it," Carlton said strongly. "Now I just don't know."

"What changed your mind?"

"Sitting in that courtroom every day, Douglas went a long way toward convincing me that Roland couldn't have done it."

"That's his job."

"I know."

"He's supposed to make you doubt the prosecution's case."

"Well, that's just what he did. He called their case a theory mixed with fact. And the brother ran it down."

"At least he hired a brother to defend him."

Carmen stood and gathered her things. "You mind if I go out the gate, Daddy? I just can't face Mother right now. And I know she's sitting right there in the living room, facing the basement door." Once again the tears flowed from Carmen's eyes. "Waiting, just like she used to when we were kids."

"I understand, baby girl. I'll tell her you said good night."

"Thank you, Daddy." Carmen kissed her father on the cheek. "Good night."

"Good night, baby girl. It sure is good to have you home. Call me in the morning, and maybe I'll take you to breakfast."

"I was thinking maybe I'd drop in and see Detective Benjamin in the morning before I go to see the lawyer. What's his name?"

"Marcus Douglas."

JUSTICE

"Marcus."

"Yes, Janise."

"Carmen Taylor is here to see you."

"The model?" Marcus sat straight up in his chair.

"Yes, the model."

"Why is she here to see me?" He straightened his tie.

"She is Desireé Ferguson's sister. You wanted her to give a deposition on her sister's state of mind prior to the murder. But she couldn't get away."

"Yeah, yeah, yeah, I remember. Didn't you cancel that?"

"I must have overlooked it. I'm sorry."

"Don't worry about it, Janise. I'll see her. She does know the trial ended yesterday, doesn't she?"

"Yes, she does, but she'd still like to see you."

"Well, send her right in."

Marcus stood up to receive Carmen; his heart beat a little faster, and he felt the palms of his hands were a bit damp. Janise swung the door open and ushered Carmen Taylor into the office.

"Marcus Douglas, Carmen Taylor," Janise said, then quickly closed the door behind her.

Marcus wiped his right hand against his pants and came from behind his desk to greet her. "Ms. Taylor, it is an honor to meet you," Marcus said as he bent at the waist and kissed her hand. It was a little overwhelming for him to be kissing the hand of somebody famous. She was more beautiful in person than any of the many pictures he'd seen of her. He started to tell her this, but he didn't want to seem like just another fan. A buster at a loss for words in the presence of the big-time model.

Carmen felt a chill run through her when Marcus kissed her hand. "Thank you, Mr. Douglas. It's nice to meet you." She looked Marcus in the eye. *Roland hired a good-looking brother to defend him. A good-looking brother with no ring on his finger,* Carmen thought.

Marcus smiled as politely as he could, trying to contain his excitement. He extended his hand toward one of the chairs facing his desk. "Please, Ms. Taylor, have a seat."

"Thank you."

"First let me apologize for not letting you know that your deposition was no longer necessary."

"To be honest, it would have been nice if you had. I traveled a long way to get here just to be told that my deposition isn't necessary and that the trial is over."

"Yes, well, the judge moved the trial date and things moved a lot faster than anyone could imagine with a case like this. But, once again, Ms. Taylor, I am very sorry for any inconvenience this has caused you." He paused for a few seconds, cleared his throat, then moved on. "Now that that's out of the way, tell me what I can do for you."

"I'm not exactly sure what you can do for me, Mr. Douglas. But what I want is for somebody to account for my sister's murder."

"I'm sure that you know that Roland Ferguson was found not guilty of the charges."

"Found not guilty thanks to your brilliant defense, from what I'm told."

"I was just doing my job, Ms. Taylor."

"Yes, Mr. Douglas, I'm sure that you were. But that doesn't change what I want. Mr. Douglas, I've been to see the assistant district attorney and the detective assigned to the case."

"Ms. Izella Hawkins and Detective Paul Benjamin."

"Right, and both of them assured me that the case isn't closed, and they would do everything in their power to see to it that the guilty party is brought to justice."

"That sounds like Izella."

"She even turned it into a photo opportunity. She had cameramen and a film crew waiting outside the office for me when I came out. They got her little 'we'll get him' speech on film."

"That sounds like Izella too. She's planning to run for DA. It will probably be on the news at six and eleven."

"I'm sure."

"What about Benjamin? What did he have to say for himself?"

"Not much. Pretty much the same thing; he said he had some leads he was gonna follow up on, but there wasn't too much they could do."

"He's right. If they arrested somebody else now for the murder, his lawyer would take the outcome of this trial and build his defense around it. Benjamin would have to take the stand and answer how the investigation led him to arrest and try Ferguson for a murder he was found not guilty of, and how that same investigation could lead him to another conclusion. It would damage his credibility as a witness and make the prosecution's case that much harder to prove. It's possible that they might pursue that option, but unless the killer just drops in their lap, it's not very likely."

"My father said the same thing. Not in as much detail, but the same thing. I asked him how this could happen. He said they had the killer but you got him off."

"I'm just a defense attorney, Ms. Taylor. It was a jury of his peers that found him not guilty."

"I understand that, Mr. Douglas. It doesn't change anything."

"I don't understand what you want from me, Ms. Taylor."

"A little bit of justice for my sister, Mr. Douglas. That's what I'm asking for. If Roland didn't kill her, fine. Somebody did! What bothers me is that nobody is interested in finding out who."

Marcus looked at Carmen; he could see the pain in her eyes. He wanted to do something to help her but knew there was nothing. "There's nothing I can do for you, Ms. Taylor."

Carmen looked angrily at Marcus and then turned away from him. "I understand, Mr. Douglas. But I assure you that I'm gonna do whatever it takes to find out who killed her."

"I understand."

"Do you, Mr. Douglas? Do you really? Have you ever lost somebody you loved and you just wanted to know what happened and why?"

Now, why she wanna go and say that? Marcus thought. She could have said anything else but that. Anything else Carmen could have said would have been met with a polite answer, followed by "I can't help you." But that he couldn't dismiss so easily. The fact was, he had lost somebody.

Marcus got up from his desk and walked over to the wet bar. Carmen watched Marcus quietly as he walked. She looked at the expression on his face and knew that she had hit a nerve.

"Can I offer you a drink, Ms. Taylor?"

"It's a little early in the day for me. But it's been that kind a day. So, I'll have Bacardi, if you have it. On the rocks, please."

Marcus filled a couple of glasses with ice, then poured Bacardi for Carmen and Hennessy for himself. He handed Carmen her glass and returned to his seat behind the desk.

"You know, it's funny you should ask me that . . . have I ever lost somebody."

"Have you?" Carmen smiled at Marcus.

He took another sip of his drink and smiled back at her. He took a minute to admire her beauty before he answered. "An old client of mine was in trouble. Well, I won't bore you with the details, but to make a long story short, she died in my arms."

"I'm sorry to hear that. Were you two very close?"

"I'm sure it's nothing like you and your sister. But, yes, we got to be very close during the time we had together. I spent the next year asking questions. Just trying to get some-body, anybody to get it to make sense to me. I ended up going to New York and hiring a private investigator to tell me what I guess I knew all along. She knew too much. So she had to die because she wanted out."

"So you do understand."

"More than you know, Ms. Taylor."

"So you'll help me?"

"I've been planning on taking a little vacation anyway." Marcus thought for a moment before he spoke again. "Yes, Ms. Taylor, I'll be glad to help in any way I can." He picked up the phone. "Janise, pull the summary notes on the Ferguson case, and give them to Ms. Taylor on her way out, please."

"I'll have the file ready for her," Janise replied. "Should I take the crime-scene pictures out first?"

"Definitely. And ask Garrett to call me at home tonight."

Marcus turned his attention back to Carmen. "What I'd like you to do is look over the notes from the case. Pay particular attention to the investigation. Let me know if you think there's something that the police might have missed. That will at least give us a place to start. I'll tell Janise to give you access to any documents you want to see."

"That sounds like a good idea," Carmen said as she stood up. "I want to thank you for agreeing to help me. I really appreciate it. I was beginning to think that nobody cared who killed Desireé."

Marcus took a card from the holder on the desk and wrote his home phone number on it. He got up and handed it to Carmen. "You're welcome, Ms. Taylor. I know how you feel," he said, and escorted her out of his office. "That's my number at home. Call me if you think of anything or if you have any questions. Where are you staying, by the way?"

"I'm staying at the Marriott by the airport."

Marcus gave a nod of acknowledgment, then extended his hand. "And now if you'll excuse me, it's been a long couple of months. I'm going home."

SORTING OUT
THE DETAILS

The drive home through downtown traffic was brutal. Marcus pushed Lee Morgan's *The Gigolo* into the CD player and loosened his tie. Of all the days Marcus picked to go home early, he would pick a day when the Braves were playing the New York Yankees in an afternoon doubleheader. "This is no way to start a vacation." Once he got on I-20, traffic began to thin out and Marcus relaxed and thought about where he could go on vacation. He tossed around a few places. Aruba, Puerto Rico, the Mediterranean, Africa maybe, but he wasn't really feeling any of those places. This would be his first vacation in three years and the first time in several more years that he'd be going by himself. Thinking about vacationing alone started him thinking about Randa. He thought again about the places that he'd considered going and realized he'd been to each place with Randa. "For once can you think about something else?"

Once Marcus finally arrived at home, he poured himself a glass of Hennessy and sat down in his favorite chair. He reached in the drawer of the end table and pulled out a pack of cigarettes and lit up. Smoking was something else he owed to Randa. He had quit smoking for her, five years before he caught her cheating. After that, puffing a Kool seemed to make things easier. Marcus turned the television to CNN, and before he knew it, he was asleep. The phone rang, bringing him out of his nod. He answered, "Hello."

"Hello, Marcus, this is Randa. Did I wake you?"

"Yes, I guess you did," Marcus replied, trying to shake himself out of it.

"I'm sorry. So, congratulations on winning your case. I saw you last night on the news. You handle the press very well."

"Thank you, Randa. What can I do for you?"

"I told you, Marcus, I just want to talk."

"Talk about what?"

"About us."

"There is no us, Randa. There's you and there's me. You killed us," Marcus said bitterly. "All there is between us now is business."

"Business."

"Yes, Randa, business. I have sold all of our property, liquidated all our assets. Everything is sitting in an escrow account. You get a substantial monthly income. My lawyer has made you offer after offer, and you've turned them all down."

"Marcus, I'm tired of talking to Duck."

"Duck? Who is Duck?"

"Your lawyer. Have you ever watched him walk? He waddles like a fat duck."

"Anyway, Randa, what more do you want from me?"

"It's not the money," Randa said, and let out a little giggle. "It was at first, but now I realized it's not what I want."

"So what do you want?"

"I want the one thing you haven't offered! I want my hus-

band back. That's what I want, Marcus. Don't you understand that I love you?"

"You love me? That's funny. Is that what you were doing
in bed with that man? Showing me how much you loved
me?"

"Marcus, that was a mistake. I know that now. Everybody
makes mistakes."

"Yeah, right."

"It just happened."

"I'm sure it did. What, were the two of you just lyin'
around naked and you *just happened* to fall on top of him?"

Randa didn't answer.

"I thought so. How could you, Randa?"

"I'm sorry, Marcus."

"I just bet you are. How long was it goin' on?"

"It was just that one time."

"That's not what the neighbor woman told me."

"Oh Lord, what does she have to do with this?"

"After you left to take your boyfriend home and left me
sitting on the steps like a fool, the neighbor woman walks up
and says, 'I'm glad you finally woke up. And don't let her
tell you that this was the first time.' I was so embarrassed, on
top of feeling stupid. If the damn neighbor woman knew, the
rest of the block did too. Maybe even the whole subdivi-
sion."

"That bitch."

"Oh, she's a bitch? You fuck another man, but she's a
bitch. In our house! In the bed we made love in that morning! And then you had the nerve to drive him home in the
Benz I paid for! And she's a bitch. Give me a fuckin' break,
Randa."

"I'm sorry, Marcus."

"Sorry don't get it done. Not this time, Randa. I don't
know why we're even talking about this."

"Because we never have talked about this. This is the conversation we should have had a year ago. But you ran off behind some woman. You were probably sleeping with her all along."

"For your information, I never slept with Yvonne."

"You really expect me to believe that?"

"I don't give a fuck what you believe."

"Are you two still *together?*"

"No, we're not still *together*. She's dead."

"She didn't die of AIDS, did she?"

"No, she was murdered."

"Why?"

"None of your damn business."

"All right, all right, no need to bite my head off," Randa said, and then she took a deep breath. "Marcus."

"What?"

"I love you."

"You said that."

"Do you still love me?"

"What difference does that make?"

"It makes a difference to me."

Marcus had no answer.

"Marcus, as much as we meant to each other, after all the things we shared together, the least you could do is answer my question. Can you honestly say that you don't still love me?"

"It doesn't matter."

"It matters to me."

Marcus got up from his seat and walked to the bar without answering.

"Marcus, are you still there?"

He poured himself a glass of Hennessy and shot it down before pouring another one and returning to his seat. "I'm still here," Marcus said, and lit a Kool.

"You never did answer my question."

"What question was that?"

"Can you honestly say that you don't still love me?"

"I did answer you. I said it doesn't matter."

"It does matter. It matters to me."

"Yes, Randa, I do love you. And maybe that's why it's so hard for me to talk to you. Why I haven't moved on from this. Maybe once it's over, I can finally put you and all this behind me." Marcus took a drag and blew the smoke out.

Recognizing a change in his breathing, she asked, "What's that I hear? Are you smoking again?"

"Yes," he said, blowing the smoke into the phone to be sure she heard it.

"When did this happen? You were doing so well."

"I started, let me see . . . I started smoking a little more than a year ago. I believe it was the day that I came home and found my wife pullin' her hair out ridin' another man's dick," Marcus said calmly.

"I guess I deserved that," Randa said quietly. She knew she was fighting a losing battle, so she decided a change of tactic was in order. "Are you seeing anybody now?"

"Why do you want to know?"

"I'm just asking. But I know you're not seeing anybody seriously."

"How do you know that?"

"Maybe I have a spy in your office."

"Well we both know who that is. Ms. Tiffanie Powers, Attorney at Law, and she'll be fired in the morning."

"You're not really gonna fire Tiff, are you?"

"Watch me."

"That still doesn't answer my question."

"Okay, since you seem to already know, I have somebody I see every now and then."

"Every now and then? As much as you love doin' it, Marcus, I know every now and then ain't cuttin' it."

"I believe that falls under the heading of my business. You gave up your rights to being concerned about how much I'm getting a long time ago."

"Well, I'm not seeing anybody on the regular either. I tried to date for a while, but I realized that it wasn't what I really wanted. What I want is my husband back."

"Well, Randa, you're old enough for your wants to hurt you."

"And it does hurt me, Marcus. Every morning I wake up and you're not beside me, it hurts. Every morning I wake up and I can't make love to you, it hurts me. And I know that I have nobody to blame but myself."

"That's the first bit of truth I've heard from you tonight."

"No, it's not. I was telling the truth when I said I love you."

Marcus responded to her comment with silence.

"Marcus, I love you and you love me. That's some place for us to start. And maybe with time we can put this behind us. Go back to being happy. Get back to the way things used to be. Do you remember how good it was between us?"

"Yes," Marcus replied, remembering how good Randa made him feel sexually.

"How we used to make love every morning?" Randa said, tempting Marcus. "And twice before bedtime?"

"I remember, Randa. Which reminds me—how could you fuck another man in the same bed we just made love in? Did you at least have the decency to change the sheets?"

This time it was Randa who answered with silence.

"You see, Randa, everything you say and everything I feel always leads me back to the same point. And I just can't seem to get past that. And I don't think I ever will."

"In time, Marcus, I hope you open up your heart and forgive me."

"In time, maybe."

"What about now?"

"Excuse me?"

"What about right now?"

"Have you lost your mind?"

"No, I haven't lost my mind. I want you, Marcus. I want to see you. I want to make love to you."

"Like I said, you're old enough for your wants to hurt you."

"But you can ease my pain, Marcus. Only you can ease my pain. Can I see you?"

"When?"

"Now."

"No."

"I know you still love me. You said so yourself. You know you still want me. I can hear it your voice."

"No, you don't."

"Come on now, Marcus, I didn't just meet you. I could hear your longing to be inside me."

"You're wrong," Marcus lied.

"Tell that to somebody who doesn't know you. Can I come by and make love to you, Marcus? I promise that I won't say a word. I'll just take off my clothes and make love to you."

"No."

"Please, Marcus. Just talking to you, hearing your voice, has made my body ache for you."

"No, Randa."

"No strings attached. Just straight-up sex."

"No, Randa, this is not going to happen."

"I'm on my way."

"I won't be here," Marcus said as he hung up the phone. The question now was, was she really on her way? He knew Randa to be a woman who went after want she wanted. She was on her way, no doubt. Randa was on her way to use her formidable sexuality to make her point. They belonged together. They were two halves of the same whole. But those days were long gone. Marcus finished his drink, then went in the bedroom and lay across his bed. Now he had a question for himself: Was he going to allow her to do it? If he chose to be honest with himself, he'd have to admit that he wanted her. That Randa was right when she said that every-now-and-then shit wasn't cuttin' it. It was great for not allowing anybody to get close to him, but it did nothing to satisfy his healthy sexual appetite.

For him the decision was easy. Randa betrayed everything they were. She took everything from him that day. And a good fuck wouldn't change that. He got up from the bed before thoughts of seeing Randa come through the door naked changed his mind. He quickly went into the closet and pulled out a suitcase. He threw a few things in the bag, then carried it unzipped to the bar and threw in a bottle of Hennessy. Marcus zipped up his bag and was on his way out the door when he remembered that he told Carmen to call him at home if she had any questions. He put his bag down and went to the phone. He dialed 411.

"Directory assistance. What city?"

"Atlanta."

"What number?"

"Airport Marriott."

"Hold for the number. 404-555-7900. I'll connect you at no charge."

"Thank you."

"Airport Marriott, how may I direct your call?"

"Carmen Taylor. I don't know what room she's in."

"Hold, please."

Marcus looked at his watch. He didn't know where Randa lived or how long it would take her to get there. But he knew this was taking too long. He asked himself why he didn't just leave and call from his cell phone, especially since that was the number he was about to give her. "Hello," Carmen finally answered.

"Good evening, Ms. Taylor. This is Marcus Douglas. I hope I'm not disturbing you?"

"No, Mr. Douglas, you're not disturbing me."

"I'm calling to give you my cell phone number. I'm not going to be home for a couple of days."

"Are you going out of town?" Carmen asked, sounding a little disappointed.

"No, Ms. Taylor. I'm just going to a hotel for a couple of days."

"Get away from annoying reporters, huh?" Carmen said, feeling relieved.

"Annoying, yeah, something like that." Marcus looked at his watch again, walked toward the window, and looked out. "Ready for the number?"

"Ready."

"770-555-5359."

"Okay, that's good to know, especially since I was just about to call you."

"Did you have a question?"

"Yes. I went over the list of people the police questioned and read their statements, and I was wondering why the police never talked to Suzanne Collins?"

"Who is Suzanne Collins?"

"Suzanne was Desireé's best friend. I think it's a little odd that the police could investigate her murder and not talk to her best friend. I take it you didn't either?"

"No, Ms. Taylor, this is the first time I've heard her name.

Ferguson didn't mention her, and she never came forward on her own."

"Well, she doesn't live far from here, and I was thinking about going by there and talking to her."

"That sounds like a good idea, Ms. Taylor. You're serious about this, aren't you?"

"Very serious. I have to know what happened to my sister."

Marcus looked out the window again. "Need some company?"

"You took the words right out of my mouth. I thought that you might do a little better at asking questions than I would. You know, being a lawyer and all," Carmen said, allowing her voice to drop.

Marcus picked up on her tone but was unsure what to read in it. So he filed it away in the back of his mind. "Well, I'll pick you up in about forty minutes."

"Sounds good."

Marcus hung up the phone quickly and headed out the door. He got in his car and drove out the driveway. He had just reached the corner and was about to turn when he saw Randa's Benz barreling down the street.

SHARE YOUR PAIN

After receiving the folder from Janise, Carmen immediately returned to her hotel room and started reading. As she read, Carmen tried not to think about the description of the crime scene, but her mind painted vivid images. "Who could have done this to her?" She had accepted the fact that Roland had killed her sister and would be punished for the crime. But all that had changed. Carmen read every piece of paper in the folder and made notes of her questions. There weren't many. Overall, she thought the investigation was pretty thorough, as far as Roland was concerned. But there didn't seem to be much investigation of Desireé.

Carmen had been reading for hours before she remembered that she had promised her parents that she would come by. And as much as she knew that they needed to talk, "Not now," Carmen said out loud to herself. Revisiting all the old emotions would only distract her from what she was trying to accomplish. When Carmen finished reading Detective Benjamin's statement, she closed the folder. She looked over at the clock on the nightstand. Carmen lay across the bed and began to think about her sister. Then it hit her. "Marcus!" she said, jumping up from the bed. He would be there to pick her up in twenty minutes, and she was nowhere near ready to go. Dressed in her old comfortable robe and slippers, she definitely didn't want Marcus to catch her like this. She grabbed some clothes out of her bag and headed for the bathroom. After a quick shower, she began to get dressed. When the phone rang, Carmen answered. "Ms. Taylor, there's a Marcus Douglas in the lobby to see you. Shall I send him up?"

"No. Please tell Mr. Douglas I'll be down shortly," Carmen replied, zipping up her jeans and stepping into her heels. She put on a dab of Escape and checked her hair in the mirror on her way out the door.

When she reached the lobby, Carmen looked around until she saw Marcus and then started for him. When Marcus saw her coming, he rose to his feet to greet her. He couldn't help but be taken as Carmen approached, turning men's heads as she passed. "Steady boy, she's way out of your league," Marcus said to himself.

"Hello, Mr. Douglas. I'm sorry I kept you waiting," Carmen said, extending her hand to Marcus.

Marcus accepted her hand, thinking, *Seeing you was worth the wait*, but instead he said, "Don't worry about it, Ms. Taylor. It wasn't that long. So, where are we going?"

"Suzanne lives in Hampton," Carmen said as they left the hotel. "You know the way or do you want me to drive?"

"I don't mind driving. My car is right over here." He unlocked the passenger door and held it open for Carmen.

"Thank you." Once they were in the car and away, Marcus said, "Did you read anything else that you had questions about, Ms. Taylor?"

"Yes, I did. But would you mind just calling me Carmen?"

"Only if you'll call me Marcus."

"Deal; Marcus it is. When you say 'Ms. Taylor,' it sounds

too much like my old economics professor, Mr. Weuhausen. 'Ms. Taylor, can you summarize Paul Samuelson's theory of equilibrium?" Carmen laughed as she imitated her old professor.

"Well, since you put it that way," Marcus said, laughing at her impersonation. "I wouldn't wanna do that. Carmen it is. By the way, what is Paul Samuelson's theory of equilibrium?"

"It's a situation in which the forces that determine the behavior of some variable are in balance and thus exert no pressure on that variable to change; the actions of all economic agents are mutually consistent. It's a concept meaningfully applied to any variable whose level is determined by the outcome of the operation of at least one mechanism or process acting on countervailing forces. For example, equilibrium price is affected by a process that drives suppliers to increase prices when demand is in excess and to undercut each other when supply is in excess—the mechanism thus regulates the forces of supply and demand."

"Oh."

"I'm glad that's settled," Carmen said with a smile. "And to answer your first question, yes. But it's more a comment than a question."

"What's that, Carmen?" Marcus asked. Now he felt funny saying it.

"That the investigation seemed to be more about proving that Roland did it than it was about who killed Dez."

"That was a major point in my defense of Ferguson. That and the time line, of course. But their investigation focused squarely on him from day one," Marcus said, and glanced at Carmen. She was looking directly at him, so he looked away quickly. "How often did you and your sister talk?"

"We talked every day."

"Did she tell you about her and Rasheed?"

"She did. Her new play toy." Carmen giggled.

"Did you talk to her the day of the . . ."

"Murder. The day of the murder. You can say it, Marcus. I'm not gonna fall apart. I did my crying a year ago and again last night. I can deal with this."

"No matter where it leads?"

"I said I could."

"Okay, Carmen, did you talk to your sister the day she was murdered?"

"Yes, but just for a minute. Dez was on her way out when I called."

"And nothing was wrong. She didn't say anything?"

"No. Just that she would call me the next day."

"Did Roland know about her and Rasheed?"

"She said that he knew about all her toys."

"Toys? She'd had more than one?"

"Yes," Carmen said reluctantly. "Dez always had somebody. But Roland loved her, and that was something he accepted about her. Dez was much younger than Roland when they got married. She married him for money and position. And don't look so surprised. If you didn't already know it, I know you at least thought about it."

"The thought had crossed my mind. So tell me about Desireé and Roland. Tell me what you know about their relationship. How'd they meet?"

"Dez met Roland at a fund-raiser for some candidate for Congress. I don't remember his name, probably because he lost. They were married six months later."

"Fund-raiser? I figure Ferguson for a contributor. But what was your sister doing there? Was she a campaign worker or was she a contributor too?"

"No, Marcus. Dez was never interested in politics. Dez was there looking for a man. She and Porsche Temple used to get themselves invited to those types of things all the time."

"Who's that? Another girlfriend?"

"Yes, and the police didn't talk to her either. And before you ask, I don't have any idea where to find her. Anyway, Dez had seen Roland at a few of these affairs and noticed that he always came with a different woman. Dez figured that they were escorts."

"Was she right?"

"She never said if they were or not, and to be honest, at the time I didn't care."

"I take it that you didn't approve of her lifestyle?"

"I just always thought she could do better. Dez was *always* smart. She graduated from Spellman. She could have done anything she wanted to. But she decided it was easier to live off her looks and her body." Carmen let out a little laugh. "She was so pretty."

"Not as pretty as you," Marcus said quickly, smiling at Carmen as he drove.

"I'll take that as a compliment." Carmen smiled back.

"It was meant to be one."

"Well, thank you for the compliment, Marcus. But I always thought she was the beautiful one in the family. Not just physical beauty. Dez was a beautiful person. She was the type of person who everybody loved. She had that kind of personality. She made you love her. I'm not saying that my sister was perfect. She had her faults, but we all do. And she had her share of hang-ups." Carmen glanced over at Marcus, deciding if she was going to continue her thought out loud. "I'm at the center of one of her old hang-ups. Me and Dez were always very competitive growing up. Rivals almost."

"The older, prettier sister," Marcus said.

"The one who everything always came easy to. It got better when I left Spellman and went to New York. After that she didn't feel the need to always compete with me. It made it easier on both of us."

"So Roland was her easy way. How'd he feel about her?"

"He loved her. Dez was twenty-two, fresh out of college; he was in his late forties, recently divorced. When I met him, he said that Dez made him feel reborn. And he went on about how beautiful and full of life she was."

"How old was Ferguson when they married?"

"I think she said he was forty-nine. Maybe that's why he didn't mind her having toys."

"Maybe, but if it was me, even if I knew and accepted it, inside it would always bother me. The woman you love with another man. That would give him the motive to commit murder," Marcus said, sounding cold and distant. Carmen looked curiously at him.

Marcus thought about Randa. What if he found out that Randa had always had somebody, a toy? The neighbor woman sure hinted at the possibility. If things had happened differently that day, could he have killed both of them in a violent rage? He thought back to when Roland Ferguson first approached him about taking the case. Marcus was still numb. It had only been two months since he returned from his quest for answers about Yvonne's death. He and Randa were in the heat of battle via their lawyers. He was intrigued by Roland's case. Marcus felt sort of a kinship with him. He remembered imagining what it must have felt like to kill your wife. "A pretty compelling motive for murder. But that's probably what the police thought. No need to look any further. Izella probably thought this was a slam-dunk. But there's got to be more, and we're gonna find it."

"Let's hope it's right around the corner. This is your exit."

They turned onto Rocky Creek Road and pulled into the

driveway. Marcus and Carmen got out and rang the doorbell. Not too much time passed before a woman answered the door. "Yes?"

"I'm sorry to bother you. My name is Carmen Taylor. Desireé Ferguson was my sister and—"

Before Carmen could finish, the woman reached out and hugged her and practically pulled Carmen inside. "Carmen, please come in." Marcus followed behind them. "I'm Helen Watts, Suzanne's sister-in-law. Your sister used to talk about you all the time. She was so proud of you." Helen led them into the living room and offered them a seat; then she sat down on the couch next to Carmen. "I want to tell you how sorry I am about your sister."

"Thank you," Carmen said. "This is Marcus Douglas."

Helen looked closely at Marcus. "I thought I recognized you. You're the one who let that bastard get away with it." Marcus started to say something. "And don't go tellin' me about no damn time line, 'cause I don't wanna hear it."

"So you think he did it?" Carmen asked.

"Who else could have? Who else would do something like that?"

"A jury found Mr. Ferguson not guilty. And you still think he's guilty, Ms. Watts?" Marcus asked.

"A man like that, rich and powerful, has a way of gettin' the things he wants done. If he didn't do it, he knows who did."

"That's what we're trying to find out," Carmen said. "Mr. Douglas has agreed to help me find out who did it. The police don't seem to be interested."

Helen looked angrily at Marcus, and then she turned to Carmen. "So, what can I do for you, Carmen?"

Carmen sat forward in her chair. "Well, I was going over the police reports and I noticed that the police never talked to Suzanne."

"We were hoping that we could talk to her, Ms. Watts," Marcus said, and Helen gave him a dirty look.

"You don't know, Carmen?" Helen asked, looking curiously at Carmen.

"Know what?"

"Suzanne is dead. She died two weeks before Desireé. I thought you knew?"

"Oh my God, no, Dez never told me. I'm sorry," Carmen said, reaching out for Helen's hand.

"Your sister never mentioned it to you?" Marcus asked.

"No, Marcus, she didn't," Carmen said sadly, and then she turned to Helen. "How did she die?"

"They found her dead in her office. They don't know how she died. They were still investigating," Helen replied sarcastically.

"How is Frank taking it? I know he must be crushed."

Once again Helen looked curiously at Carmen. "Frank's dead too. He took Suzanne's death very badly. He was frustrated with the police not being able to tell him how she died. I guess it got to be too much for him, because he went to her grave site and shot himself."

"I'm sorry for your loss, Ms. Watts. Can you tell me how long after his wife died that your brother committed suicide?" Marcus asked.

"Two weeks."

"Two weeks?" Marcus asked, and he looked at Carmen.

"I believe it was the day before Desireé was murdered."

"Helen, we're sorry to have bothered you. I am so sorry. Frank was a good man. Did the police ever talk to you about a connection between their deaths and Desireé's?" Carmen asked.

"No."

"I wouldn't think they would," Marcus said as he stood up. "Sorry to have bothered you, Ms. Watts."

"Why not?" Carmen asked. "Why don't you think they would ask about a connection?"

"Because Frank committing suicide wouldn't appear to have any connection to Desireé," Marcus said, and started for the door. "Let's go, Carmen. We've taken up enough of Ms. Watts's time."

Reluctantly Carmen stood up and followed Marcus to the door. They apologized once again and said good night. Once they were in the car and drove off, Carmen asked Marcus why he rushed her out of there. "Because it was time to go. Helen couldn't tell us any more, and all we would have done by continuing to ask questions is upset her."

"Okay, I guess you're right. But you do think there's a connection, right?"

"Could be a coincidence."

"It's more than a coincidence, Marcus. I'm sure of it."

"Is that what your years of investigative experience tells you?"

"Well . . ." Carmen smiled.

"Look, Carmen, it may be just a coincidence, but maybe not."

"Well, what are we gonna do now?"

"We investigate, Carmen. The best thing to do is to find out more information about how they died."

"How are we gonna do that?"

"I know a private investigator who does work for me sometimes. Ex-cop, still has some contacts in the department. I'll talk to him, see what he can find out. You have any idea why Desireé wouldn't tell you that Suzanne was dead?"

"No. I wouldn't think she would keep something like that from me."

"What are you doing tomorrow, Carmen?"

"Nothing. Why?" Carmen asked.

"I was thinking about paying a visit to your brother in-law. Wanna tag along?"

"Of course I do. What time?"

"I'll pick you up about noon. That too early for you?"

"No, it's not too early. I'm always up at the crack of dawn anyway. And this time I promise I'll be ready. What do you wanna talk to Roland about?"

"I want to ask him about Suzanne."

"You think he'll talk to us?"

"Why shouldn't he talk to me? I'm his lawyer. Besides, he should be glad to help find who killed his wife."

"I'll be ready," Carmen replied, but she was no longer smiling.

"What's wrong?"

"Dez and Suzanne had been friends for years. Now they're both dead," Carmen said quietly. She said nothing else on the way back to her hotel, and Marcus let her have her space.

UNTOUCHABLE

After dropping Carmen at her hotel, Marcus checked into a Residence Inn. Once he was settled into his room, he called and left a message for Connie Talbert and requested to see Roland in the afternoon around one. Marcus poured himself a drink, then lifted the phone to check his messages. Randa had called to say that she was sorry about everything in general and that she was mad about not getting to his house fast enough. "But I still think we need to talk. Maybe we can meet somewhere, in public. I know you won't call me. So I'll call you." *To delete this message, press seven.* Marcus quickly complied.

The next message was from Garrett Mason. Garrett used to work for the Atlanta police, but he got caught up in a corruption scandal. Marcus defended him. He was eventually cleared of the charges, but the damage was done. He quit the force and went into business for himself as a private investigator. Garrett had done some work for Marcus, and over the years they'd become friends. He returned the call.

"Hello."

"What's up, Garrett? This is Marcus."

"Congratulations, Mr. Big-Time Lawyer. Here's hoping that this will create a financial boom for both of us."

"Thanks. How's it goin' with you?"

"Goin' good. Busy, but busy gets you paid."

"You working on something now?"

"Yeah, working on an embezzlement case. Real high-tech stuff."

"High tech? What do you know about high tech?"

"Enough to know that I don't know anything about it. And enough to know I needed to hire someone who did."

"You hired an operative? You, Mr. Go-It-Alone Mason? Say it ain't so."

"Not this time, Marcus. I hired a chick named Jamara Deneè. And, Marcus, she is so damn fine."

"She any good? As an operative, I mean."

"She can get in there and hack with the best of them. But you know I know how good she is."

"Where'd you find her?" Marcus asked.

"Her probation officer recommended her."

"She's on probation?"

"For embezzlement."

"I thought you said she was good?"

"She is."

"If she's so good, how'd she get caught?"

"She got cocky," Garrett said. "Hit the place she worked. But before that, she was hackin' into companies through their Web sites. Hittin' them a little here, a little there. Enough to buy herself a five-bedroom house and a couple of cars. The house and the cars are in somebody else's name. Some old friend of the family who lives in the islands somewhere. But she was smart; she kept her apartment and her old Toyota, and when she went to the apartment, it was always in the Toyota."

"How's she workin' out?"

"She's all up in it. Got her working undercover at the company. I'm doin' my thing on the outside. It's working, man," Garrett told Marcus. "This could open up a whole line for me, especially with the clientele you 'bout to have access to."

"You got time to look into something for an old friend?"

"Sure, what you got?"

"I need you to find out all you can about a Suzanne and Frank Collins."

"What's the deal with them?" Garrett asked.

"She was found dead in her office. He was so frustrated with the investigation that he shot himself at her grave site," Marcus explained.

"Who's the client?"

"Carmen Taylor."

"Carmen Taylor? Where have I heard that name before?"

"She's Desireé Ferguson's sister."

"The model?"

"Yes, Garrett, the model."

"What's she like?" Garrett asked excitedly.

"She's very nice."

"That's not what I meant. Is she fine?"

"As hell. She is so beautiful that it's intimidating. My palms got all sweaty when I met her. And I find myself getting tongue-tied when she looks at me. She has such beautifully piercing eyes and a big pretty smile. Garrett, you just don't know."

"Maybe you'll introduce me."

"Maybe."

"That is unless you're planning on keeping her to yourself?"

"What do you care? You're married," Marcus said.

"My being married is irrelevant," Garrett replied.

"Not to Paven. She would think it's very relevant."

"Anyway. You at her or what?"

"No. She's way out of my league."

"She's just people. And besides, you may not have noticed it yet, but you're a big-time lawyer now. Been on TV and shit. Women will be linin' up to get next to you. So maybe it's her who's out of your league," Garrett said. "So what does the late Collins couple have to do with her?"

"The woman was Desireé Ferguson's best friend. Carmen was going over the case file and noticed that the police never talked to her. I'm just looking for any connection."

"Okay, I'll check on it. But what does it have to do with you? They found Ferguson not guilty."

"True, but somebody killed her sister. She wants to know who. Police don't seem interested in reopening the case, so she asked me to help her."

"Marcus, you're not gonna run off on another wild-goose chase, are you?"

"No, Garrett. I'm not gonna try to investigate this on my own. But I coulda used you the last time."

"Like I told you then, that black-bag stuff wasn't nothing either one of us needed to get involved in. All the time and money you put into it, and for what? For somebody to tell you what I told you already. People in that game don't retire, they get retired. Permanently."

"Lighten up, Garrett, I said I wasn't gonna do anything. And if we get any fresh leads, we'll turn them over to the police."

"I'm glad to hear you say that. You do the lawyer thing and leave the investigating to me."

"I did call you and ask you to do just that, didn't I?"

"Just checking."

"Don't worry about me, Garrett."

"I'll call you tomorrow and let you know what I found

out," Garrett said, and hung up the phone. After which Marcus fell asleep thinking about Carmen. Thinking about Desireé Ferguson's brutal murder. And then Randa creeped into his dream.

Marcus had just picked up the papers off the printer when he thought he heard a noise. He turned around and walked up the steps straight to the bedroom and opened the door. There was Randa, in bed with her lover, bucking like a wild colt and screaming out in passion. Marcus stood there, watching. He couldn't move. Then he looked down and realized that he had a golf club in his hand. He gripped the nine iron tighter, and his eyes narrowed as he walked slowly toward the bed, still unnoticed. He raised the club above his head and once again he couldn't move. He started to swing, but he couldn't move.

Randa moaned loudly, "That's the spot!"

Marcus felt the anger well up inside him. He swung the club and hit Randa in the head. Randa's blood squirted across his face. The impact of the blow knocked her off the man and onto the bed. Marcus walked slowly around the bed as the man grabbed his pants and headed for the door. He stood over Randa as she looked at him with terror in her eyes, trying to speak, but no words came out. He raised the club again. Randa finally screamed, "I love you!"

Marcus shot straight up in the bed, looking around and wondering where he was. The nightmare was over, but his heart was still pounding, and his T-shirt was drenched in sweat. He sat there for a moment, breathing hard, trying to gain his composure. As he began to calm down, he tried to come to grips with his nightmare. It seemed pretty obvious. But did he want to kill Randa? His cell phone rang before he could give more thought to an answer. "This is Marcus."

"Hi, Mr. Douglas, this is Connie Talbert, assistant to Roland Ferguson. I'm returning your call."

"Good morning, Connie. How are you?"

"I'm doing just great, Mr. Douglas. How about yourself?" Connie asked.

"I'm okay," Marcus lied, not wanting to tell Connie he just dreamt of killing his wife. "I was calling to see if Mr. Ferguson had time to see me this afternoon about one?"

"That would be fine. He's in the office this afternoon, and he'll look forward to seeing you then."

"Excellent. Then I'll see you at one," Marcus said, and hung up the phone. He gave some thought as to whether he was blindsiding Ferguson by not mentioning that he was coming with Carmen Taylor. Not that it should matter; he of all people should want to know who killed his wife. All the same, Marcus was interested to see how he'd react. Because when it got right down to it, he didn't know whether Ferguson killed Desireé or not. He'd never even asked him. His job was to defend him of the charges and get him off. That was the dilemma Marcus faced as a defense attorney. "Guilty people are entitled to a defense too," he'd always say.

The phone rang again. "This is Marcus."

"Good morning, Marcus," Janise said. "I hope you don't mind, but Connie Talbert called and said you wanted to see Ferguson this afternoon. Said she tried you at home and didn't get an answer. So I gave her your cell phone number."

"Yeah, that was fine, Janise. She just called me."

"Where are you?"

"I'm at the Residence Inn."

"Why, Marcus?"

"Just wanted to get away from the phone. It was ringing off the hook," Marcus lied.

"It wouldn't have anything to do with Randa, would it? The only reason I ask is that she called for you first thing this morning."

"It has nothing to do with Randa," Marcus lied again.

"Which reminds me, is Ms. Tiffanie Powers, Attorney at Law, in this morning?"

"Yes, she is. You wanna speak to her?"

"No, just tell her she's fired."

"Excuse me?"

"Tell her that her services are no longer required. Turn all her work over to Simon."

"Are you serious? You're firing Tiffanie?"

"I haven't decided yet."

"Now I know you're lying. This is about Randa."

"What makes you say that?"

"'Cause when I told her that you weren't in, she asked to speak to Tiffanie."

"Nevermind, Janise. I'll handle it myself."

"You're the boss." Janise laughed. "Enjoy your vacation."

"Bye, Janise."

Marcus got up and laid out a suit to wear. He paused a moment to think about what Carmen would be wearing. And how she'd look in it. He could think of worse ways to spend his vacation. Marcus smiled and headed for the shower. If he was going to be at the hotel for a while, he would have to stop at the house to pick up some more clothes. He stopped in his tracks. *No. I'm not gonna hide from Randa. I need to face her. Get it over with. She'll just keep coming until I do. I'm goin' home.* Marcus shaved, showered, and got dressed. He packed up his suitcase and checked out of the room. On the way to the Marriott, he thought about what Garrett said. Model or not, she was just people, no better, no worse. In spite of his nervousness, Marcus had enjoyed being with her the night before.

Would she even be interested in a guy like me? Maybe if I just relaxed, maybe she'd take more than a professional interest in me. Nah, she probably doesn't date black men.

Marcus arrived at the Marriott at five minutes to noon to

pick up Carmen. He went into the lobby, heading for the desk. Much to his surprise, sitting in the lobby waiting patiently was Carmen, and she looked incredible.

Carmen woke up at six, just as she did every morning. Before too long, she was dressed in sweats and heading for the treadmill in the hotel's gym. Two and a half miles later, she returned to her room. Carmen called room service to order breakfast, a cup of coffee, and half a grapefruit. While she ate, she flipped through the paper, only to find herself on page three. It was a picture of her standing next to Izella Hawkins. The caption read ASSISTANT DISTRICT ATTORNEY HAWKINS PROMISES JUSTICE IN THE FERGUSON CASE.

Once she finished eating, Carmen gave some thought to what she would wear. She wanted to be stunning without being overdressed. She wanted to look her best when she confronted Roland. Carmen wasn't entirely convinced of his innocence. And she wanted to look her best for Marcus. She wasn't about to pretend that she didn't find him attractive. Marcus could be a welcomed change. *Maybe if he wasn't so stiff.* Carmen shrugged it off and padded her way to the shower, dressed, and headed for the lobby.

When she saw him coming, Carmen stood up and started walking toward him. She was wearing a red Douglas Hobbs dress that complemented her features. "Good morning, Marcus."

"Good morning, Carmen. I hope you haven't been waiting long?"

"No, I had just sat down."

"You look magnificent, Carmen," Marcus commented enthusiastically as he walked alongside her.

"Thank you, Marcus. I was only trying to look stunning." Carmen shook out her hair and laughed. She smiled at Marcus.

Marcus wanted to say something clever, but he was too caught up in her smile to think of anything. So he just smiled back.

Atlanta Life Insurance was located in the high offices on Auburn Avenue. As always, traffic on the downtown connector was terrible, so Marcus and Carmen arrived late. Once they made it to the office, Carmen picked up a copy of *Essence* and made herself comfortable on the sofa. Marcus walked over to the desk and was greeted by the receptionist. "Good afternoon, can I help you?"

"Good afternoon. Marcus Douglas to see Mr. Ferguson, please."

"Would you mind signing in?" The receptionist called for someone to escort them to Roland's office. Once their escort arrived, he led them to the desk of Connie Talbert. When she saw Marcus coming, Connie stood up. Her eyes became as round as oranges when she noticed that Carmen was walking beside him.

"Carmen!" Connie exclaimed as she rushed up to Carmen, giving her a big hug. "It's so good to see you! It's been so long."

"How are you, Connie?" Carmen asked, trying to free herself from Connie's vicelike grip.

"Oh, I'm doing just fine. I didn't know you were in town. What brings you here?"

"I'm here to see Roland." Carmen paused and glanced at Marcus. "With Mr. Douglas."

"Oh," Connie said as if some of the enthusiasm seemed to have been drained from her. "Well in that case, if both of you will follow me, please." Connie led them into a small conference room. "Mr. Ferguson is on a call, but he knows you're here, and he'll be with you as soon as he's off," she said, closing the door behind her.

"What'd you think about that?" Carmen asked.

"About what?" Marcus replied, taking a seat at the table.

"That reception."

"Seemed like Connie was real glad to see you."

Carmen held up her hand. "Me and Connie aren't that tight."

"She did seem surprised that you were here with me, but that's to be expected. So relax, Carmen. There aren't bad guys around every corner."

"Maybe just around this one," Carmen commented as they made themselves comfortable in the conference room, where Roland kept them waiting until almost two-thirty. The door swung open, and Roland entered the room. "Marcus, how are you?" Roland said, stopping to shake his hand.

"I'm fine, sir. How are you?"

"Not bad for an old man. And Carmen, this is a surprise. When did you get in?"

"I got here Tuesday night. I came to give a deposition for your trial."

"I wish I had known that you were in town. You could have come by the house. I had a few friends over," Roland said as he took a seat at the conference table. "Carmen, I never did get a chance to tell you how sorry I am about Desireé. I know the two of you were very close."

"Thank you, Roland."

"You know, Carmen, sometimes I don't know if I can go on without her. There were times during the past year that I wished she were there to tell me that everything would be all right. That we'd get through this together, like we did everything else," Roland said sadly. "I don't really think anyone could understand that, Carmen. Except you."

"I do understand, Roland," Carmen said sincerely. "I've found myself thinking the same thing. I feel so alone without Dez."

Roland reached out his hand to Carmen. "I know that this might not be my place, but if you ever feel the need to talk, I hope we can be there for each other. We've both suffered such a terrible loss." Roland took off his glasses and placed his hand over his eyes.

"Some days it's harder to deal with than others." Carmen looked at Roland as he shed a few tears, and her attitude softened. She had come there that day prepared for an angry confrontation with the man responsible for her sister's death. She was going to tell him, point blank, that she knew that he killed Desireé and she would see him rot in hell for it. *But look at him*, Carmen thought. *He's hurting*. Marcus looked at Roland and then to Carmen, still holding hands; now both were crying.

"I'm sorry, Marcus," Roland said, wiping his eyes. He put his glasses back on. "Sorry if we embarrassed you."

"No need to apologize. Like you said, both of you have suffered a terrible loss. I should apologize for intruding."

Roland cleared his throat and dabbed his eyes with his handkerchief. "That's no reason for me to act unprofessionally; I mean, really, crying in front of my lawyer. So, tell me, what brings you two to see me? I wasn't aware that you two knew each other."

"Actually, we met only yesterday," Carmen said. "To be honest with you, Roland, I was very upset when my father told me that you were found not guilty. I was sure that you did it. I'd talked to the police and the DA and neither of them seemed to have any intention of pursuing this any further."

"Yes, I know. I spoke with Ms. Hawkins and Detective Benjamin yesterday, and I got the same impression." Roland paused. "Somebody killed Desireé and they don't care. You were right, Marcus—no high-profile trophy, no interest."

"It seems that way," Marcus said.

"I had an appointment to see Marcus, and after we talked about it, he agreed to look into it on my behalf."

"That's an excellent idea, Carmen. Since Marcus is intimately familiar with the details of the case, perhaps his investigator, what was his name?"

"Garrett Mason."

"Yes, yes, Mason. Perhaps he can uncover something that the police weren't able to. Well, Marcus, I want to help in any way that I can. And don't spare any expense; I'll gladly cover your fee. I just want some answers," Roland said, looking at Carmen. She nodded in agreement. "Tell me what I can do to help."

Carmen started to speak, but Marcus cut her off. "I just wanted you to know what I was doing. I didn't want you to feel like my working for Carmen was a conflict of interest."

"Nonsense. Finding Desireé's killer is my only interest."

"Can you think of anybody who may have wanted to kill Desireé? I know you've already talked to the police about this in your first interview, but that was almost a year ago. Maybe since that time you've remembered something."

"I can't think of a soul who would want to harm her. I've racked my brain, trying to think of a reason for anybody to do such a thing."

"How much do you know about Rasheed Damali?"

"Not much; he was a friend of Desireé's. I met him a few times, but I couldn't tell you much about him."

"Know anybody who might?"

"Not that I can think of. I'm sorry, I'm not much help, am I?"

"That's all right, Roland. I know this must be difficult for you to talk about. I think we've taken up enough of your time," Marcus said as he rose to his feet and nodded at Carmen.

"Sorry I wasn't much help. If you have any more questions, Marcus, please call me at home. We're all family here," Roland said as he got up to show them out. Since she was now the only one still sitting, Carmen got up too. "No need to be so formal."

"There is one more thing you can help us with. Carmen was looking at the case file, and she noticed that the police never talked to Desireé's friend Suzanne Collins." Carmen was confused by the way Marcus posed the question. He knew Suzanne was dead. "Carmen thought it was odd, seeing that they were best friends."

"You don't know. Carmen, Suzanne is dead. She died some time before Desireé did."

"No, Roland, I didn't know that. Dez never mentioned it to me," Carmen said, following Marcus's lead. "Which is strange, because you know we used to talk every day. Maybe we weren't as close as I thought."

"Desireé took Suzanne's death very badly. She practically threw the police out of the house when they told her about it. She didn't want to believe it. She was in denial about it. She wouldn't talk to me about it. I had to literally drag her to the funeral. So, please, Carmen, I can assure you that there was nobody closer to Desireé than you. She loved you so much. And she was so proud of you. So you get that thought out of your head," Roland said as they reached the elevator. Roland put his arms around Carmen.

"Thank you, Roland. You take care of yourself," Carmen said.

"Are you going back to Europe soon?"

"No. I'm thinking about staying here for a while," she said, and glanced at Marcus.

"Maybe we can have dinner some time," Roland said.

Carmen smiled. "I'd like that."

It was obvious to Marcus that Roland had touched Carmen's heart. He could see it in her eyes. They said nothing to each other until they reached the car. "Well, what did you think?" Carmen asked as they drove away.

"I don't know. I've never seen Roland so . . . so passionate."

"Are you kidding? That was vintage Roland. He was always very passionate about Dez."

"I'm not saying that he's not. I've just never seen him like that, is all I'm saying. I spent the better part of a year with the man, and this is new to me."

"You heard what he said, no reason to act unprofessionally, 'I mean, really, crying in front of your lawyer,'" Carmen mused.

"What did you think of his explanation about Suzanne?"

"That was vintage Dez." Carmen laughed a little. "I remember we used to have a dog named Mercedes. Dez loved that dog. He was part of the family. One day Mercedes got out of the house and got hit by a car. For months after that, Dez was in denial. She wouldn't admit the dog was dead. Every day she'd put food out for him. My father would have to come behind her and throw it away. She'd talk to Mercedes, and this went on for months."

"What brought her out of it?"

"My mother. Dez said she was goin' for a walk and called for Mercedes to come with her. I guess my mother had had enough. She yelled, 'Desireé Marie Taylor, if you say one more word to that dead dog, I'm taking you to a psychiatrist', and that did it. Dez never mentioned Mercedes again."

"Yeah, when your mama calls you by your full name, you know it's serious. What's your middle name, Carmen?"

"My middle name is Aneale. It's a family name. My grandfather's name was Neal. My mother's middle name is Aneale and so is mine."

"What's your mother's name?"

"Dominique. You'll meet her."

"Dominique. I like that name."

Carmen rolled her eyes and looked away. "So what do we

do now, Marcus?" she asked as they approached the connector.

"Not much to do until I hear from Garrett. So, after I drop you off, I was going to go home and take care of some unfinished business," Marcus said, thinking about having that long-overdue talk with Randa.

"Believe me, I can understand that. I have some things I need to put behind me too," Carmen mused, thinking about her mother. "But I'm not quite ready to do that just yet. So, since you're gonna drop me off"—Carmen frowned and rolled her eyes—"I guess I'll go back to my room and call some old friends. Maybe I'll try to find Porsche Temple."

"That sounds like a good idea. Call me later on tonight; hopefully I'll have heard from Garrett and we'll compare notes," Marcus said without taking note of Carmen's apparent disappointment with his plan for the evening. The cellphone rang. "This is Marcus Douglas."

"Marcus, this is Garrett. I got some information about Suzanne and Frank Collins. Meet me at your office and I'll lay it all out for you. Oh, and Marcus, is the client with you?" Garrett asked excitedly.

Marcus looked at Carmen while she stared aimlessly out the window. "Yes, she is."

Carmen glanced back at Marcus. "What?"

"You are gonna bring her with you, right?"

"I can be there in half an hour." Marcus smiled at Carmen, who was once again staring out the window. *She is beautiful,* Marcus thought.

"Yeah, yeah, I'll be there," Garrett said. "But you are gonna bring her?"

"Half hour it is, Garrett," Marcus said, then ended the call.

"What is it?" Carmen asked.

"Garrett has some information about Suzanne and Frank."

"What did he say?"

"He's gonna meet me in my office in half an hour."

"Oh," Carmen said in a manner that reflected her mood.

"You wanna hear what he has to say?"

"You know I do," Carmen said, and the life returned to her smile. Marcus smiled back at her, making a mental note of her change in mood. He attributed it to her enthusiasm about the case. Carmen watched as he got off at the next exit and headed for his office, totally unaware that she had her eye on him.

2 NO U

Marcus opened the car door for Carmen and extended his hand to her. She accepted and stepped out of the car. *His hands are so warm and soft,* Carmen thought for a moment. She stood in front of Marcus and looked in his eyes. "Thank you, Mr. Douglas," she said, finally releasing his hand.

"We're back to Mr. Douglas, huh?"

Carmen smiled. "No, I just like a gentleman, that's all."

"My father raised me to be a gentleman," Marcus said as they walked. "I had two older sisters, and my father required that I treat women with respect."

"A very wise man," Carmen flirted.

They entered the office, and the first person Marcus saw was Tiffanie Powers. "Marcus, can I talk to you for a minute, please?"

"Your office, five minutes," Marcus barked as he walked past her on his way to speak to Janise. "Is Garrett here yet?"

"Not yet."

"Let me know when he gets here."

Marcus led Carmen into his office and asked her to wait

there for him while he went to talk to Tiffanie. He knocked casually on her door as he walked in. Tiffanie jumped to her feet. "Sit down, Tiffanie. This won't take long."

"Marcus, I just wanna say—"

Marcus held up his hand to stop her. "Tiffanie, I'm not going to tell you what to do with your social life or try to tell you who you should be friends with."

"Marcus, I—"

"But, if I ever hear your name mentioned as the source of information about my personal life, I swear, Tiffanie, I will fire you. I don't care how good a trial lawyer you are."

"Marcus, I'm sorry—"

"Save it, Tiffanie," Marcus said as he turned to leave her office.

"Marcus, wait." Marcus turned around. "I want you to know that I'm sorry about this, and it won't happen again. Everything I am, I owe to you. You hired me right out of law school. You saw the lawyer in me that even I didn't know existed. I wasn't trying to get in your personal business, but when you disappeared for months, some of us were, you know, concerned, that's all. But Marcus, Randa really does love you. All she wants to do is talk."

"Thank you for being concerned, Tiffanie. By the way, watch your billing before somebody complains."

"I will, you can go to trial with that," Tiffanie said with a smile as she watched Marcus walk out of her office and rejoin Carmen. She was glad that she had seemingly dodged a bullet. When she arrived at the office that morning, she had been greeted by Janise. Who, Tiffanie noticed, seemed a bit more excited than usual to see her when she came in.

"Good morning, Janise," Tiffanie had said wearily.

Janise smiled and simply said, "You're fired. Your services are no longer required. Turn all of your work over to Simon."

"What?" Tiffanie dropped her briefcase.

"That's what Marcus told me to tell you."

"Are you serious?"

"That's what I asked him." Janise was enjoying it just a little too much. But she knew impact was important if she was going to make her point.

"What did he say?"

"He said that he hadn't decided yet. Then he said 'never-mind; I'll handle it myself,'" she mimicked, trying her best to sound like Marcus.

"Did he say why?"

"No. But I can tell you why. That is, if you really wanna know?"

"Of course I want to know. At least I'll be prepared, Janise. Tell me."

Janise looked around the office and motioned for Tiffanie to come closer. "You need to stay out of Marcus and Randa's business."

Tiffanie didn't think Marcus would fire her. But she couldn't be sure. As of today, Randa was cut off from any more information about Marcus. She had no doubt that Marcus would fire her if it happened again. Keeping Randa up on what color tie Marcus was wearing with which suit wasn't worth her future. Like everybody else, Tiffanie saw the possibilities that would open up as a result of the Ferguson case. She knew she was a good lawyer and was glad to hear that Marcus thought so too.

The wait wasn't long before Garrett came in the office all smiles and walked straight up to Carmen. He reached for her hand, bent slightly at the waist, and kissed it. Marcus shook his head and laughed quietly. "Ms. Taylor, my name is Garrett

Mason. It is an honor to meet such a beautiful woman. I'm just sorry that it has to be under these circumstances."

Carmen accepted the gesture in stride but looked at Marcus through the corner of her eye the entire time. "Well, thank you, Mr. Mason. It's a pleasure to meet you as well."

Garrett kissed her hand again.

"You two want me to leave and give you some time alone?" Marcus asked.

"No," Carmen said quickly, and louder than she needed to. Carmen eased her hand out of Garrett's. "That won't be necessary."

"Well in that case, Garrett, what you got for us?"

"Suzanne Collins, real estate agent, dealt exclusively in the residential properties starting at five hundred thousand. She worked out of a small office in Dunwoody. Just her and a secretary. According to the secretary, she left Suzanne working and when she came in the next morning, she found her, naked."

"Naked?" Marcus asked, unbuttoning his top shirt button and loosening his tie.

"That's what I said, naked, bent over, facedown at her desk. There were bruises all over her upper torso. And there was quite a bit of internal bleeding," Garrett stated, glancing at his notes.

"Was she raped?" Marcus asked.

"There was evidence of"—he paused and looked at Carmen—"of vaginal penetration, but there was no trauma associated with it, so it's believed that the sex was consensual. Rough sex that went too far, maybe."

"What was the cause of death?" Marcus asked.

"The internal bleeding."

"Wait a minute," Carmen said. "Her sister-in-law told us that they hadn't assigned a cause of death. That's supposedly the reason why Frank killed himself, because he was frustrated with the lack of progress in his wife's investigation."

"The reason the investigation was going so slowly was that her husband, Frank, wouldn't allow her body to be autopsied. After he died, her family gave the police permission to exhume the body and perform an autopsy. They're not calling it murder because there isn't enough physical evidence to support it. No sign of forced entry. No sign of a struggle, no skin under her nails or abrasions on her hands. Her clothes were folded neatly on a chair near the desk. So she was down for whatever was goin' on, at least the sex. They had no suspects, except Frank. They thought maybe Frank did it and that's why he wouldn't let them autopsy the body."

"What about him? What's his story?" Marcus asked.

"He was the interesting one. Old Frank worked for Hudson Financial Corporation as an account manager. The only other thing I can tell you was that they found his body laid out across his wife's grave with a thirty-eight slug in his head. And that it was ruled a suicide."

"What makes that so interesting, Garrett?" Marcus asked. He felt Carmen's eyes on him, but she looked away quickly when he turned to look at her.

"There were no records in the files. I talked to the detective assigned to the case, and even the notes he made were gone from his desk. When he asked his lieutenant about it, he got a polite 'I'll look into it'. I can follow up with him, see if he got curious enough to find the file on his own," Garrett said as his cell phone rang. "Garrett Mason." While he talked on the phone, Marcus and Carmen sat quietly looking at each other until Garrett got off the phone. "I gotta go, people. That was Jamara. She's got something to show me."

"Jamara Deneè, that's a pretty name," Marcus said, smiling. Carmen rolled her eyes and looked away. "I'm looking forward to meeting her one day."

"I'll be sure to tell her. Anything else you need me to do?"

"I know you got something else goin' on, but see what you can dig up on Rasheed Damali." Marcus glanced at Carmen. "Start looking into his relationship with Desireé."

"I'm on it," Garrett said, standing up to leave.

"We'll walk out with you," Marcus said, following Garrett out of the office. "Carmen, are you ready?"

Carmen gathered her things and followed them out to the parking lot.

"Good-bye, Ms. Taylor. I hope I get the chance to see you again," Garrett said, and once again kissed her hand.

"Bye, Garrett. I'm sure I'll see you again." Carmen smiled. Garrett got in his truck and drove off. Marcus opened the car door for Carmen; she thanked him and got in. Once Marcus put on his seat belt, Carmen said, "So, here we are again."

"Seems that way." Marcus nodded.

"I guess you'll be going to take care of your unfinished business now?"

"I guess, but I'm hungry," Marcus replied, and Carmen smiled in anticipation of an invitation. "I haven't had a thing to eat all day. I guess I'll stop and pick something up on the way."

"Hmm," Carmen mumbled. She was hoping he'd ask her to have dinner with him, and the disappointment was apparent in her voice. "You don't cook?"

"Not at all. Best I can do is boil water for hot dogs. What about you—can you cook?"

"I love to cook. I just don't get a chance to cook as often as I'd like to," Carmen said.

"Maybe you'll cook something for me before you leave."

"Maybe."

"What are you gonna do now?"

"You can take me back to my hotel; I'll find something to do."

Marcus picked up the tone of her voice. "Would you . . . maybe you could have dinner with me?"

"Well?" Carmen played it. "I haven't eaten since early this morning either. But I don't want to get in the way of you takin' care of your unfinished business."

"Believe me, I would much rather spend that time with you."

"Are you sure? 'Cause I don't wanna be a bother. I mean, you've been very nice to me, and I know you said you were going to take a vacation."

"Carmen, really. I want to."

"Okay." Carmen's eyes lit up. "You talked me into it. Where do you wanna go?"

"I don't know. Where do you wanna go?"

"You know where I haven't been in years?" Carmen paused. "The Sundial. It used to be one of my favorite places."

"That's one of my favorite places, too, so it's settled."

Marcus drove to the Plaza Hotel on Peachtree and International. The valet parked his car and went inside the hotel. "Wait a minute." Marcus stopped to button the top button on his shirt and adjust his tie.

"Here, let me do that," Carmen said. Marcus tried to stand completely still while he looked at Carmen as she fumbled beneath his chin. "There, pretty as a picture."

"Thank you, Carmen." Marcus stepped away nervously and headed for the glass elevator to the Sundial restaurant and lounge located on the seventy-second floor. The building was round with a revolving floor that allowed its patrons a beautiful and full aerial view of the entire city while they dined.

The hostess escorted them to a table, and shortly there-after their server arrived, took their drink and food orders, and blended discreetly into the background. Carmen turned to Marcus. "Do you think there's any connection between what Garrett told us about how Suzanne and Frank died and Dez?"

"Not really. What it sounds like is Suzanne was into whatever she was into, and it got out of hand. Frank fell apart when he found out about his wife and shot himself."

"But we really don't know that. There could be a whole lot more to it. Think about it, Marcus; the police tried to in-vestigate Suzanne's death, but Frank wouldn't let them au-topsy the body. I know Frank; he probably wasn't very cooperative. They tried to talk to Dez, and she throws them out. Then Frank kills himself; then Dez is killed, and they ar-rest Roland for her murder."

"I see where you're going with this," Marcus said. "So if there was more to Suzanne's death, the two people who could have told them anything were dead."

"Which leaves it right where it is, with the police not call-ing it murder and with them not having any suspects."

"Okay, so let's speculate," Marcus offered.

"Okay," Carmen said as their drinks were served.

"Let's start with Frank. Suppose he and Suzanne were having rough sex and as a result, Suzanne died. What con-nection does that have to Desireé?"

"Doesn't seem like any, but what if he didn't do it?" Carmen asked.

"All right, let's say Suzanne could have known whoever it was, since there were no signs of forced entry. Maybe she was seeing somebody else."

"Dez could have known who it was, and that would have given him a reason to kill her."

"That's true; it could have."

"Or it could be something that Frank was into."

"It could be, Carmen," Marcus said. "But how do we know it had anything to do with either of them? There's one possibility that you don't seem willing to entertain."

"What's that?" Carmen frowned.

"That it could be something your sister was into. Her killer might have been one of her other toys."

"But I think if something like that was going on, she'd tell me," Carmen said.

"How can you say that? Her best friend might have been murdered and she didn't tell you. She could have been in denial about that too."

"All right, Marcus, all right," Carmen said, loud enough to get the attention of the people at the next table, who glanced over at them. She took a sip of her Bacardi and thought that maybe there was a lot about Desireé that she didn't know. Although they talked every day, Carmen hadn't been to Atlanta in two years. Prior to that, her visits were infrequent. "I have to accept that maybe I didn't know her as well as I thought I did. It's just hard for me to do that."

"I'm glad you see that. Carmen, I know how important this is to you, but don't let it consume you. Believe me, that's something I know about," Marcus said quietly. "I allowed it to take over my life."

"You're not quitting on me, are you?"

"No, I'm just getting started and so are you. Tomorrow morning I'll go to Hudson Financial. Bill Hudson and I are members of the same health club. I'll try to find out what Frank was working on. What you have to do is get to know who your sister was. Find out the things about her that no one would tell the cops."

"I know somebody who might know where to find Porsche."

"That's a place to start. But you have to do more than that."

"Like what?" Carmen asked.

"Since you and Roland are all friendly and sharing pain, find out if he still has Desireé's stuff and go through it. See if you can find any kind of address or phone book. Talk to all of those people," Marcus suggested. "Did she ever send you any e-mail?"

"Yes, why?"

"If she's like everybody else, I'm sure she forwarded you jokes. See who they came from and who she sent things to. E-mail them and see what you can find out."

"I could tell them that I'm putting together a pictorial memorial and ask them to send me their memories of her."

"That's a great idea, Carmen."

"I was thinking about doing that anyway," Carmen said sadly. "I was going to use some of the pictures my father has of her."

"Do you know who her toys were?" Marcus asked.

"I think I remember some of their names, but I'm not sure. I'm not sure of anything about Dez anymore."

"Whatever you can remember would be helpful. You know, if you had been here, you could have been a big help in the investigation a year ago. Did you ever talk to the police?"

"No." Carmen sat back in her chair. Thinking that maybe if she hadn't left right after the funeral, the police would have talked to her. Maybe they would have looked into all the things Marcus had suggested. She took another sip of her drink and gazed out the window. "I just love the view from here," she said, sensing the need to back herself out of the topic at hand.

"Yes, the view is spectacular," Marcus said, looking at Carmen. *But the spectacular beauty here is you,* he wanted to say, but didn't. "On a clear night, you can see as far as Stone Mountain."

"I used to come here to think," Carmen said to him. "I'd sit here for hours, drinking Cokes and looking out at the city. This is the first time I've come here since I first left Atlanta. The skyline's changed a lot in ten years. I'd almost forgotten what a beautiful city this is."

"Why did you leave?"

Carmen looked down, avoiding eye contact with Marcus. "I needed to get away from here," she said, fiddling with her napkin. Then she looked at him. "To be honest with you, Marcus, I had a big fight with my mother."

"Over what?"

"It's a very long story. Nineteen years long, to tell the truth. So, to make a long story short, she was very hard on us. It wasn't abuse. She didn't beat us any more than she needed to or anything like that. And now that I'm older, I can see that she was just trying to give her daughters all the advantages that she never had. But at the time, she seemed like the meanest woman in the world. So the older I got, the more we'd bump heads."

"I'll bet the two of you are a lot alike."

"That's me, *Dominique's baby*," Carmen said playfully. "I thought that was my name for the longest time. When you meet her, you'll see. I look just like her. Same eyes, same smile, complexion, hair, all from her."

"Nothing from Daddy?"

"I have my father's height and his wonderful disposition." Carmen smiled brightly.

"You got along with your father a lot better."

"How could you tell?"

"The way your face lit up when you mentioned him," Marcus said, and smiled at Carmen.

"We were Daddy's girls. He was our sanctuary from Mom."

"So what did you and *Dominique* fall out about?"

"In my quest to do everything she told me I couldn't, I started hangin' out."

"Dominique doesn't seem like the type who would let you hang out."

"She wasn't. But me and Dez had it down to a science. By the time we got to high school, my mother stopped picking us up and driving us everywhere. But that was only after Daddy told her she was embarrassing us. Anyway, we were involved in every extracurricular activity there was. And that gave us a reason to be out of the house."

"What'd you do with that newfound freedom?"

"Get high. Me and my boyfriend. I had a thing for thugs back then. We smoked a lotta weed, drank a lotta rum," she said, raising her glass. "Sniffed a little coke sometimes. We went everywhere together. My mother couldn't stand him." Carmen looked at Marcus for a second or two before continuing. "So one Friday night we're hangin' out; I was in college at Spellman, living on campus when this happened. That night we didn't have any weed. So my boyfriend says he knows this guy, a friend of his uncle, and he always has weed. So we go to this guy's house, and we're sittin' around listening to music and gettin' high. As soon as we leave, the police arrest us."

"What for?"

"Turns out the guy was dealin'. So we go to jail and I call my mother. Well, of course, you know she loses it. She says, 'I oughta leave you there; it will teach you a lesson.' And she did; I spent the weekend in jail. I called my father at work on Monday, and he came and got me out. She never told him or Dez where I was. After that, things got worse between us, so I dropped out of school and moved to New York."

"That was kinda cold. Her leaving you in jail, I mean," Marcus said quickly.

"That's what we fell out about. Maybe I just need to forgive her so I can move on, because now I can see all the things she was trying to teach me. If I wanted to be honest with myself, I know I wouldn't have done half the things I've done, wouldn't have felt the need to graduate if it wasn't for her. She told us to get an education 'cause you couldn't live on your looks. But here I am, living on my looks. Seems like neither me nor Dez listened to that one," Carmen said sadly.

"I thought you said you dropped out of college?" Marcus asked.

"I went back a year later."

"What school did you go to?"

"Cornell University, bachelor of economics," Carmen said proudly.

"Impressive."

"Where'd you think I graduated from, the Barbizon School of Modeling?"

"Yes, I mean no. Well, I just . . . what I meant was . . ." Marcus stuttered and smiled.

Carmen smiled back. "Do I make you nervous, Marcus?"

"Very."

"Why?"

"It's your eyes, Carmen," Marcus said, and stared into her eyes.

"My eyes? What about my eyes makes you nervous?"

"I'm sure you know this, but you have very beautiful eyes. They're piercing."

"How do you mean, piercing?"

"It's like they cut right through me."

Carmen smiled playfully at Marcus and leaned toward him. "Does it hurt when I look at you?"

"No," Marcus answered nervously. "It's like your eyes

reach inside me and demand my undivided attention. You're beautiful, Carmen. I mean, look around us. Everywhere we've been, everybody is looking at you."

"That's because I'm a model."

"A supermodel, you mean."

"No, I'm not. I'm just a model."

"What's the difference?" Marcus asked.

"The difference is nobody knows my name. It gives me a certain anonymity, and I like it that way. They recognize me; I look familiar to them, 'cause they've seen me before. People stop me all the time and say they think they know me, but they just can't figure out from where."

"That's not it, Carmen, it's your eyes. Like they're speaking a language all of their own."

"My eyes do all that to you? Well," Carmen said, and began digging in her purse. She pulled out her sunglasses and put them on, "maybe this will help you feel more comfortable." She started weaving her head from side to side like Stevie Wonder while singing "Isn't She Lovely." Marcus laughed hard, almost to the point of tears. "Oh, so you do laugh."

"Yes, Stevie, I do, just not like this, and not in a long time," Marcus said, still laughing. Carmen took her shades off and returned them to her purse as the server arrived with their meal. Grilled Cervena venison loin for Carmen and fire-roasted rib eye of angus beef for Marcus.

"So why haven't you laughed like that in a long time?" Carmen asked, picking at her meal.

"I guess I haven't had anything to laugh about."

"And why is that?"

"I'm a workaholic."

"So am I," Carmen said. "But I still sneak in a good laugh every now and then."

"I know, you're right, Carmen, and all I can do is make

excuses for not having fun. And to be honest with you, I'm not having *any* fun. But I have been working on the case."

"The case is over, Marcus."

"It was until you came along."

"Oh, so I'm bothering you? Why didn't you just tell me? Oh yeah, it's my eyes, my piercing, demanding eyes." Carmen laughed. "Well, my eyes demand that you relax, be yourself. Don't be nervous around me. I promise I won't bite you. I only bite when the moon is full. Once you get to know me, you'll find out that I'm just people."

"That's what Garrett said."

"He's right. So get to know me, Marcus. And give me a chance to get to know you. Not Marcus Douglas the lawyer, but the real person."

From that point on, Marcus tried to relax, no longer intimidated by her beauty. Well maybe just a little. While they enjoyed their meal, they talked and got to know each other. Marcus did tell her that he was going through a divorce, yet he resisted the temptation to pour his heart out about it. Talking to Carmen caused him to realize that the only way he was going to move past it was to talk to Randa. *Maybe I just need to forgive Randa and move on.*

Listening to Marcus talk, Carmen knew he had passion. She felt it coming from him. For her part, Carmen let her guard down too. But she carefully steered the conversation away from Desireé or her family.

"So you're a workaholic, huh? What do you like to do?" Marcus asked.

"Work."

"Sensible answer, but it really doesn't speak to the question. So, I'll rephrase it. When you are not working, what does Carmen enjoy? Or is your life consumed with being Carmen Taylor the model?"

"Okay, since you put it that way, my favorite color is

black; my favorite food is shrimp, favorite dessert is cherry cheesecake. I enjoy reading the most. Going to the movies is a close second. I'm a romantic to the bone. I love being surrounded by scented candles and incense. I love taking long walks to nowhere in particular. I'm a sucker for interesting conversations, and I love going to plays. I also absolutely love the ballet, but I haven't been in quite a while. Is that a better answer?"

After dinner, they went upstairs to the lounge to listen to the Moses Davis Trio. The remainder of the evening was filled with music, cocktails, and lots of laughter and good conversation. Marcus found Carmen to be quite funny. Carmen still thought he was a little stiff, but she liked him. After years of dating fakes and flakes, Marcus was real people, and that to her was a good start. He eased his arm around her, and she accepted the gesture by laying her head on his shoulder. Marcus glanced down at Carmen and couldn't think of a better way to start his vacation.

When Marcus and Carmen left the plaza, they walked slowly back to the car. Talking and laughing, Carmen even gave Marcus a playful shove when he told her how bad her Stevie impression was. Marcus fought the urge to slide his hand into hers when it brushed up against his.

"I'm not ready to go back to the room yet. I'm having too good of a time," Carmen said.

"What do you want to do?"

"You know what else I haven't done in years, Marcus?"

"What's that, Carmen?"

"I haven't been dancing in years."

"Neither have I."

"Can you dance?"

"I used to go dancing all the time back in the day. At least five nights a week. I closed plenty of spots in those days."

"Really?" Carmen asked, not bothering to hide her disbelief.

"Yes, really."

"Somehow I find that hard to believe. I just can't picture you being a club king and dancing the night away."

"You'll see. I may not have been in a professional dance company, like some people, but I used to dance my ass off. You see I haven't got any left," Marcus joked, glancing down over his shoulder toward his behind.

Carmen laughed. "I don't know, Marcus. I think you still got a little ass. Emphasis on the word *little*, however," Carmen said with a smile as she got in the car. "But what's there is cute."

"Anyway," Marcus said, and closed the door. Once they were in the car and away, he asked, "What kind of music do you like?"

"I don't care; you pick the place. I chose the restaurant."

"Do you like reggae?"

"Me like reggae music, mán," Carmen replied, knowing that her West Indian accent was much better than her Stevie impression. "It make me wánt to dance all night, ya know."

"Good. I know a place," Marcus said, and drove Carmen to Dan Starks in Decatur, where they danced until they could hardly stand up. After which he took Carmen back to her hotel and saw her safely to her room.

"Good night, Marcus." She kissed him on the cheek. "I enjoyed our day together."

"I did too. We'll have to do more of this."

"I'm sure we will." Carmen kissed him on the other cheek. "I'll call you tomorrow."

Marcus watched, almost breathlessly, as Carmen unlocked her door and disappeared inside. He left there hoping that it was more than just a friendly kiss.

OLD LOVES

Although it was well past three in the morning when she kissed Marcus good night, Carmen was up at seven to begin her daily routine. While she put in her time on the treadmill, Carmen thought about her agenda for the day and a lot about Marcus. When she got back to her room, Carmen picked up the remote, flipped on the television, and called room service to order breakfast. While she ate, she watched the local news to catch the weather report. It was overcast outside, and it looked like it was going to rain. The lead story was about the death of an FTC investigator, John Heard. He was found by his wife at his desk in his home office. His death was ruled a suicide after ingesting sleeping pills and vodka. *Maybe he found out something about his wife too,* Carmen thought. She gave some thought to what Marcus had said about Frank and Suzanne Collins's deaths being just what the police considered it, rough sex gone terribly wrong. Maybe she was looking for something that simply wasn't there. She would have to come to grips with the idea that exploring her sister's lifestyle could be the only thing that would lead her and Marcus to the killer. *And what if it does lead me to the killer—what am I going to do then?* Carmen turned off the television and got in the shower.

The first thing on her list was to call Roland to see if he still had Desireé's things. "Ferguson residence," Melissa, the housekeeper, answered.

"Good morning, Melissa, this is Carmen Taylor. How are you?"

"I'm fine, Ms. Taylor. Mr. Ferguson said you were in town. Hold on a minute; he's right here," she said, and handed the phone to Roland.

"Good morning, Carmen. You just caught me walking out the door; I was on my way to the club," Roland said, and went toward the door.

"Well, I don't want to keep you. I had a question, a request, really."

"What is it?"

"This may sound strange, but I was wondering if you still had any of my sister's things?"

"I still have all her things," Roland said as he sat down in a chair by the door. "I just couldn't bring myself to go through them. Why do you ask?"

"I've been really feelin' Dez since we talked yesterday, and I thought it might, you know . . ."

"You thought it might make you feel closer to Desireé. Carmen, I understand completely. You are more than welcome to come here anytime. Like I said, I'm on my way out, but I'll tell Melissa to let you have the run of the house."

"Thank you, Roland. This really means a lot to me. There's one more thing. I was thinking about making a pictorial memorial to her, and I'd appreciate your input."

"Of course, Carmen, I'd be honored, but I really do have to run. If you're still here around four, we can have dinner together and talk about it."

"I was going to my parents' tonight," Carmen lied. "But we'll get together soon."

With that out of the way, Carmen devoted her attention to finding Porsche Temple. To accomplish this, she would have to find Denny Barnes. If anybody could find Porsche, it was Denny. He was Carmen's first real boyfriend, her first love.

They met one afternoon while she was shopping at the Underground with her mother. Denny saw Carmen and tried to approach her, but Dominique ran him off. So Denny followed Carmen until she was out of her mother's sight and then he slipped her his number. Carmen called him as soon as she got home. They were so very different. Carmen, a straight-A student. Denny never went to school. Denny was well on his way to being a weed-smokin', gun-totin' thug. He showed her a side of life she'd only heard about. He was a member of a gang, he smoked, he drank, but in spite of what Denny was, he was in love with Carmen, and she loved him. When it began, Carmen saw it as a way to rebel against her mother's control. Dominique despised Denny and all he represented. Denny was exactly the type of boy she'd tried to keep her daughters away from. They went together from tenth grade until Carmen dropped out of Spellman and moved to New York. Seeing "Denny Boo," (as she called him,) was always, if nothing else, interesting.

Finding Denny would be easy. It was just a simple matter of calling his mother and asking. Mrs. Barnes had become a second mother to Carmen during the years when Carmen's relationship with Dominique was strained. Carmen dialed the number, amazed that she still remembered it after all these years.

"Good morning," Mrs. Barnes answered.

"Good morning, Mrs. Barnes, this is Carmen. How are you?"

"I could complain, Carmen, but ain't nobody wanna hear about my bad back. They just wanna tell me about their arthritis."

"Well, now that you mention it," Carmen said in a frail-sounding voice, "my arthritis has been givin' me trouble here lately."

"Stop it, girl. You still crazy. How you been, Carmen?"

"Well, my big toe swelled up this morning, so I know it's gon' rain today." Carmen laughed. "Let me stop before you hang up on me."

"And you know I will if you get to actin' silly."

"I'm doing fine, Mrs. Barnes, but is your back really hurtin' you?"

"No more than it did yesterday and no more than it did the day before that. But it's nice of you to ask, and it's so nice of you to call. Are you in town?"

"Yes, I got in on Tuesday."

"Well, you make sure that you stop by here before you run back out of town."

"Actually, I was thinking about staying a while. I'll try to get by there this week, but I need a favor."

"Denny's new cell phone number is 678-555-7543. That is what you wanted, ain't it?"

"You know me too well, Mrs. Barnes."

"Well, if you do move back here, maybe you could talk Denny into gettin' a real job."

"Still livin' that thug life, huh?"

"How they say it, he thugged out."

Carmen couldn't help but laugh. "I'll try, Mrs. Barnes, but you know Denny don't listen to nobody but Denny."

"You just talk to him; he'll listen to you. Now let me go, Carmen. My show fixin' to come on. You come see me now."

"Maybe I'll get Denny to bring me by on Sunday for dinner."

"That'll be the day."

"Bye, Mrs. Barnes," Carmen said, and hung up. She dialed Denny's number.

"Hello." Denny answered.

"What's up, Denny Boo?"

"Ain't but one person call me Denny Boo. What's up, Carmen? You in town? Let me come scoop you up, take you to lunch."

"Which question you want me to answer?"

"All of 'em!"

"Well, let me see." Carmen paused. "I'm fine. Yes, I'm in town, staying at the airport Marriott. And no, you can't come scoop me up."

"Why not?"

"I have a lot to do today."

"You know you'd have a better time hangin' out with me. Remember the last time you was here? We had a good time, right?"

"Yes, we did," Carmen replied. "And I never did thank you for showing me such a good time. You were the perfect gentleman."

"Gentleman? Only to you and don't tell nobody 'bout it either. It's bad for my rep."

"Your secret's safe with me, Denny Boo. But there's a price for my silence."

"Anything you need."

"I need to find Porsche Temple. Do you know where to find her?"

"What you want with that skank trick?" Denny asked.

"I'm trying to talk with some of Dez's friends."

"Yo, Carmen, I never did say how sorry I was about Dez. The way you bounced in just for the funeral and back out of town, didn't hardly nobody have a chance to say nothing to you. But I understood that; you and Dez was tight. I know you were trippin'. And knowing you, you probably tried to bury yourself in work."

"That's exactly right."

"Do I still know my Baby Carm, or what?"

"So, do you know where to find her, Denny Boo?"

"She was trickin' for this guy named James Martin."

"Porsche's a prostitute?" Carmen asked in shock.

"Can't everybody be a big-time model or marry no rich man, like you and Dez. Somebody gotta be a ho. But she was a high-price ho, if that makes a difference. She was doin' a little runnin' too."

"Runnin'?"

"Drug runnin', baby. Once a month, her and Martin used to drive to Miami, pick up their shit, and come back. But all that ended when Martin got killed in a car jackin'. I ain't seen Porsche in a while. Let me see if any of these niggas know where to find her. Hold on, Carmen." Carmen held while she thought about Porsche running drugs and turning tricks. Denny returned to the line. "Don't nobody know where she live at. But you can find her at either Goose Bumps or Pleasers. She got girls shake dancin' at both them spots."

"So she's not a drug-runnin' prostitute anymore; now she's a pimp."

"Yeah, whatever," Denny said. "When I'ma get to see you?"

"When was the last time you had Sunday dinner with your mother?"

"I couldn't tell you the last time. Why?"

"'Cause your gonna take me there. I promised her that I would come and see her."

"No can do, Carm. Goin' to DC for a few days."

"I'll let you off this time. But call me when you get back. Maybe I'll let you come scoop me up and feed me when you get back."

"A'ight." And with that, Denny hung up. Carmen took a deep breath and proceeded to get ready to go to Roland's house. She grabbed the biggest purse she had and was out the door. When she arrived at Roland's house, a cold chill came over her as she drove up the long driveway to the house. She thought she saw Desireé standing in the doorway, waving as she did on Carmen's visits to the house. As she got closer, Carmen could see that it was Melissa, the house-keeper, who had been with Roland for fifteen years. Melissa was a black woman, forty-six years old, but you couldn't tell it by looking at her. She looked like a woman in her early thirties, late twenties maybe, but that was stretching it.

When Desireé and Roland were first married, Desireé thought that there was something going on between them. But in time, she told Carmen that nothing could be further from the truth. Carmen got out of her car and walked toward the house as the rain began to fall. Melissa gave Carmen a little hug and rushed her into the house and out of the rain. After chastising Carmen for not having an umbrella or any-thing to cover her head, Melissa showed her to Desireé's room. Carmen walked into the room and was taken aback immediately by how much the room looked like Desireé's room at their parents' house. She stopped and looked around. "This is their bedroom?"

"No, Ms. Taylor. Mrs. Ferguson preferred to sleep alone sometimes, and besides," Melissa said as she walked to the closet and opened it, "she needed the closet space." Melissa

walked up to Carmen and stopped right in front of her,
closer than Carmen was comfortable with. Melissa smiled at
her in a way that made Carmen uncomfortable. "Make yourself comfortable; stay as long as you want. If you need me,
just use the intercom," she said, pointing to the device on the
wall. "Will you still be here at four, Ms. Taylor? I'm preparing uccelli scappati for Mr. Ferguson. He was hoping you
would join him."

"No, I'll probably just be here an hour or so," Carmen
replied as Melissa started to leave the room. "By the way,
what is uccelli scappati?"

"It's broiled veal and bacon on a skewer with a pinch of
rosemary, served with gravy," Melissa answered as she left
Carmen alone.

"Oh, with a pinch of rosemary," Carmen said with attitude. "Like I should know what uccelli scappati is," she said,
shaking her head and locking the bedroom door. Carmen
first walked into her sister's closet. It was like looking at
racks at Saks Fifth Avenue. She touched a few things, then
came out of the closet and sat down on the bed. That's when
she saw them. Standing on the dresser were three framed
pictures, each of her and Desireé. The first was of them at
the pool in the backyard as kids. Carmen remembered that
right after the picture was taken, Desireé pushed her into the
deep end of the pool and she almost drowned. The second
was taken before they went to their first debutante ball. The
night of her first kiss. Her eyes began to water as Carmen
picked up the third picture. It was taken on her last trip to
Atlanta. That was the last time Carmen saw Desireé.

She cried.

Maybe this isn't such a good idea, she thought, wiping
the tears from her eyes. *I need to find what I'm looking for
and get out of here.*

Carmen opened the dresser drawer and went through it. In the back of the bottom drawer, Carmen found a stack of letters Desireé had banded together. She put them in her bag and moved on to the desk in the corner of the room by the French doors.

Carmen opened the doors so she could hear the rain come down while she waited for the computer to boot up. She liked listening to the rain. It made her feel at peace with herself, and she needed peace as she rifled through the desk drawers. Carmen found Desireé's phone book and flipped through it before putting it in her bag. When the computer prompted her for a password, Carmen slumped down in the chair. She tried Desireé's birthday; that didn't work. Since their old address was her password, she tried that; no joy.

Come on, Dez, what's your password?

Carmen sat back and sat up just as quickly. Carmen typed *mercedes* on the keyboard. The desktop icons began to pop up.

Thanks, Dez. Carmen rambled through her purse, pulled out a thumb drive, and plugged it into the USB port on the tower. Carmen logged into Desireé's e-mail and forwarded all the mail in Desireé's in-box to herself. She would read them all later. She clicked on START, DOCUMENTS and looked at the last fifteen files Desireé had opened. They were all Word documents. Carmen began copying the files in her document folder to the thumb drive, then opened the first document. It was a letter to Roland, telling him that she was going to meet India to see a play and have drinks and that she would be home after one. Carmen checked the file's properties; it was created, modified, accessed, and printed two days before Desireé was murdered. Then Carmen noticed a file named "Hi big Sis.doc." She opened it.

It read:

From inside the soul of
Desireé Taylor Ferguson

Hi, big sis,

I bet you're surprised to be reading a letter from Desireé Marie Taylor, when you talk to her every day, but I wanted to tell you about some things that have been on my mind, things I don't get a chance to say or can't say because I'm not always alone when we talk. Especially since you're in Europe and we talk at such weird hours. But the main thing I want to tell you is that I miss you. I understand why you live where you live. Your mother is a trip, but I miss my best friend, the only real friend I ever had. Everybody around me is so phony to the point that they make me feel phony. I don't love and my so-called friends just use me for money and my body. But you know there's nothing new or unusual about that.

I need you, Carmen. I need your strength. I need Carmen the sneak. ☺ There's so much I have to tell you, about me and about what's going on around here these days. I think somebody is

The letter ended there. Carmen quickly checked the properties; it was created, modified, and accessed at 6:47 P.M. on the day Desireé was murdered. Carmen closed the document and glanced over at the pictures on the dresser.

You were trying to tell me.

Carmen fought the urge to cry again and took the drive from the port, turned the computer off, and left the room. She ran down the steps as fast as she could in heels and a tight skirt, and ran right into Melissa.

"I didn't think you'd be up there long. When my sister died and I had to go through her stuff, it took me a month and I cried every time," she said, walking Carmen to the door. "But you come back any time you want to. Take all the time you need."

It was still raining quite hard when Melissa opened the door. She handed Carmen an umbrella and a matching scarf. "Take these; they were Mrs. Ferguson's favorite. She wouldn't want you to get wet."

"Thank you," Carmen said, and was crying before she could finish tying the scarf. Melissa hugged Carmen and kissed her on the cheek. She ran to her car and sat there for a while.

Once she pulled herself together, she made the drive back to her hotel. Carmen broke out her laptop and logged onto the Internet. She made a mailing list of the people who sent Desireé e-mail and named it "friends of Desireé Ferguson."

To: friends of Desireé Ferguson
From: Carmen Taylor <carmentaylor@carmen taylor. com>
Subject: Remembering Desireé Ferguson
Hello friends,
I am Carmen Taylor; Desireé Ferguson was my sister. I recently saw some of the pictures that my father had taken of Desireé and I thought his pictures were an excellent tribute to her. But pictures need words. In the coming months I will begin compiling a pictorial memoir to my sister. If any of you, her friends, would like to contribute some memory of Desireé, a story, a poem, kind words, or a picture you'd like to contribute, please e-mail me. It is my desire to create something that is simply Desireé. So keep it real.
Carmen Taylor

With that out of the way, Carmen flipped through the pages of Desireé's phone book. *Axle Grant, Robert Pettibone, Ira Stinson, I remember those names.*

Carmen lay across her bed and began to read the mail that she took from her sister's drawer and the files she'd copied from her computer. By a quarter to four, it had stopped raining and Carmen was tired of reading and tired of being cooped up in that room. She hated living out of her suitcase, and she was beginning to miss cooking for herself. She decided to look for someplace to move to.

A furnished one bedroom, maybe.

Carmen picked up the paper and headed for the door. She would look through the classified section once she was out of the room. She opened the door. "Hello, Carmen," Dominique said, standing in the doorway. "I was just about to knock."

"What are you doing here, Mother?"

"I knew you wouldn't come to see me. Can I come in?"

"No, Mother, you can't come in. I was just about to leave. I can't spend another minute in here," Carmen said, closing the door. She gently pushed past Dominique and began walking down the hall. "I was about to go hunt for a furnished one bedroom." Carmen stopped and turned to face Dominique. *Maybe I just need to forgive her and move on.* "Why don't you come with me, Mother? You always did have good taste."

"I would be honored, Carmen," Dominique said. Her face lit up the hallway.

"Good. You drive."

"You still don't like driving, do you?"

"I hate it, Mother. And traffic has gotten so bad here. I don't know how you stand it."

"Like everything else, you get conditioned to conditions."

Once they were in Dominique's car, Carmen looked at the ads for furnished condos.

"Here's one: Virginia Highlands, fully furnished, one bedroom with a den, one bath. 'AVAILABLE IMMEDIATELY,' it says in capital letters. I guess that was to get my attention. Maybe the owner will be motivated enough to do a week to week."

"Why do you need a condo?"

"I may be here for a while."

"You know you can always stay at the house. Your father and I would love to have you."

"Mother, I need my space, and I like my privacy."

"I didn't come here to argue with you. It's just an offer. You can stay there until you find something."

"Thank you, Mother," Carmen said, realizing she was getting defensive.

"And you need to start calling me Dominique. Every time you call me 'Mother,' it makes my flesh crawl. It's like you hate me."

"I think that's why I started doing it."

Dominique smiled at Carmen. "I was hoping that if you called me Dominique, maybe we could start over and maybe we could become friends."

"I'd like to try, Dominique. But I need to talk to my mommy one more time first. I want you to know that I'm sorry for all the pain I've caused everybody. And to thank you, Mommy, for all that you tried to do for me."

Dominique's eyes began to water. "Thank you for saying that, Carmen. It means a lot just to hear you say that."

Carmen was silent for a few seconds before she spoke again. "I talked to Denny today."

Dominique sucked her teeth. "How is he?"

"Still doing the same thing. You did the right thing leaving me there."

"I am sorry about that, Carmen. I never meant to drive you away."

"It was the right thing to do, even if it didn't seem that way at the time. I had to get away from Denny. You were right all along, about everything. But I was just too young and naïve to see it. Everything I know that matters, I learned from you or I know because of you, Mommy."

CARPE DIEM!

Marcus parked his car in the visitors parking area and ran to get out of the rain. He shook the rain off his jacket and proceeded to the reception area. "Good afternoon, my name is Marcus Douglas, and I'd like to see Bill Hudson," Marcus said to the receptionist, and handed her his card.

"Do you have an appointment?"

"No, I'm an acquaintance of his, and I'd like to speak with him. I won't take up much of his time."

"Would you mind having a seat, please?" she said to Marcus, and smiled flirtatiously. Marcus winked back and sat in the waiting area. It wasn't long before she called him back to the desk. "Mr. Douglas, Mr. Hudson is out of town, so if it's all right, Mondrya Foster is going to talk to you."

"And who is Mondrya Foster?" Marcus asked, leaning on the counter.

"She is executive vice president of operations for Hudson Financial," a female voice said from behind Marcus. He turned around and smiled at her as she continued. "Her major duties include maintaining domestic and international sales, and managing sales forecasts and the sales pipeline, provid ing monthly updates to the CEO and CFO," she said, and ex tended her hand. "Hi, I'm Mondrya Foster."

"Marcus Douglas. It's a pleasure to meet you, Ms. Foster," he said, and accepted her hand.

"I'm sure Doris has told you, Mr. Hudson is out of town So is there anything that I can help you with?"

"I'm sure that you can," Marcus said, and smiled a Mondrya.

"If you'll follow me, then. I'll give you the fifty-cent tou on the way to my office."

"Please, lead the way."

"Hudson Financial is an international, full-service finan cial firm, which provides brokerage, investment banking and asset management services to corporations and individ uals around the world. Our core services include sales, re search, and trading for individuals and institutions. We provide underwriting, advisory and specialty financing fo corporations, mutual-fund services, futures, and asset man agement. We offer clients a full range of investment prod ucts, including stocks, bonds, mutual funds, CDs, insuranc and annuities, and services such as advice on retiremen planning, asset allocation, portfolio management, and othe services for affluent investors," Mondrya explained as she led Marcus into her office. He gave an appreciative nod on her summary of the business. Once she was seated, she asked, "What can I do to help you today, Mr. Douglas?"

"Ms. Foster, I'm an acquaintance of Mr. Hudson. Actually we go to the same club, and I wanted his help with some thing."

"Is it something that I could help you with?"

"You had an employee who committed suicide recently."

"Two, actually," Mondrya said quickly.

"I'm sorry?"

"We've had two employees commit suicide recently. Coleman Wilson, one of our senior executives, and Frank Collins, one of our account managers."

"I wanted to ask about Frank Collins. As you probably know, I represent the interests of Mr. Roland Ferguson. At the request of Mr. Ferguson and Carmen Taylor, the victim's sister, my staff and I are now conducting an independent investigation into Mrs. Ferguson's death."

"I see. What can I do to help? And what does it have to do with Frank?"

"Mr. Collins's wife, Suzanne, was a close friend of Mrs. Ferguson."

"It was a shame about the two of them. They were very nice people."

"Did you know them personally, Ms. Foster?"

"Mondrya, please, and yes, before my promotion, I was Frank's group manager. I'd met his wife several times. I may have even met Mrs. Ferguson at one of Suzanne's parties, but I can't say for sure."

"Do you mind if I ask you a few questions?"

"No, not at all," Mondrya said, taking out a pad and pen. "Do you mind if I take notes?"

"Not at all." Marcus smiled. "What did Mr. Collins do here?"

"Frank worked as an account manager. Our account managers work closely with clients to develop a customized plan that meets their long-term financial goals and objectives. They offer exclusive access to products and an array of quality financial products and services."

"Was he still reporting to you at the time of his death?"

"I was already in a new position by that time. And if I remember correctly, that happened when Frank was transitioning to a new role himself. So he would have made a direct report to Mr. Hudson."

"What was his new position?"

Mondrya turned to her computer and clicked a few times. "To develop and execute plans to integrate software and Internet-based technologies into our services. Recruit, hire, lead, and perform staff evaluations. Measure and report on key initiatives; use data to identify and implement improvements. Achieve commitments: revenue, productivity, service quality, net income."

"Impressive. All that information."

"It's the secret of my success, availability of information," Mondrya said, and smiled. "When I started here fifteen years ago, right out of college, I was just a skinny black girl with a degree in finance. They hired me as a receptionist, and I made my way from there."

"Receptionist to VP."

"There were some stops along the way: analyst, financial planner, group manager." She shrugged as if her accomplishments were no big deal.

"But there was a time when Mr. Collins did report to you?"

"Yes. We have two teams of about eighteen members a piece, each under the leadership of a group manager, and each managing portfolios with credit lines up to ten million dollars."

"Mr. Collins managed portfolios like that?"

"For as many as twenty clients."

"Any problems you know of?"

"Frank was doing an excellent job; all of his clients were pleased. And he had some hard-to-please clients." Mondrya paused and looked at Marcus. "That's why he was promoted."

"How long was this before his wife died?"

"Two weeks, maybe. After that he went to pieces. It was sad to watch a friend go through that."

"Did he talk much about the details of his wife's death?"

"He didn't; there were a lot of rumors, but there always are."

"Like what?"

"Like he raped and killed her himself or that she was having an affair with—" The phone rang. "Excuse me, Mr. Douglas; my husband," Mondrya said, and turned away. "Instruct our broker to execute that order as quickly as possible at the best price available," she said, and hung up the phone. "I just love it when he calls for investment advice."

"This your family?" Marcus asked, picking up the picture frame from her desk.

"Yes, those are my two sons, Zaviere and Keenan. Zavi is seventeen and Keenan is twelve. That's my husband, Amar. Handling them is truly a labor of love."

"I'm sure that you handle them in the same manner you do your career."

"I wish. With this new project, I barely have time to sleep."

"What are you working on, if you don't mind me asking, Mondrya. And by the way, that's a very pretty name."

"Thank you, Marcus. And no, I don't mind telling you. My current project is to develop and implement strategic and tactical plans to offer and deliver services to small and middle-market businesses. Develop, close, and integrate business and portfolio acquisitions. And in addition, I have to develop and implement distribution using multiple channels."

"How do you plan to accomplish all that?"

"Through direct sales, direct marketing, Internet, alliances. It won't be hard. But it will be time-consuming."

"You have to learn to rule the day or the day will rule you. I try to rule every day."

"Carpe diem," she said with a smile.

"Excuse me, what does that mean?"

"*Carpe diem* is Latin. It means seize the day."

"Thank you for the translation. Are you fluent in Latin?"

"No, that's the only Latin I know," Mondrya said, and her phone rang again. "Excuse me again, Marcus. Mondrya Foster." While Mondrya talked, Marcus concluded that he had gotten all the information from her that there was to get. "Good, Gloria, I'll see you next Monday night at Starbucks. Six is good for me," Mondrya said, ending the call; then she turned her attention back to Marcus. "I'm sorry, Marcus, lawyer this time."

"I know how annoying those lawyers can be, so I won't take up any more of your time."

"I hope I was able to help you, but somehow I don't think I was."

"What makes you say that?"

"You're looking for, fishing really, for some connection between what happened to Frank and his wife and Mrs. Ferguson's murder."

"You've given me some interesting information."

"Interesting, maybe. But nothing I've told you, and I think I've told you quite a bit, would seem to be of interest to you. It might be if you were investigating Frank and Suzanne."

Marcus smiled and got up from his chair. "But it was still a pleasure talking with you, Mondrya."

"It was a pleasure talking with you as well, Marcus. And feel free to talk with anyone else you like. Just coordinate the interviews with the receptionist."

"I don't think that will be necessary. You've told me what I needed to know. If I have any more questions, can I call on you again?"

"Please do, and when you see Mr. Ferguson, tell him I said hello and that I wish him well. He probably won't re-member me."

Marcus sat down. "You know Roland Ferguson?"

"Yes, I worked very closely with him during the time of the merger."

"Merger? What merger?"

"There was a proposed merger between Hudson Financial and Atlanta Life. But the deal fell apart at the last minute. We had the press release all ready to go and everything."

"Who backed away from the table?" Marcus asked.

"Ferguson."

"What would be gained by such a merger?"

"The stock holders wanted to know that too. Wait a minute, you can read all about it. I still have the press release that never went out." Mondrya printed a copy and handed it to him. Marcus read the date. January 1995. *Desireé was still in high school, no connection there.* "I don't think you'll find anything you can use in that document. I would have given it to you sooner if I thought it was important."

"Do you mind if I keep this anyway?" Marcus asked, rising to his feet again.

"Be my guest." Mondrya shrugged.

"Mondrya, it's been a pleasure talking with you."

"Likewise, Mr. Douglas."

"Marcus, please."

"You know, I may not have been any help to you, but when I sit and think about it, there are some things I may be able to look into. If I get something you can use, I'll call you."

"That is more than I could have hoped for," Marcus said, smiling as Mondrya escorted him out of the office.

By the time Marcus left the building, the rain had stopped. He got to his car and tried to call Carmen, but she wasn't in her hotel room. His next stop was the library. Armed with the press release he'd gotten from Mondrya, Marcus went to check to see if Desireé's death began in January of 1995. He checked the microfiche of the *Atlanta Journal Constitution* for information on the merger. He cross referenced Roland Ferguson and Bill Hudson. Marcus found a story dated July 1993: PROPOSED MERGER BRINGS NEW CAPITAL TO STRUGGLING BROKERAGE. The story detailed a list of ill-advised moves and bad investments made by Hudson Financial during the mid-1980s. The article went on to say that the influx of much-needed capital was the only thing that market analysts predicted would save the cash-strapped brokerage. Another dated December, 1994: ATLANTA LIFE, HUDSON FINANCIAL MERGER DEAD IN WATER. That article quoted unnamed sources as saying that Roland Ferguson pulled out of the deal at the eleventh hour. It quoted Roland as saying, "There's something rotten at Hudson Financial." When asked to elaborate, Roland declined to comment, then later denied making any such comment, offhanded or not.

Marcus tried to call Carmen again, and once again got no answer. He wondered what it was that made Roland pull out at the last minute. Could Mondrya have known why he pulled out and not mentioned it? *Why not ask her?* Marcus thought as he left the library. He got out her card and dialed. "Mondrya Foster, please."

"I'll connect you; one moment, please."

"Mondrya Foster."

"Ms. Foster, Marcus Douglas."

"That didn't take you long, Marcus," Mondrya said to him. "I've got somebody on the other line. Can you hold?"

"Sure." Marcus's mind wandered back to Carmen. Where was she, and what was she doing?

"Marcus, thanks for holding. So, twice in one day, huh? To what do I owe the honor?"

"I was wondering if you knew why Ferguson pulled out of the merger at the last minute."

"That was a long time ago, Marcus. I was still an analyst

then. High-level information like that would have never fil-
tered down to my level."

"But you had to be one of the top analysts to get pulled
into a project team like that."

"You're right, I was one of the top analysts."

"I know it's been a while, Mondrya, but try to remember—did any of the project team members find anything that
may have caused Ferguson to pull out?"

"I just don't remember, Marcus. And besides, Ferguson
had his own team of analysts that he brought in to work with
us. We used to call them the analyst analysts, because all
they did was go over our work." Mondrya laughed. "I haven't
thought about that for a long time. It's funny how your mind
works. Give me a day or two to see what else I can remember."

"Why don't we get together for lunch on Tuesday to talk
about it?"

"That sounds like a real plan to me. A very strategic and
tactical plan, if I might add. And I should know, being a
strategic and tactical planner."

Marcus laughed a little. "What makes you say that?"

"You, my dear Marcus, are looking for an ally here. So
you get me interested in what you're doing, without actually
knowing what you're doing, and let my natural curiosity take
over. You'll need to hear what I have to say, and I'm more
likely to speak freely in a comfortable environment, away
from the office. Where you'll ply me with good food and al-
cohol. I was a psychology major before I switched to finance."

"Ms. Foster, you're beginning to interest me," Marcus said.

"I'm sure my husband won't be as flattered by that as I
am. But tell me something, Marcus."

"What's that?"

"How do you know you can trust me?"

"Because, trust isn't the real issue here. If there is something going on, your telling somebody that I'm investigating this will draw whoever or whatever out of the closet."

"Well, for reasons of my own, I'll meet you at eleven-thirty on Tuesday." She paused slightly, but spoke again before he could respond. "On second thought, why don't you pick me up here and we'll go to O'Charley's at Crescent Centre."

"I'll be there. I'm looking forward to seeing you again, Mondrya."

"Something else my husband won't be flattered about. We'll talk on Tuesday; good-bye, Marcus."

Marcus dialed Carmen's number again and still got no answer. He started his car and drove out of the library parking lot. He thought for a minute about who would know why Ferguson pulled out, then dialed his phone. "Connie Talbert."

"Good afternoon, Connie. This is Marcus Douglas."

"How are you, Mr. Douglas?"

"I was wondering, how long have you worked as Mr. Ferguson's assistant?"

"Eighteen years this October."

"Then you knew the first Mrs. Ferguson?"

"Yes, I did. But if you're thinking that Janet had something to do with this, forget it. Janet lives in Nairobi, happy as a clam to be where she is, with what she has. She did very well in the divorce."

"Thanks, Connie; just kickin' around some options," Marcus lied. He knew where the first Mrs. Ferguson was and what she left with. As he drove, Marcus tried Carmen again. Still no joy. He hung up and punched in another number; it was well past six in the evening. He hoped she hadn't gone for the day. "Mondrya Foster."

"Mondrya, it's Marcus again."

"Are you trying to tell me something, Marcus?"

"No, Mondrya, I'm not trying to tell you anything. Although you are a very beautiful woman, you're a very beautiful married woman. And I have nothing but respect for that. But I didn't call to flatter you, not this time. I was wondering if one of the analysts analyst was named Connie Talbert?"

"Yes, Lord, she was the analyst analysts analyst. Always looking over everybody's work. She used to get on our nerves. Why, is that important?"

"Maybe. I'm just trying to get the whole picture. By the way, you guys don't look cash-strapped anymore. What happened?"

"A group of private investors came in and made a successful presentation to the board of directors." Her comment processed quickly through his head; then he stored it, thinking that he'd be able to tie that information in somewhere later down the road.

"Thanks, Mondrya."

"So, I'll talk to you in, say, about fifteen minutes?"

"Anything's possible, so I'm not ruling it out. But this time for sure, have a nice weekend." Marcus parked the car and got out, dialing the phone again.

IN THE LATE NIGHT

"Hello," Carmen finally answered.

"Hello, Carmen. This is Marcus. How are you?"

"I'm fine, Marcus. I have got so much to tell you and so much to show you."

"I guess you had a good day?"

Carmen thought about the time she had just spent with her mother. They hadn't healed all their wounds, but they made a good start. "I had a good day."

"Let me take you to dinner and we can talk about what made this day so great," Marcus said, entering the elevator.

"I'm sorry, Marcus." Carmen smiled. "I just came back from dinner. My mother and I ate at Atlanta Grill. Have you eaten there yet?"

"No, I can't say that I have."

"I'll have to take you there; the food was great."

"I thought you were going to cook for me?"

"And I still will; just not tonight. But if you're not too busy this evening, stop by. I have a lot to share with you."

"Okay, I'll see you soon. I can just order something from

room service," Marcus said as he got off the elevator and started down the hall.

"Sounds good. I'll see you when you get here," Carmen said, then hung up the phone. She looked around the room. The bed was covered with the letters she had taken from Desireé's room. After reading each one, Carmen had separated them into piles. She waved her hand at the bed, dismissing the piles, and started for the bathroom, thinking that she would straighten up later. She was startled by a loud knock at the door. "Who is it?"

"It's Marcus." Carmen glanced down at her watch before she opened the door. "Did I take too long?"

"That was quick," Carmen said, smiling as she stepped aside to let Marcus in. *Glad to see he has a playful side.* "Come on in."

"I was downstairs when I called. I didn't wanna come up unannounced and uninvited. I've been calling you for a while now."

"I just got here. I haven't had a chance to do anything."

"I see this," Marcus said, standing over the bed. "I guess this is your spot?" He pointed to the one blank spot on the bed. "What is all this anyway?"

"These are the letters I found. Dez had them in the back of one of the bottom drawers in her room." Marcus started to comment. "Before you ask, quote, Mrs. Ferguson preferred to sleep alone sometimes, unquote."

"Roland?"

"Melissa, the housekeeper."

"Okay."

"Anyway, I read all of the letters, the big pile is letters and postcards I sent her. But before we get into what's in the rest of them, I want you to read a letter Dez had started to me on the day she was murdered," Carmen said, placing her laptop in front of Marcus. Carmen opened Microsoft Word and clicked on "Hi Big Sis.doc." Once the document was open, Carmen looked on as Marcus read the unfinished letter without comment.

"Well?" Carmen asked.

"Very touching that she would write this to you or at least have started it, but I know that's not what you're talking about. A few things stand out and others just raise questions. I assume that you have the answers, which is why you wanted me to read this first."

"Well, Marcus?" Carmen asked anxiously, wishing he'd get to the point.

"First off, it says Desireé Taylor Ferguson in the heading, but in the first line she's Desireé Marie Taylor. She seems unhappy with her life, and she has been keeping things from you for various reasons." Marcus looked at Carmen with questioning eyebrows, then continued. "'Carmen the sneak' jumped off the page at me." Carmen smiled shyly then transitioned him away from probing before he could get started.

"I wish she would have finished that last sentence. Doesn't it just scream 'I think somebody is trying to kill me'?"

"In retrospect, yes, but only because we have the benefit of knowing that she was murdered. But that's not the most interesting thing I see. This is not a complete sentence." Marcus pointed at the screen.

"What's not?" Carmen asked, and glanced at the screen. "Okay, so she didn't use perfect English. Loosen up a little, Marcus. I've been known to forget a modifier or two. And *but* has started a lotta things for me." Carmen smiled.

"I'll bet your butt has started quite a few things, but that's not what I'm talking about."

Marcus went into Options on the Tools menu, then clicked on Spelling & Grammar. He removed the check in the box that read "Hide Grammatical Errors in this Document," and clicked OKAY. "See it now? See the green line? 'I don't love'?

It's obvious that there are two spaces between those words. Like the name of the person she doesn't love has been deleted. My guess is it said 'I don't love Roland', and Roland deleted it."

"There's no way he could have; it had a password."

"You got in, Carmen."

"I guessed her password," Carmen said, pushing out her chest with pride. Marcus blinked and inhaled deeply.

"That computer's been sitting there for a year. If he wanted to get in, a password wouldn't stop him. Carmen, your brother-in-law is a very resourceful man."

"You're starting to think he did it, aren't you?" Carmen asked.

Marcus decided not to comment further on his thoughts. It was his turn to direct the conversation. "It does leave me with one big question."

"Here it comes." Carmen rolled her eyes upward.

"What's up with the 'my so-called friends just use me for money *and* my body. But *you know* there's nothing new or unusual about that.' That's what I wanna hear about," Marcus said, smiling as he picked up the menu for room service. "Come on, give it up, Carmen."

"Marcus, there was a *whole* lot that I didn't know about my sister. Well, I knew, but I didn't know how deep, until today. Remember I told you that I rebelled against my mother's control by hangin' out and gettin' high? Well, Dez had a different type of rebellion. Sex."

"Sex," Marcus repeated, but didn't lift his eyes from the menu.

"While I was gettin' high to escape, Dez was having sex. I remember telling her that when I smoked weed, I couldn't hear Mommy trippin', and she looked at me and said, 'I know what you mean Carm; when I'm doin' it and it's good, I don't hear her trippin' either. I couldn't have been more

han sixteen and still a virgin then, and here's my little sister
ellin' me how good sex is."

"Sex is escapism in its highest and most beautiful form."

Carmen looked away from Marcus, not wanting to meet
his glance. She pointed to one of the piles of letters on the
bed. "Most of those letters and just about all of the e-mails
are sexually explicit. Poems, short stories." Carmen paused.
"Thank-you notes."

"Who are they from?"

"Most of them are from Robert Pettibone, or they're
poems that she wrote for him. He was one of her toys. I
found her phone book and I called him, but the number is
disconnected. I saw two other names that I remembered,
Axle Grant and Ira Stinson. I called both of them, but I didn't
get an answer. Dez went out with somebody named India the
night before she was murdered. I left a message for her."

"Anything else?"

"I sent out that e-mail. But now I'm afraid to read what I
get back. I know where we can find Porsche Temple. So if
you're going to order something, order it now, 'cause we
have some place to go tonight," Carmen said, and looked at
Marcus. "That is if you don't already have something to do."

"Where are we going?"

"Porsche has girls dancing at two clubs—Pleasers and
Goose Bumps."

"You want to go to Pleasers and Goose Bumps? Do you
know what kind of places those are?"

"They're strip clubs, I know. But that was the only thing I
could find out about her."

"Anything else?"

"Yes, but it's not business. So, tell me about your day."

"It's no smoking gun, but I found a connection between
Ferguson and Bill Hudson."

"Bill Hudson of Hudson Financial?"

"Roland was involved in a merger with Hudson. But he pulled out of the deal at the last minute."

"That sounds like it could be something."

"Yeah, but it was in the mid-nineties. I'll keep on it, see where it leads," Marcus said as he put down the room service menu. "There's nothing on this I want."

"Well, what do you wanna eat?" Marcus looked at Carmen and smiled. "What?" Carmen asked.

"Nothing, Carmen." Marcus laughed. "I don't know what I want. But if we're going strip-club hopping, I do want to go by the house and change my clothes."

"Do you have any food at your house?"

"I got some hotdogs. I'll nuke a couple."

"See, I was thinking about making you something real quick while you changed clothes, but I guess you'll just have to wait until tomorrow."

"What's happening tomorrow?"

"If you don't have any plans, I'm having a *very* small housewarming party and I can cook for you."

"A housewarming?"

"Yes, a housewarming. I really don't like living out of a suitcase. And I've been thinking seriously about moving back here. So I rented a condo," Carmen said, looking at Marcus, who was smiling all over himself. "On a week-to-week basis for the time being."

Week to week or not, Marcus was happy that she was thinking about staying. Right then and there, he planned to give her as many reasons as he could to stay. "Anything in particular got you thinking that way?"

"I'm tired of being alone, Marcus."

On the way to Pleasers, Carmen wondered, *What will this be like? Is it gonna smell foul or fishy in there? Are people gonna think I'm gay if I gaze at the women too long?* When Marcus and Carmen arrived, Carmen quickly assessed the place. The lighting was soft, not quite dark, but dark enough to cast a mysterious hue over the room. The stench she expected didn't exist; the room smelled like a mixture of cigar and cigarette smoke instead of stale body parts. Carmen was immediately swept up by the music. It was loud, high-energy rap with a contagious beat.

No sooner had they taken a seat than one of the dancers approached their table. Marcus's eyes grew wide. She was a thick redbone with juicy lips, wearing a black teddy over her wide hips. She glanced at Carmen as she passed on her way around the table to Marcus. She stepped in between Marcus's legs and put her arms around his neck, resting her healthy chest against him. "My name is Peppermint; you wanna dance?" she whispered in his ear.

Marcus looked at Carmen out of the corner of his eye. "Not right now, but you make sure you come back," Marcus said, reaching in his pocket for a dollar bill. Almost without looking, Marcus carefully folded then placed the bill in her garter. "And could you send us a waitress?"

"Sure, baby." She kissed Marcus on the cheek and moved on to the next table.

"I see you've been here before?"

"What makes you say that?"

"You weren't even looking when you put the dollar in her garter. And she was all over you like you were a regular customer or something."

"Watch, Carmen. That's what all the women are doing. They go from table to table asking men if they want a table dance. Like they're doin'." Marcus pointed to the table next to theirs, where two dancers were removing their outfits to table dance. Carmen leaned forward to look around Marcus, then shook her head.

"Where's the ladies' room?"

"What?" Marcus yelled, completely distracted by the dancer on stage. Not to mention the two who were dancing at the table next to him.

"I said, where's the ladies' room? I guess I have to be naked to get your attention in here."

Marcus looked at Carmen and then around the room. "That's not true. You are much better looking than any of these women. They have to walk around naked to compete with you. And even with your clothes on, a lot of these men are looking at you," Marcus said, and continued filling his eyes.

But it's your attention that I want. "Marcus! Where's the ladies' room?"

"I don't think there is one, at least not that I've ever seen. Ask one of them," Marcus said, pointing in the direction of the dancers as they passed. Carmen got up and approached one of the dancers. "Excuse me, is there a bathroom I can use?"

The dancer led Carmen into the dressing room. Carmen felt comfortable there. The women reminded her of models getting ready for a show. Which they were.

"Don't I know you?" Peppermint asked Carmen.

"I don't think so." Carmen smiled.

"You look real familiar; you sure I don't know you?"

"I just have that type of face. People tell me that all the time," Carmen said, walking up to Peppermint. "My name is Carmen Taylor."

"They call me Peppermint for obvious reasons, but my name is Paula M. Dent."

"That kinda rhymes with Peppermint."

"It sorta do," Peppermint said, looking at Carmen. "I ain't tryna be funny, but you just don't look like the type to be up in a spot like this. But who am I to judge?" Peppermint shrugged.

"I'm looking for somebody. Do you know Porsche Temple?"

"Yeah, I know her. She got Misty and Chocolate strung out on her and dancin' here in the afternoon." Peppermint stood up from a small vanity where she was seated. "But they're all gone now," she said as she walked out of the dressing room. Carmen visited the ladies' room before starting back to her seat. Marcus was half-smiling, leaning on the table, and enjoying the dancer on stage while looking at all the other women walking around or performing table dances. *At least I know he ain't gay.* Before she reached Marcus, she bumped into Peppermint again. Carmen smiled deviously.

"Peppermint, how much is a table dance?"

"Five dollars."

Carmen got a twenty-dollar bill out of her purse and handed it to her. "Do you see that guy there?"

"You mean the one you're with."

"Yeah, get one of your friends and y'all go dance for him."

"I'll get Wet."

"What?" Carmen was a little taken aback.

"Wet, that girl over there. She calls herself Wet," Peppermint said, pointing to a woman who had the same build as she did; her dark skin was covered with baby oil.

"I'm not even gonna ask you why she calls herself Wet, girlfriend."

Peppermint put the twenty in the fat bank roll she had spun around her garter and went to get Wet to dance for Marcus while Carmen returned to her seat. "Nobody came to take your drink order yet?" Carmen asked, standing by the table.

"Not yet," Marcus replied without even looking at Carmen.

"I'm going to the bar to order. Hennessy, right?"

"Thank you, Carmen."

"I wouldn't want to interrupt you," Carmen said, and headed for the bar. As soon as Carmen was out of the way, Peppermint walked up to the table with Wet and they began removing their clothes. Marcus did a double take and started to say something, but Peppermint put her titties in his face. "The lady at the bar paid for this," she whispered, gently pushing Marcus back in his chair. He looked over at Carmen; she waved and he waved back but quickly refocused his attention on the entertainment before him. Carmen shook her head and got another dancer to bring Marcus his drink. He tipped her and she danced for a while, then moved on. Carmen rejoined Marcus at the table and watched him. She was surprised at how much she enjoyed watching his body movement as he consumed Peppermint and Wet with his eyes. When the dancers dressed and moved on, Marcus leaned close to Carmen. "Thank you, Carmen."

"You looked like you were enjoying yourself."

"I'm a bit of a voyeur," Marcus admitted.

"I always wanted to see what goes on in these places," Carmen told him.

"What do you think?"

"Well, it wasn't what I was expecting."

"What were you expecting?"

"I expected it to be, you know, wild with men screamin' and hollerin' and grabbin' women as they walked by. Which they are. And I expected it to stink."

"Stink?"

"Yep, I just knew it was gonna be stank up in here."

"So, do you see Porsche Temple anywhere?" Marcus asked.

"Peppermint said that she's got two young girls dancing

here in the afternoon, but they're gone. So you wanna try Goose Bumps now?"

"Let's go," Marcus said, and followed Carmen out of the club. On the way downtown, Carmen turned up the music and seductively rotated her upper body. "What do you think, Marcus? You think I could be a dancer?"

Marcus ran his tongue over his lips. "Carmen, if you danced there, all the women would hate you, 'cause you'd be makin' all the money. But if you really want to know, I know some spots that have amateur night."

"Sorry, pal, wrong sister. In one of her letters, Dez described for Robert Pettibone how she would come to his apartment in a trench coat with lingerie under it and dance for him and his friends for his birthday."

"Nice present. You wouldn't do that for a man, Carmen?"

"For my man." Carmen swayed from side to side with the music. "If I was in love with him," she flirted, looking into his eyes. "I'd do anything he wanted. But not for all his boys."

"That's good to know."

"Why is that?"

"I'd like to think of you as a private dancer."

"An extraordinary private dancer."

"Are you really?"

"I'm a very good dancer."

"Yeah, I saw how you were moving last night."

"Like I said, I was part of a small dance troupe in New York. I've taken ballet, tap, African, and modern dance," Carmen said as they pulled into the parking lot at Goose Bumps. Marcus came around and opened the car door for Carmen. "Thank you, Marcus. Oooh, there she is going into the club now."

Once they were inside, Carmen looked around for Porsche

while Marcus found himself a good seat, wondering if Carmen would send more dancers his way while he waited. Carmen found Porsche sitting at the bar. "Porsche!"

"Carmen?" Porsch said; looking at her strangely. "Carmen Taylor! What are you doin' here?"

"Looking for you."

"For me? Well you found me!" She hugged Carmen briefly. "You're lookin' good, Carmen. Sit down. What you drinkin'?"

"Bacardi on the rocks."

"Reggie, get her a Bacardi on the rocks and bring me another double. So, how you been, Carmen?"

"I'm good, Porsche. How you doin'?"

"I'm doin' better than I was, but, girl, you lookin' real good," Porsche commented again, staring at Carmen. She exhaled heavily and shook her head. "I tell you what, you were the last person I was expecting to see and looking for me. First of all, how did you find me here?"

"Denny told me you'd be here."

"What you looking for me for?"

"I wanted to talk to you about Dez."

"What about Dez?"

"I wanted to know if you talked to her any time before she died?"

"No. I hadn't talked to Dez for a couple of months before she died. We didn't fall out or anything like. I was going through some shit. But I'm doing better now."

"What was wrong?"

"Hitting that pipe, Carm. That rock had me fucked up for a while. Had to go to rehab. That's where I met Denise."

"Who's Denise?"

"Simone, the one dancin' on stage now." Carmen turned to look. "If Denny told you I'd be here, I know he told you what I was doin'. How is Denny anyway?"

"He's doin' fine."

"Tell him I said hey."

"Can you think of anybody else Dez might have talked to before she died?"

"Dez kept her personal business to herself. Only other person Dez really talked to was Suzanne, and she's dead too. I'm sorry I'm not any help, Carmen," Porsche said as Simone joined them at the bar and kissed Porsche on the cheek. "You know, if there was something I could tell you about Dez, Carmen, I would," Porsche said with tears in her eyes. "I loved Desireé. I miss her so much. I know you miss her too." Porsche hugged Carmen, and Simone smiled at her. "I gotta go, girl, but I'd like to get together sometime before you leave. How long are you staying?"

"I might be here for a while."

"Where are you staying?"

"I'm moving to a condo in Virginia Highlands tomorrow."

Porsche handed Carmen a card. "That's my number; call me soon. It was so good seeing you again, Carmen," she said, hugging Carmen again and kissing her near the lips before she walked off. Simone winked and blew Carmen a kiss before following Porsche into the dressing room. Carmen stood at the bar for a second before finishing her drink and rejoining Marcus.

"You ready to go?" she asked. Marcus stood up, finished his drink, and followed Carmen out the door. Once they were out of the club and in the car, Carmen turned to Marcus. "Maybe it's my imagination, then again maybe not, but I think I was just propositioned on the down low."

"You girls were looking quite chummy over there, with all that kissing and hugging y'all were doing."

"I'm surprised you noticed."

"What's that supposed to mean?" Marcus turned on the radio and started to move to the beat.

"You were practically drooling over Simone. But I don't think you're her type. Not the way she was kissing on Porsche and winking at me. I thought something was in her eye."

"Let's face it, Carmen, everybody wants you," Marcus said playfully. "The young and the old, the rich and the poor, males and females, blacks, whites, Puerto Ricans."

"Everybody just a freakin'."

"Good times are rollin'."

"I think not, Marcus. That ain't my type of bump and grind." She smiled at Marcus, moving her upper body slowly and seductively.

Marcus watched her move. Her eyes closed, feeling the music flowing through her. "Carmen Taylor, you are really beginning to pique my interest."

"That's good, Marcus Douglas, because you began to interest me some time ago," she replied, dancing each word, moving closer to and then away from Marcus.

"You've had my undivided attention since you walked into my office. Everything you've done since has just made me more focused."

"So, do you mind if I ask you a personal question?" He felt the piercing of her eyes.

"Go ahead. Ask me anything you'd like."

"I know you're married and getting a divorce; what I need to know is, are you seeing somebody now? I don't like crowds."

"No, I haven't been serious about a woman since I left my wife."

"What broke y'all up?"

"I caught her in bed with another man."

"Oh." Carmen abruptly stopped dancing. "I'm sorry."

"Carmen, please." He reached for her hand. "You don't need to apologize."

"I shouldn't have asked. I know that must hurt you."

"It did and still does. But a friend of mine made me see that I needed to forgive her and move on."

"This friend of yours seems pretty smart."

"Yes, she is very smart and very pretty," Marcus said gently. "Lately I've been feeling a lot better about that whole situation. I know that has everything to do with being with you. So, please, don't interrupt my private dance. Please don't stop."

Carmen smiled. "Too late. The song is over."

"But that doesn't mean you have to stop dancing. I like watching you move."

WHY LEAVE US ALONE

Marcus heard the doorbell ring, but he thought it was part of his dream. In his dream, he and Carmen were back at Goose Bumps. He was the only customer, and Carmen was the only dancer. He thought it was a little strange that a doorbell would be ringing at a strip club, but it was a dream, a good dream, so he tried to get back to it. When he heard the bell ring again, he cursed and rolled over. The clock said 1:05 A.M. *This better not be who I think it is,* he thought as he angrily got out of bed. On the way to the door, Marcus indulged himself in the fantasy that it was Carmen at the door, but he knew better. First of all, Carmen didn't know where he lived, but fantasy was a good thing. The doorbell rang again, only this time it was coupled with loud banging. At that point, he knew it wasn't Randa. *Randa would never bang on the door—she might break a nail.*

Marcus looked out the window and saw Garrett's truck crookedly parked behind his BMW. *What does he want at one in the morning?* He opened the door. "Wassup, Marcus!"

Garrett said, and wandered in. "Glad you opened the door. I was about to get ugly out there."

"Come on in, Garrett, make yourself comfortable," Marcus said sarcastically, seeing that Garrett was already inside and on his way to the couch. "What you wanna get ugly for at one in the morning?"

"I'm tryin' to figure that one out myself, Marcus. Why would I get ugly?" It was obvious that he had been drinking, but he wasn't drunk. "I was starting to think you had a woman up in this mug," Garrett said as he plopped down on the couch.

"Suppose I do?"

"Then you'd have to set her out!" Then he whispered, "Is it Carmen?"

"No. Nobody's here, Garrett."

"If Carmen ain't here, she should be. I can tell she's diggin' you by the way she looks at you."

"I know. We talked a little about that tonight." While Garrett went on about how he could size up any woman and about how fine Carmen was, Marcus thought about her. After they left Goose Bumps, Marcus drove Carmen back to her hotel. They stood outside the hotel, laying the foundation of a new relationship. Carmen showed Marcus a few of her old dance routines to prove she still had it. Marcus was mesmerized by Carmen's smooth, yet erotic, movements. For over an hour they laughed, talked, and made plans to meet for dinner at Carmen's new condo at seven the following evening. "Hold up, Garrett. I know you didn't come here at one in the morning to tell me how fine Carmen is."

"No, partner, I needed somebody to talk to."

"Why don't you go home and talk to your wife, then?"

"I can't do that."

"Why not?"

"Paven left me."

"What?"

"I didn't stutter. I said, Paven took the kids and left me. I got home around nine tonight, and the house was dark, but I didn't think much of it. I just figured somebody had come and picked them up. When I got inside the house, Paven was sitting at the dining room table. She was leaving me a note."

"What did the note say?"

"She didn't have to finish it; I was standin' right in front of her."

"What did she say?" Marcus asked Garrett.

"Garrett," Paven said, startled by his sudden appearance. "I didn't think you'd be home so early." Garrett walked up to her and tried to kiss her, but Paven resisted. "Garrett, sit down. There's something we need to talk about."

"What's the matter, Paven? Are the kids all right? Where are they anyway?"

"They're fine. They're at my mother's."

"What they doin' over there?"

"Garrett, sit down, please."

Reluctantly Garrett sat down at the table and waited to hear what Paven had to say. "I . . . ," Paven said, and looked away. "Garrett, the kids are at my mother's because I'm leaving you."

"What do you mean, you're leavin' me, Paven?"

"I can't say it any plainer than that. I'm not happy with us, Garrett."

"Why?"

"You're never here, for one."

"I have to work, Paven. You know there aren't any set hours in what I do. I gotta work to make a good life for you and the kids."

"I know that, Garrett, but do you ever think about what

that is doin' to us? To your children? We need you here with us sometimes too. They need their father, and I need my husband."

"I am here for you, Paven. Everything that I do, I do for you."

"You're not understanding what I'm sayin', Garrett. You are and always have been a good provider. You've always taken good care of us. We've never wanted for anything, but I need more. Your son will be fourteen years old soon, and he needs his father to set a positive example for him."

"So now I'm a bad influence on him, huh?"

"No, but the only example you are setting for him is that he should work all the time."

"Right. A man's gotta work to take care of his family, otherwise he ain't no man. My father worked two, sometimes three jobs. We didn't have everything we wanted, but he made sure that his kids had what they needed."

"That's exactly what I'm talking about. This whole mentality you have about it."

"What you talkin' 'bout, woman?"

"That mentality that says, as long as the bills are paid, then everything is all good."

"Well, ain't it?"

"No, Garrett, it ain't all good. Not for us. Not for me. I feel like a prisoner in this house and a slave to the children."

"Nobody told you that you had to sit here all day, talkin' on the phone, watchin' them stupid soap operas and that gotdamn meddlin'-ass Oprah Winfrey. That's probably what this is about. What, was that the topic of yesterday's show?"

"Oprah doesn't have anything to do with this! This is about us, Garrett, you and me!"

"All right, Paven, all right. We're not gonna get where we need to be by yelling at each other. I'm sorry if I haven't been here. I'll do better, Paven. I'll work less and spend some more time here with you and the kids, I promise."

"Garrett, this ain't the first time we've talked about this. And every time you promise me that you'll change. That you'll spend some time with your children and pay me some attention. And we get dinner and a movie, once. Then it's back to the same old Garrett."

"This time—"

'And you always say, 'This time, baby, things will be different,' but they never are. So what's gonna make this time any different from the last time?"

"This time I know you're serious." Garrett laughed.

"This ain't no joke, Garrett," Paven said, and took a swing at him. "I need some time away from you, away from this house to think about what I'm gonna do. I need to do something for myself. I don't do anything for me."

"So what, you want a divorce now?"

"I don't know. I just need some time to sort things out. To decide what I want to do for myself. And you need to think about whether you want to be an active member of this family."

"We can both do that right here. Let's try to work this out together. In the same house. Why you gotta leave?"

Paven got up from the table. "I just have to, Garrett."

"I love you, Paven."

"I love you, too, Garrett. That's why I have to go," Paven said, and walked out of the house. Garrett followed her out to the car.

"Can I at least call you?"

"Of course you can call me, Garrett. I expect you to call. I have your children; I would be very disappointed in you if you didn't call and talk to your children. I need to know that you want to be a part of their lives."

"Do you have any money?"

"I'll be all right."

"No," Garrett said, reaching into his pocket, "I ain't gonna have my family freeloadin' on nobody." Without bothering to count it, Garrett handed Paven all the money he had on him. "That should hold you a while; should be about three hundred there. I'll bring you some more tomorrow."

"Thank you, Garrett."

"For what?"

"For not making this ugly."

Paven got in the car and drove away, leaving Garrett standing alone in the driveway wondering how he ever let things go so far.

Garrett got up from the couch and walked over to the bar. "Mind if I fix myself a drink, Marcus?" Garrett asked while he poured.

"Go ahead."

"You want one?"

"Make it a double," Marcus said. "I'm sorry to hear about you and Paven. What are you gonna do now?"

"I'ma drink your Henny, that's what I'ma do," Garrett said, handing Marcus a filled glass.

"I mean about Paven?"

"Look, Marcus, Paven's gonna do what she's gonna do. I can't change who I am or what I do. I love my baby and I want her to come home, but this is something she's gotta work out for herself."

"That's a pretty enlightened attitude for a brother."

"Yeah, sounds like I been watchin' that gotdamn meddlin'-ass Oprah Winfrey, too, don't it?" Garrett laughed.

"You a trip. But you know Paven is right. You're always

working, so you're never home. I've never seen you take a vacation and go anywhere. Women need attention."

"Didn't nobody pay a woman more attention than you paid Randa and look how that turned out." Marcus looked at Garrett but didn't say anything. "Sorry, Marcus. I shouldn't have said that."

"You're right, you shouldn't have. But, shit, you're right. Ain't no denying that."

"I think you paid her too much attention. And you didn't give her enough to do. Shoulda pumped some babies into her."

"Like them four you pumped into Paven?"

"Touché," Garrett said as he raised his glass and drained it. "You want another?"

"No, still working on the first one."

"Well, man up," Garrett said, standing in front of him, waiting for his glass. Marcus drained his glass and handed it to Garrett. "Thank you. On second thought, get dressed. Let's get the fuck outta here."

"And go where?"

"Let's go watch some girls."

"Did that already tonight," Marcus replied as he got up and went into his bedroom to get dressed.

"Where'd you go?" Garrett yelled while he poured the drinks in plastic cups.

"Pleasers and Goose Bumps," Marcus yelled back.

"Who'd you go there with?"

"Carmen," Marcus said as he came out of the room.

"Playa, if that ain't the stupidest thing I ever heard, I don't know what is."

"What do you mean?"

"You took the finest muthafucka in town to a titty bar?" Garrett paused. "She ain't no lesbian, is she?"

"No, and I quote, 'That ain't my type of bump and grind,' unquote."

"I feel better just knowing that. Now, why did you take her to a titty bar?"

"I know you've been tied up with your other case. And now with you and Paven having problems, your time is gonna be even more limited. So we've been doing a little investigating on our own."

"I thought we agreed to leave the investigating to me?"

"Garrett, if Carmen Taylor asked you to go with her to a strip club so she could talk to a friend of her sister's, what would you say?"

"I'd say, you want me to drive?"

"I rest my case," Marcus said as they walked out to the car. While Marcus drove, he brought Garrett up to speed on what little progress they had made on the case. "Did you find anything out about Damali?"

"Not really. He's a real mystery man. Nobody knows anything about him. Desireé was paying for the apartment he was staying in. Neighbors say he was quiet and kept to himself, like they always do. The car he was driving was stolen in Texas, but the Texas police don't have anything on him. No match on his fingerprints."

"Who identified the body?"

"Ferguson. When he identified his wife's body, the cops asked him to identify the other body."

"What about their relationship?"

"Another big zero. Nobody knows anything about them. Where she met him, where they went together. Other than Roland's testimony at the trial, nobody even knows how long they'd known each other."

"I really appreciate you for what you're doing. I know you've already got a full plate."

"What you want me to do, Marcus?"

"First chance you get, take a run at Porsche Temple. I'll call you tomorrow with a phone number for her. Or we might just catch her at Goose Bumps."

"She dance there?"

"No. Dig this. She got three girls dancin' for her. Two at Pleasers and one at Goose Bumps."

"So this Porsche Temple woman is mackin' these girls?" Garrett shook his head and smiled. "What kind of freaky shit you got yourself into, Marcus?"

Marcus looked over at Garrett, shrugged his shoulders, and started laughing.

"I may have to free up a little more time for you on this one."

LET'S BE FRIENDS

By eight-fifteen, Carmen was packed and on her way to check out of her room. On the way to her new condo, she stopped by a grocery store to pick up some cleaning supplies, shelf liners, and a pair of rubber gloves. When she arrived at the condo, Carmen dug her key out and got busy with cleaning, lining her shelves and drawers, and putting away her clothes.

After she was settled in, Carmen sat down on the bed and looked around the room. She glanced over at the dresser and began to think about the three pictures that Desireé had on her dresser of the two of them. She decided to ask Roland if she could have them. Carmen showered, dressed, and headed to the Cingular store; twenty minutes later, she walked out with a new phone. Once the phone was activated, she called Roland. Naturally Roland said yes. He told Carmen that he felt it was time that somebody went through Desireé's things and asked Carmen if she would do it because he still didn't feel up to it. Carmen told Roland that she would come by later that morning with Dominique. Then she called Dominique and asked if she wanted to come with her. She excitedly accepted the invitation.

After two hours of sorting through and organizing Desiree's things, both mother and daughter had burned out. They agreed to come back another day to finish. They told Roland that they were leaving and settled on a day to come back to complete the task. Roland thanked them for coming and walked them to the door. When she got outside, Carmen saw that her car was gone. "What happened to my car?" she asked.

"I had Connie send somebody by to return it, Carmen," Roland replied, and handed her a set of car keys. "Those are the keys to Desiree's car," he said, pointing to the gold Mercedes parked where the rental car had been. "You can drive that while you're here."

"I can't take these, Roland," Carmen said while she tried to hand Roland back the keys. Dominique elbowed her in the side and gave her a look.

"Please, Carmen, there's no point in you spending money on a rental, especially if you plan on being here for a while. You can drive it for as long as you're here or until you get something else."

Carmen reluctantly accepted the keys and drove Dominique home. "When somebody offers you the keys to a Mercedes, Carmen, you say thank you."

"I just feel kinda funny driving her car."

"Do you feel funny about taking her pictures?"

"No, but that's different."

"What's the difference?" Dominique asked.

"Those are pictures; this is a car."

"Only difference is dollar value, Carmen. They both belonged to your sister. If there's something you want, you should take it."

"I would feel too weird wearing her clothes."

"I agree," Dominique said. "We should donate all of it to the church charity. But I don't think we need to donate all of Desireé's jewelry to Reverend Fredrickson's wife."

"Or his girlfriend," Carmen threw in. "Okay, I'll keep the car, 'cause to be honest with you, this bad boy does drive real smooth."

"See, I did teach you common sense." Dominique smiled at Carmen.

"Anyway, thank you for coming with me, Dominique. I don't think I could have done it by myself."

"Thank you for asking me. I asked Roland if he wanted me to do it after the funeral, but he refused. He got a little hostile about it."

"I guess he wasn't ready to let go."

"At the time, I thought that he was trying to hide something," Dominique said, causing Carmen to think about the seemingly deleted words from the letter Desireé was writing her.

On her way back to her condo, Carmen left another message for India, the woman who Desireé had gone out with the night before her murder, and left her cell phone number. It was getting late in the afternoon, and it looked as if it would rain. Carmen still needed to shop if she planned to cook dinner for Marcus.

She gave some thought to what she was going to cook. *Something French so he'll know that I have mad cooking skills.* Carmen had the butcher pick out a good-size boneless pot roast and asked him to slice four thin pieces of salt pork. Then she went down the produce aisle to pick up onions, carrots, bay leaf, thyme, and two potatoes. All she needed now was a can of tomato paste, and on to the checkout line. Then she went by the liquor store to get a bottle of red wine to serve with dinner, Côtes du Rhône, and a domestic Cabernet to cook with. Carmen also picked a bottle of Bacardi for the house and a bottle of Hennessy for Marcus.

When she got back to the house, it was almost four o'clock. If she wanted the roast to be done by seven, she would have to get started. She changed into a pair of shorts and a big T-shirt and got busy in the kitchen. Carmen found the sharpest knife in the drawer and began to cut the potatoes into slices. Then she cut two carrots into one-inch pieces and sliced two onions. With that done, she looked for a big heavy pot and lined its bottom with the salt pork. She arranged the carrots and onions, threw in a pinch of thyme and one bay leaf over the salt pork, and placed the pot roast in the bed of vegetables. Carmen poured in two cups of the Cabernet, added a little salt and pepper, and covered the pot. Once it came to a slow boil, Carmen turned down the gas and left it to simmer for the next three hours.

With time on her hands before Marcus arrived, Carmen decided to set up her laptop in the den and read some more of the documents she'd downloaded from Desireé's computer. The first was another letter that Desireé had written to her dated two years before she died.

From inside the soul of
Desireé Taylor Ferguson

Dear big sis,
I don't know why I keep writing you these letters, seeing that I never mail any of them. That may have something to do with the fact that I never finish them. I may actually finish one, one day. But I wonder sometimes why you continue to write me, knowing that I never write you back. But I'm glad you do write me. Getting letters and postcards from you from all over

the world makes me feel like I'm right there with you.
Now I know you're thinking, "There goes Desireé, bitin'
on my life again. Didn't she grow out of that years
ago?" Well, believe me, I have, but the fact of the mat-
ter is, I would gladly trade my life for yours. But that
would mean that you would have to have this life, and
I wouldn't wish this life of lies I lead on anyone.

Today I contemplated suicide. DON'T CALL THE
AIRLINE. I would never actually do it. I'm too much
of a coward to take my own life. But now I think I under-
stand why so many people consider it and why some
do it. I know you'll say, "Dez, think about all the things
you have to live for. Your friends and your family. You
have everything you ever dreamed of. Why do you
want to die?" Because I am not happy with my life. It
is filled with disappointment and pain, because I don't
have any control of it. So today I asked myself what
was the point of life if you can't live it the way you
want to. And if I'm not living my life the way I want to,
is that really living? I'm not really living; I'm just ex-
isting from day to day, waiting to die. So if that exis-
tence will only be filled with more disappointment and
pain, then why wait to die? Bearing that pain, day
after endless day, waiting to die. Why not die now?

I thought that marrying rich was the answer to all
my prayers, but it's not. Maybe what I really wanted,
all I ever dreamed of, was to be loved. I know Roland
loves me, but I don't love him. I want to be loved by the
person that I love. So I seek love in the arms of others
like Robert, who only wants to use me, and never find
the love I seek.

With her eyes welling up with tears, Carmen frantically
opened another document, looking for more letters written

to her. She opened document after document, looking for the words "Hi big sis" until the phone rang. Carmen composed herself enough to answer. "Hello," she said, still wiping the tears from her eyes.

"Carmen?"

"Yes."

"This is India Carter; I'm returning your call."

"Yes, India, thank you for calling me back. I'm Desireé Ferguson's sister."

"I know who you are." Carmen could hear the smile in India's voice. "Dez talked about you all the time. I've always wanted to meet you, but Dez could never get us together when you were in town. And now here you are calling me," she said excitedly.

Carmen laughed a little. "Yeah, what a coincidence, huh? I was calling to see if you would talk to me about my sister."

"I'd be glad to. When can we get together?"

"Anytime that's good for you."

"Where are you staying?"

"I've rented a condo on St. Charles off of North Highland."

"Really. Well, I'm not too far from there. I'm in Little Five Points. I could be there in ten minutes."

Carmen looked at her watch; she had plenty of time before Marcus would arrive for dinner. "That's fine, India. I'm cooking dinner for a friend tonight, so we can talk while I get things ready."

"See you in a few," India said, and hung up the phone.

Carmen turned off her laptop and prepared to meet India. She thought about changing into something a little more presentable, but she just wasn't feeling it. Carmen was still quite shaken by Desireé's letter. With each word, she felt her pain. *Why didn't you tell me, Dez? I would have been there for you if I knew you were in that much pain.*

As promised, India rang the doorbell exactly ten minutes later. Carmen opened the door for a tall, dark-skinned woman dressed in white shorts and a white nylon blouse. It was obvious to Carmen that India wasn't wearing a bra, as she could see her dark erect nipples pressing against the fabric of her blouse. "Carmen?"

"India. Please come in." Carmen led India into the living room. "Have a seat, and thank you so much for agreeing to talk to me."

"Thank you, Carmen. And it's no trouble at all," India said as she sat down on the couch and crossed her legs. "Like I said, I always wanted to meet you. I would have preferred to meet you in a more social setting, but this is fine. I like what you've done with this place."

"Actually, it was like this when I got here; I just moved in today. I don't like living out of a suitcase, so I got this place until I find something more permanent."

"So, what can I tell you about Desireé?" India asked.

"How long did you know Dez?"

"We'd known each other for three years when it happened."

"Were you two very close?"

"I'd say we were," India said, and smiled. "I thought Desireé told you about me?"

"No, I'm sorry, Dez never mentioned you to me."

"Really? I was sure she had." Carmen could see a little hurt in India's eyes. "Well, even though she didn't tell you, we were very close," India said.

"I know she had planned to meet you the night before she was murdered."

"You mean before Roland killed her," India said.

"How do you know Roland killed her?"

"Who else would have?"

"That's what I'm trying to find out. Did you meet her that night?"

"I did. We had dinner at the Food Studio. Then we went to the Alliance Theater to see a play. I can't remember the name of it; it was terrible. We had drinks at Justin's, and then we went back to my place to"—India smiled at Carmen—"To talk."

"You were one of the last people to talk to her, then?"

"Yes, I suppose I was."

"Was she upset, or did she say anything that was unusual?"

"No. Desireé was her usual vibrant self. And even if something was bothering her, she would never let on. That's just how she was. She always wanted everyone around her to be happy. And Desireé had a way of making people feel good," India said, and put her hand on Carmen's thigh. Carmen gave India a look that made India move her hand away, but only after she allowed it to linger across Carmen's skin. "You really don't know anything about Desireé, do you, Carmen?" Before Carmen could answer, India said, "Desireé and I were lovers."

Carmen's eyes were now wide open, along with her mouth, which she quickly closed.

"Desireé and I met at a pool party at my house. We got together a couple of days later and made love by the pool," India said, apparently enjoying the fact that she was making Carmen uncomfortable. "She came with Roland, but when he was ready to leave, Desireé made up some excuse and she stayed. She told me afterward that Roland knew why she wanted to stay."

"Roland knew?" Carmen asked in surprise.

"Yes, Carmen." India laughed lightly. "Roland knew all about me and Desireé. We've made love while Roland watched. He liked to watch me make love to Desireé."

"He just liked to watch?"

"Roland is impotent. She said he got off on watchin' people make love to her."

Carmen held up her hand. "Would you like a drink, India? I sure need one right about now."

"Anything you have is fine," India said, and giggled.

"All I have is Bacardi and Hennessy," Carmen said, getting up from the couch.

"Hennessy on the rocks is fine." India smiled and repositioned herself on the couch so she could watch Carmen walk away as she went for the drinks. Carmen poured herself a shot of Bacardi and drank it down on the spot before pouring herself another one, this time on the rocks, and a Hennessy for India. Carmen checked on her roast and returned to the living room and handed India her glass. When she sat down, she noticed that India had undone a couple of buttons on her blouse, exposing her cleavage. India took a sip of her drink. "I know this is a little overwhelming for you to find out all this about Desireé."

"I think we can definitely mark that down as an understatement."

"Desireé was a very sexual woman. With very strong desires."

"I've always known that she was," Carmen said; then she tried to clear it up. "That she was very sexual, I mean."

"But you didn't know that she was bisexual or that Roland was impotent and liked to watch, did you, Carmen?"

"No."

"Have you ever made love to a woman, Carmen?" India asked as she inched just a bit closer to Carmen and put her hand on Carmen's thigh.

"No, India, I haven't," Carmen replied with attitude. "And I'd appreciate it if you took your hand off my thigh."

"I'm sorry," India said, slowly removing her hand. She smiled. "I could make you feel things that a man can't."

"Can you really, India? And just how might you do that?"

"I know what a woman wants. What she needs, and I'm very good."

"Yes, I'm sure you are. But you know something, India? There is something to be said for penetration."

"I can give you that too," India eagerly told Carmen.

"Yes, I'm sure you can. But there's nothing like having real dick. Feelin' its warmth and its smooth texture when it slides in and out of me," Carmen said, slowly turning the tables on India. Now it was India who began to squirm. "To feel my man's dick throb when he gets excited, because I know I'm really throwin' this pussy at him. And there's nothing better than feelin' his shaft expand and his head swell when he explodes inside me." Carmen smiled at India. "It just makes me cum in ways that a woman never will."

"Oooh, stop it, Carmen. You're making my clit hard."

"You started it, girlfriend."

"I see that your sexuality is just as strong as Desireé's. She was always very descriptive about how she wanted to be satisfied too."

"Maybe, but the difference is, I like feelin' some dick in me after I get my clit licked."

"So do I, honey, and so did Desireé," India agreed. "She and I have shared a man too."

"I thought you said Roland was impotent?"

"He's not the only dick in town."

"Did you two ever share Rasheed Damali?"

"Yes." India frowned.

"Why do you say it like that?"

"I didn't like him."

"Why?"

"Because Desireé was in love with him."

"Were you in love with her?"

"Yes."

Damn, Dez, you just had all these women sprung. "Can you tell me anything about him?" Carmen asked.

"Like what?" India asked.

"Like, was he involved with somebody or something that could have caused her death?"

"No."

"Well, what can you tell me about him?"

"Only that she loved him."

"You know where he was from? Anybody he knew?"

"We didn't spend a lot of time talking," India flirted.

"I guess he never brought along a fourth to y'all's threesome?"

"He wanted to once, but Desireé wouldn't have it. She said a fourth would take attention away from her. And Desireé liked being the center of attention."

"That's sounds like Dez."

"Didn't you say you had a man coming over tonight?"

"Yes, what about it?"

"All this talk has got me cravin' to feel some dick."

"And?"

"I was thinking maybe I could stay for dinner and we could all play afterward."

"I don't think so, India. That's not what I had in mind for tonight."

"Okay, then, Carmen," India said as she got up from the couch. "I'm goin' to go now. See if I can't find a couple of people to play with me."

"I'm sure that won't be a problem for you," Carmen said sarcastically, walking India to the door.

"Carmen, it was a pleasure to finally meet you. I was hoping that you and I could become friends."

"Sure, we can. You'd be fun to hang out with."

"I'm lots of fun, Carmen. Try me sometime. I just might change your mind."

"You're something else, India. Bye." Carmen closed the door and rolled her eyes. "I need another drink."

EN DAUBE

Marcus rang Carmen's doorbell at exactly seven o'clock. When the door didn't open right away, he paced back and forth in anticipation. Suddenly the door opened with flourish and Carmen stood before him dressed in a red, sculpted, single-shoulder Donna Karan dress. "Good evening, Marcus."

Marcus smiled as he looked at Carmen. "Good evening, Carmen. You look beautiful tonight."

"Thank you, Marcus. Please, come in."

"I didn't know if you wanted me to bring anything, so I brought these," Marcus said, taking his hand from behind his back and handing Carmen a dozen long-stemmed yellow roses.

"Thank you, Marcus. How did you know I loved yellow roses?"

He turned the corners of his lips down and shrugged. "I guessed."

"Well, it was an excellent guess. I want to put them in water, but I don't think there's a vase in here. I'll have to find something for them. Have a seat; dinner is almost ready,"

Carmen said on her way to the kitchen. "Can I get you a drink?"

"Thank you, Carmen."

Carmen searched through the cabinets for something to put the roses in, but all she could find was a pitcher. *That is going to look so tacky.*

She poured Marcus's drink and handed it to him.

"Thank you. This is a nice place."

"Thanks, I'm glad I found it," she said, and returned to the kitchen to finish preparing the meal. She peeked around the corner at Marcus. *That is one fine man,* she thought as she got to her task. Carmen removed the roast from the pot, placed it on the cutting board, then sliced and arranged it in the center of a serving platter. Then she arranged the steamed vegetables and potatoes around the meat. Carmen poured a can of tomato paste into the pot that she had cooked the roast and vegetables in, and left it to simmer for five minutes. She went into the dining room to light candles and dim the electric lights. Once her sauce was ready, she poured it over the meat. She took the platter into the dining room and placed it in the center of the table. Carmen went back into the kitchen to get the wine and the corkscrew. "Marcus," she said, standing in the doorway.

"Yes."

"Dinner is served."

Marcus took another swallow of his drink and joined Carmen in the dining room. Once he was seated, she turned off the living room lights and sat down. She handed Marcus the bottle of wine and the corkscrew. "Would you do the honors?"

Marcus took the bottle and read the label. "Côtes du Rhône. Excellent choice, Carmen," he commented as he opened and poured the wine.

"Are you familiar with this vintage?" Carmen said in a snooty tone.

"Isn't everybody? It's a French wine made from Grenache, Moutvèdre, and Carignan grapes."

"I'm impressed, Mr. Douglas."

"Thank you, Ms. Taylor. I'm impressed by this meal. It all looks delicious," Marcus observed as he raised his glass. "To my radiant and charming hostess."

"To my handsome dinner companion." They touched and then sipped from their glasses. "Would you like me to serve you, Marcus?"

"I would be honored." Carmen served Marcus his meal and then served herself. They ate in silence until Marcus said, "This is delicious. What do you call it?"

"Beef en daube."

"What ever you call it, it's to die for," he said, and took a sip of his drink. He looked back at Carmen. "Is something wrong?"

"No," she uttered quickly without looking up at Marcus. When she did look up, Marcus was looking in her eyes. "When you said 'to die for,' it made me think of Dez."

"I'm sorry, Carmen. Really poor choice of words."

"It's okay," she declared, reaching for his hand. "Really, I'm fine. It's just that I found another letter that she started writing me. It was written two years before she died. She would start writing me these letters but never finish them."

"What did it say?"

"It was about her contemplating suicide. She wasn't happy in her marriage, with her life. She called it a life of lies. I know if I go through all her files, I'll find more. But, Marcus, I never had any idea how depressed she was. She was reaching out to me with these letters. And it hurts me that I wasn't here for her."

"Carmen, I can't even imagine what this must be like or how hard it must be on you, but can I offer you a little friendly advice?"

"Well, you do owe me for giving you such good advice." Carmen smiled at Marcus and squeezed his hand.

"Try not to beat yourself up too bad." Marcus smiled. "You need to forgive Carmen for not being there and move on."

"That's not fair," Carmen said, jerking her hand away. "Giving me my own advice."

"At least you know it came from a good source."

"Good recovery, Marcus."

"Thank you. I'm a lawyer, you know; words are my business," he said with a bow. "Did you find out anything else today?"

"Yes." Carmen looked curiously at Marcus.

"Well, what did you find out?"

"I'm trying to think of a delicate way to put this." Carmen tipped her head from side to side. "Fuck it, there isn't one." She sat up straight and cleared her throat. "My sister, Desireé, was bisexual."

"You're right, Carmen, there was no delicate way to say that," Marcus said, shaking his head.

"I met India Carter today, one of her lovers. She told me that Roland is impotent and that he liked watching her and Dez have sex."

Marcus swallowed hard, not knowing what to say. "I tell you what, you definitely made up my mind about what I'm going to do tomorrow."

"What's that?" Carmen asked innocently.

"I'm going to spend it with you. Your days are definitely more interesting than mine."

"Why, how did you spend your day?"

"I slept through most of it."

"Why?"

"After I dropped you off, Garrett came by and we went out."

"Did he have something for you?"

"No, he just needed to talk. His wife left him."

"I'm sorry to hear that. Was he cheating on her?"

"No," Marcus lied. "He wasn't spending enough time at home."

"Sounds like she may have been cheating on him."

"Not Paven. I can't believe she would do that."

"Believe me, Marcus, a woman, any woman, will creep if she's not happy." Carmen could tell by the look on Marcus's face that he was thinking about Randa.

She was about to change the subject.

"What do you want to do with the rest of the evening?" Marcus said, saving her the trouble.

"I don't know. What do you wanna do?"

"I was going to take you dancing, but it's raining pretty hard now."

"That would have been nice," she commented, knowing that dancing wasn't quite what she had in mind for the rest of the evening. "I know what we can do," Carmen said, jumping up from the table. She turned the radio to an old-school party mix; the Funkadelic's "Knee Deep" was on. "Come on, Marcus, show me what you got."

Marcus got up and took off his jacket while Carmen moved the coffee table out of the way. They danced to a long version of "Knee Deep"; then the "Electric Slide" came on. They took turns laughing and talking about each other because neither could keep their steps together. A commercial came on, and the weary dancers took a much-needed break. Carmen refreshed their drinks. As soon as she sat down, the commercial ended, followed by the Isley Brothers "For the Love of You."

Marcus quickly rose to his feet and extended his hand. "May I have this dance?"

"Yes, you may," Carmen said, accepting his hand.

They swayed back and forth to the music. Marcus began to sing the words softly in her ear. "Oooh, you go, boy."

Carmen closed her eyes and rested her head against his chest. When Marcus stopped singing, she looked up at him; he was looking at her. They stared into each other's eyes. Carmen closed her eyes and tilted her head back as Marcus kissed her, delicately pressing his lips against hers. He drew her closer and caressed her face. Carmen opened her eyes as Marcus began to kiss a path from her lips down to her neck and then up to her earlobes.

"I never did give you a tour of the condo," she whispered in his ear as she walked backward toward the bedroom.

Marcus continued to kiss her, following her lead. She stopped in front of the bed and began to loosen Marcus's tie, slid it from around his neck and collar, and allowed it to fall to the floor. She unbuttoned his shirt and unfastened his pants. He frantically kicked out of his shoes while Carmen removed his shirt and allowed his pants to sink to the floor. She gazed into his eyes and slowly peeled his underwear away from his body. Marcus became lost in her eyes. She seemed so intently determined to accomplish her mission.

By the time she gently sat him on the bed, "For the Love of You" was over and "Hangin' on a String" by Loose Ends was playing. Carmen stepped back from the bed and slowly swayed her hips, moving to the music as if she felt it to her core. She seductively turned her back to him, then began to lower the zipper on her dress. Marcus saw the material pool around her feet but quickly focused his vision upward again to her firm round cheeks, separated by the lace of her red thong. Braless, she turned again to face him, running her fingers along her neck, over her cleavage, and down her sides while rotating her hips to the beat. Marcus's eyes burned into her bare skin. He could only gaze longingly and lick his lips in anticipation.

Still moving seductively to the beat, she put a finger into her mouth and sucked it. Marcus studied her closely as she used that moist finger to rub her stiffened nipples. His eyes appeared in danger of popping out of his head when she scooped her breasts in her palms and brought each one up to her lips. Carmen used her tongue to circle her nipple while staring directly into his eyes.

When she was completely naked, she strutted over to the bed and lay down next to Marcus. His breathing was labored as he ran his hand across her breasts. Carmen squeezed her eyes shut and prepared herself so that she could memorize his touch. He took her breasts, touched them, held them, squeezed them, and then slid his tongue slowly around her beautiful dark circles, coming close but not quite touching her nipples. Her natural reflexes took over, and Carmen's legs spread, almost begging Marcus to finger her clit. He obliged and felt it getting harder beneath his touch. Carmen moaned her approval. She reached out to him and slowly began to massage his hardening length with one hand while fondling his balls with the other.

She kissed him passionately and continued to stroke his erection. Marcus guided his tongue along her eyebrows and kissed her eyelids; then he paused to look at her face. Just inches from it, Carmen appeared even more beautiful than she had at any point since they'd met.

The sensation of hands gave way to the sensation of her lips, soft and wet, against his chest. He lay on his back, eyes closed, and enjoyed the taste of her tongue darting playfully in and out of his mouth and then across his chest. It didn't take long for her hands to glide down his sides and back to his now-throbbing hardness.

His excitement grew as he relied on only his sense of touch. The feeling seemed heightened as Carmen took him into the soft and warm wetness of her mouth. She suckled his head, then slid her tongue up and down his erection. Marcus reached for Carmen, and he watched the perfection that was her ass as she crawled, turned around, and positioned her body so he could taste her. He ran his tongue along her lips and proceeded to lick and suck her clit. She moaned her pleasure as she again lowered her head and took him into her mouth. His back arched. The movement of his tongue increased to a pace that matched hers. Moments later, her body quivered. "Sssss . . . M-M-Maar-cus, I don't want to cum yet, baby," she cried.

Carmen repositioned herself to straddle him. Marcus looked on as she lowered herself onto him, taking his erection inch by inch into the wetness between her thighs. They stared into each other's eyes as they moved in unison; each movement was agonizingly slow and deliberate to heighten their mutual pleasure.

After working that angle for a while, an exhausted Carmen rolled off of Marcus. He moved beside her and ran his hands along her back, down and around her perfect ass, and squeezed her firm thighs. Carmen spread her legs, and he began another sweet assault on her clit; he fingered it and played with her lips. Marcus got up on his knees and entered her from behind. Her pussy was so soft, so wet; he could barely control his passion. He felt her ass buck, pounding against him. He thought he'd explode when he felt the muscles inside her tighten around him.

"Harder, baby!" she cried.

Marcus complied with her request until they both collapsed from exhaustion.

Carmen smiled and touched his face; then she curled up in the fetal position. Marcus ran his hand over her shoulder and down her arm. Her skin was silky soft. He paused to admire each curve, studying each nuance of her body. Carmen began to move in response. She rolled into his arms and kissed his lips; satisfaction had found its home on her face.

He tasted her tongue. It glided slowly and smoothly over his. Marcus broke their embrace and spread her legs once again. He kissed her inner thighs and suckled the wetness between them. Carmen gripped his head, and held it in place as his tongue slithered along her lips and made circles around her clit.

Her grip grew tighter, her stomach muscles locked, and her head drifted back in quiet ecstasy. Carmen sat up and Marcus entered her. He placed the weight of his body onto his arms. Carmen's back arched; she rotated her hips in perfect unison with his, moving slowly, then fast and then slowly again. Her body began to quiver as she stretched out her legs. It was as if she anticipated his movements and matched each stroke. Their heartbeats quickened until their bodies both trembled together.

UNDERCOVER

"Good morning, Ms. Foster," the receptionist said. "You're in early today."

At eight-thirty on Monday morning, Mondrya Foster arrived at work. She usually got in around nine-thirty, but not today. Today she had things to do. After talking to Marcus about Frank Collins and the circumstances surrounding his death and the death of his wife, Suzanne, she couldn't shake the feeling that there may be something going on. She spent all weekend thinking back to the time of the merger. And it had all started to come back to her. The more Mondrya thought, the more the details of those days came into focus. She remembered that when they were selecting the team of analysts, Frank Collins was selected to be a member of the team. At the time, his selection caused quite a bit of controversy. Frank had only recently come to Hudson Financial as an account manager from another brokerage. The question the analysts posed was why would a new account manager be on a team of analysts? Mondrya remembered this specifically because it was her friend Bennett who was passed over. And then there was Connie Talbert. The analyst's analyst. *She and Frank sure hit it off quick, almost from day one. It always seemed like they knew each other.*

After she got her coffee, Mondrya settled into her office and turned on her computer. She put her phone on speaker and dialed. "IS, this is Richie."

"Good morning, Richie. This is Mondrya Foster."

"Mondrya, good morning; this is a surprise."

"I need a favor, Richie. Could you come to my office?"

"I'll be right up."

With all the questions she had about Frank, Mondrya needed to access his personnel file. Since walking into HR and pulling the file wasn't possible, the HR system on the network was her only option. But the system had safeguards, and she needed Richie to circumvent them. It wasn't too long before Richie knocked on her door. "Mondrya, how are you?"

"Long weekend, Richie. Come in and close the door. How are Mary and the kids?"

"They're all fine. And your boys, how are they doing?"

"They eat too much."

"I know how that feels." Richie laughed. "So, to what do I owe the honor of this audience, your highness? Since you moved up two floors, I don't get to see nearly enough of you."

"You know you can come by to see me any time you want to. You do have access to this floor."

"You could see me up here a lot more often if you would get Sheldon fired. Then you could use your influence to get me the IS director job." Richie paused. "But I forgot, you're a new-style VP. Nothing like your predecessor, the late Mr. Coleman Wilson, may he rest in peace. No interoffice back-stabbing politics on your watch. But I shouldn't speak ill of the dead."

"No, you shouldn't, even if it is true," Mondrya said. "But everybody was tired of that stuff, Richie."

"That's why they created that senior exec spot for him. They had to get the crazy old bastard out before he did something else stupid. Who knew all they had to do was wait a few months for him to kill himself."

"Yeah, who knew?"

"You know what was interesting?" Richie said, and made himself a little more comfortable.

"What's that, Richie?"

"Coleman killed himself on the same day as some state official."

"I remember hearing about that. What was his name again?" Mondrya snapped her fingers a few times. "John Heard, I think that was his name. Well, anyway, those days are over. No more office infighting. No more secret conspiracies. And I'm not committing suicide. So you come by any time; my door is always open."

"Yeah, well, I notice that it's not open now."

"I need a favor, Richie."

"What's that?"

"I need to look at something in the HR system."

"I can show you how to do that. It's easy, let me show you." Richie hopped up.

"Richie, I know how to access what I want to see."

"So what do you need, Mondrya?" Richie asked as he sat back down.

"Doesn't the system have an automatic trigger that sends out e-mails when non-HR personnel access the system?"

"Sure, it sends an e-mail to a predetermined distribution list, with details of who accessed the system, at what time, and what information they looked at."

"Can the system be bypassed?"

"It can; why?" Richie asked slowly.

"How?" Mondrya asked, ignoring Richie's question.

"Somebody would have to be logged in as system administrator and then it would just be a matter of turning off that option in the setup."

"Can you do that?"

"Yes."

"And if you turn it off, does it trigger an e-mail to anybody?"

"Yes."

"And who gets that?" Mondrya asked.

"You and Sheldon."

"Sheldon is on vacation and has the out-of-office auto response turned on. Anybody else get one?"

"No. Why do you want to know?"

"I told you, I need to look at something, and I don't need the whole company knowing what I'm doing. So I need you to turn off that setting. Will you do it?"

"Whose records do you want to look at? Never mind, I don't want to know." Richie got up again. "You don't mind if I do this from here, do you? Whatever you're doing, I really don't want it coming back on me."

"Not at all. I understand your need to cover yourself." Mondrya got up and let Richie have access to her computer. The minute and a half that it took seemed like forever.

"Well, it's done," Richie said, and started to leave. "Let me know when I can turn it back on."

"Sit down, Richie. This won't take long," Mondrya said, and logged into the HR system. She accessed Frank Collins's personnel file and examined each page. Mondrya wasn't exactly sure what she was looking for, but she would know it when she saw it, and she saw it on the work history page. Before coming to work at Hudson Financial, Frank Collins worked as an account manager for Dean Witter, in New York. Prior to that, he was a sales representative for Atlanta Life Insurance.

Mondrya logged out of the system and told Richie that he could reset the system. "You owe me a favor, Mondrya. It's a shame that you're a new-style VP, 'cause I really would like to be IS director."

"Richie"—Mondrya took a deep breath and looked at him—"Sheldon is a blithering idiot; you and I both know that and so do other influential people. He will eliminate himself in due time. When that happens, I know that you'll be in a very strong position to assume that role."

"Is that official or unofficial?"

"What do you think, Richie?"

"Unofficial. That sounds pretty political for a nonpolitical VP."

"You'll find out when you become IS director that perception is reality."

As soon as Richie left her office, Mondrya called the Dean Witter office in New York. "Human Resources, this is Judy; how may I help you?"

"Good morning, Judy, this Mondrya Foster calling from Hudson Financial Corporation in Atlanta. How are you this morning?"

"It's Monday, and the weekends are never long enough," she joked.

"I think we all need shorter work weeks and more vacation time."

"Ain't that the truth. What can I do for you, Mondrya?"

"I'd like to verify employment for a Frank Collins, please."

"I can help you with that."

"Let me know when you're ready," Mondrya told her.

"I'm ready."

"Oooh, your system is much faster than ours," Mondrya said. "Anyway, Mr. Collins reports being employed there from July 1993 to February 1994."

"That's correct."

"Can you tell me if he resigned or if he was terminated?"

"Company policy prohibits the release of that information."

"I understand. Here's my problem, Judy: Mr. Collins has applied for a sensitive position, and I need to know if he was terminated for any type of financial impropriety."

"Hmm, I understand your situation, Mondrya, but I hope you can appreciate the need to protect confidential information. So . . ." Judy paused.

"Yes, Judy?"

"If I were to tell you that Mr. Collins was fired for gross mismanagement of the accounts assigned to him, I could be fired. Sorry I couldn't help you. You have a nice day, Mondrya."

"You, too, Judy. And thank you," Mondrya said, and hung up the phone.

The better part of the day was filled with a boring meeting, followed by a dull corporate lunch. At least the food was good. Lunch was followed by two more boring meetings. It was three-thirty before Mondrya got back to her office. While she sat through the endless series of meaningless gatherings, Mondrya's mind was focused clearly on how she was going to proceed. She needed to access Frank Collins's records again. This time she wasn't worried about the automatic e-mails, since they all would come to her anyway. Mondrya turned on her computer and tried logging in with her old group manager password.

ACCESS DENIED

She tried to remember the system password she'd seen Richie type so many times.

ACCESS DENIED

Mondrya knew she would only have one more attempt to gain access before the system locked her out. *Think, Mondrya, think.* She thought about logging in as herself, since she had access to the system, but she definitely didn't need anybody knowing what she was looking for in the system. The HR system was one thing; the in-house brokerage system was another matter entirely. *Last chance.* Mondrya began to slowly type *WONNIEMTEL*, which was *let me in now* spelled backward, and pressed ENTER. When she saw the hourglass, she knew she was in.

Mondrya searched for all documents or entries related to Frank Collins. The system returned 39,892 items. She needed to add a variable to narrow the search parameters. Mondrya thought back to the weeks before he committed suicide. Frank had meetings with Bill Hudson on an almost daily basis. Then the promotion came. She remembered how it seemed strange to everyone that Frank wasn't happy about it at all. The daily meetings became daily arguments. *The time before Suzanne died.* She tried to remember the exact date, but it didn't matter. *New search:* get all documents or entries related to Frank Collins, last 14 months. The system returned 47 items. *Display list.*

Mondrya opened and read each document carefully. She got to a document named "CLIENT LIST COLLINS, FRANK" and another named "CLIENT LIST COLLINS, FRANK"; Mondrya thought it was the same list. The only difference was one had a space before "Frank" and one didn't. Mondrya scanned CLIENT LIST COLLINS, FRANK. *Frank's client list*, nothing she hadn't already seen hundreds of times as his supervisor. Mondrya sat straight up in her chair when she began reading CLIENT LIST COLLINS,FRANK.

"Jackpot."

When the document was accessed, the system sent the following e-mail:

To: advisory board member <advisoryboard@ hudsonfinancial.com >
From: System Administrator <sysadm@hudson financial.com>
Subject: Unauthorized File Access

This message was automatically generated and sent to the advisory board member distribution list. Please be advised somebody has accessed restricted document:

File name: CLIENT LIST COLLINS,FRANK
Was accessed by: SYSTEM ADMINSTRATOR
From Terminal Position: 136
Position Owner: Mondrya Foster

The document she opened contained a list of ten clients that Mondrya had never seen. Some of the names were in Spanish, while others had names like Benjamin Franklin and James Madison. It didn't take her long to figure out the pattern was dead presidents. Mondrya quickly printed the document. She called and left a message for Marcus, confirming their luncheon engagement for the following day: "And, Marcus, I have things that I'm sure will interest you. I'm meeting a friend at Starbucks in downtown Decatur; if you're in the area around six, stop in and join us." Then she got a file folder out of her drawer and took out her pad. At the top of the page she wrote "Notes To Marcus," then created an outline of all her observations and the conclusions. Then she came across a document named "11A2B3675C489."

Mondrya opened it and the system automatically generated another e-mail.

The system opened to an area brokerage system that she had never seen before. It prompted her to enter a password. Once again, Mondrya typed *WONNIEMTEL*. **ACCESS DENIED.** Mondrya looked at her watch and noted that it was almost five o'clock, and she would have to leave soon if she was going to meet Gloria at six at Starbucks in downtown Decatur. Mondrya inserted a CD in the drive and copied the three documents to the disk. She logged out of the system, turned off her computer, grabbed her purse, and headed for the door.

As usual, traffic on 285 was ridiculous. Even though she was late, Mondrya wanted to get the disk she had just copied out of her hands. She stopped at the Decatur post office and sent the disk, along with the client lists and the notes she made for Marcus, to her attention at Gloria's office, via priority mail. This was her insurance policy, and she would need it if it was to get out from under Bill Hudson's thumb.

When Mondrya arrived at Starbucks at six-twenty-five, Gloria Giannelli was already waiting. Gloria stood up when she saw her and waved Mondrya over to the table. "I was starting to think you weren't coming, Mondrya."

"I'm sorry. Traffic, you know how it is. I would have called you, but I left your cell number at the office."

"Well, you're here now. That suit looks very nice on you. Where did you get it?"

"Niemen's, caught it on sale." Mondrya went to the counter to order. "Caramel Macchiato, please." Once she got her coffee, Mondrya returned to the table.

"So, what did you want to see me about?"

"Because you're my friend. Can't two friends get together for a cup of coffee after work?"

"I'm sorry, Mondrya. Of course we can, but you made it sound like it was business."

"Well it's that, too."

"So, you do need a lawyer?"

"Not yet. I just need a little friendly advice. I'm thinking of filing a sexual harassment suit, and I want to know something first."

"I kinda assumed that, since sexual harassment is my specialty. Anyway, I can give you a broad legal definition of what constitutes sexual harassment. Unwelcome sexual advances, requests for sexual favors, and other verbal or physical conduct of a sexual nature constitutes sexual harassment. When submission to, or rejection of this conduct, explicitly or implicitly affects an individual's employment, unreasonably interferes with an individual's work performance, or creates an intimidating, hostile, or offensive work environment, that situation could also be deemed as harassment."

"I think I qualify," Mondrya said, casually sipping her coffee.

"Who is it?"

"I'd rather not say. Not yet anyway. What should I do now?"

"That depends; have you directly informed the harasser that the conduct is unwelcome and must stop?"

"Many times."

"The next step is to use any employer complaint mechanism or grievance system available to you. Have you done that?"

"No, I will if I have to."

"That's important, Mondrya. When investigating allegations of sexual harassment, EEOC looks at the whole record. So it is very important that you have as much documentation of the harassment as possible."

"What information are they looking for?"

"The circumstances of the allegation, such as the nature of the sexual advances and the context in which the alleged incidents occurred. That's what we'll need to go to court with."

"I understand. I have kept a record of all the occurrences. Dates, times, what was said. But I don't expect it to go that far." Mondrya smiled and Gloria wondered why. "What? Why are you looking at me like that? I've just gotten a little insurance."

"Insurance?" Gloria questioned.

"Just a little bit of information to guarantee that things go my way."

"What are you looking to get out of this?"

"Peace of mind."

"Peace of mind and money, you mean."

"Anyway." Mondrya smiled. "Have you ever met Marcus Douglas?"

"Mr. Good-Looking Attorney for the Defense? I met him once years ago at a conference."

"I'm meeting him tomorrow for lunch."

"I didn't know you knew him."

"He came to the office last week."

"What for?"

"His firm is conducting an independent investigation of Desireé Ferguson's death. I was looking into something for him, and that's how I got my insurance."

"What's that?" Gloria asked as three masked men suddenly rushed into the Starbucks carrying guns.

"Nobody move!" one shouted from the doorway. "Everybody be quiet and cool, and everybody goes home alive tonight."

"All we want is the money," the second said, shoving his gun toward the cashier's face.

The third robber moved to cover the customers. He looked

around the room, pointing his weapon. "What the fuck you looking at, bitch?" he shouted, walking over to Gloria and Mondrya's table.

"Nothing, I wasn't looking at nothing," Gloria said, shaking.

"Oh, so I ain't nothin'! You pretty bitches think y'all better than me?" He pointed the gun at Gloria. "See if you better than this." He fired one shot at Gloria and grazed her temple.

"NO!" Mondrya yelled. He turned the gun on Mondrya and fired three shots.

"What the fuck you doin'? Let's get outta here," the one by the door yelled. The three rushed out, leaving Gloria and Mondrya lying on the floor.

The paramedics pronounced Mondrya dead on the scene.

ON SECOND THOUGHT

At ten o'clock on Tuesday morning, Marcus woke up and looked over at Carmen; she was dead to the world. The day before, Carmen took Marcus to see Mrs. Barnes, her old boyfriend Denny's mother. Marcus wondered out loud why Carmen introduced him to Denny's mother before introducing him to her own parents. Carmen told him that she wasn't ready for him to meet her parents. After which they took in a movie and went dancing.

He lay next to her quietly and watched her. Even in sleep, Carmen was beautiful. The last few days with her made Randa's betrayal seem like a distant memory. He felt lucky, lucky to be with her. He eased out of bed quietly and made his way to the shower. When he got out, Carmen was still asleep. He dressed quietly and left her a note saying that he would be back around two.

Marcus arrived at Hudson Financial to pick up Mondrya Foster for lunch. He had been anxious to find out what she had that would interest him. Besides, Mondrya Foster was a beautiful woman. *A beautiful married woman. Anyway, didn't you just leave a beautiful woman sleeping in your bed?*

Marcus approached the receptionist, once again thinking how lucky he was to be with Carmen. She was so much fun to be with, and she was down-to-earth, not the phony, overly-impressed-with-her-beauty that he thought she would be. *Wrong woman; you're thinking about Randa.*

"Good morning," the receptionist said.

"Good morning. Marcus Douglas to see Mondrya Foster, please."

The receptionist took a deep breath. "I'm sorry to have to be the one to tell you this, but Ms. Foster was murdered last night."

Marcus grabbed hold of the counter to steady himself. "Murdered?"

"Yes, murdered. She was at Starbucks in downtown Decatur last night when they were robbed. One of the robbers shot her three times. I'm sorry," she said as the phone rang.

"Well, thank you anyway," Marcus said, and she waved good-bye, mouthing the words "I'm sorry" again. As he turned to leave, Marcus saw Bill Hudson coming toward him. "Marcus Douglas!"

"How are you, Bill?"

"Fair to partly cloudy." Hudson smiled. "What brings you here?"

"I was going to have lunch with Mondrya Foster."

"Very tragic. A wonderful woman like that, shot down for no reason. I was on my way to have a drink. Why don't you join me?"

"I could use a drink," Marcus said, and followed Hudson to the elevator.

Marcus followed Bill to Spring Street to a nearby strip club called Cheetah III. "I hope you don't mind drinking here, Marcus, but I like to have a little entertainment with my drink."

"No, Bill, I don't mind. I've been known to enjoy a drink or two at places like this."

"Have you even been here before?"

"Can't say that I have. I don't mean to sound politically incorrect, but I prefer to have my entertainment in color. But this might be an interesting change of pace for me."

"I know what you mean," Hudson said as he flashed his membership card to the doorman. "I've been known to go down to Magic City every now and then. One thing I'll say for them black gals there, they sure do give you a show for your money. But they usually have one or two black gals dancin' here."

Hudson led Marcus to a table near the main stage. Marcus looked around. He had been to many strip clubs before, but this was different. At noon, the place was crowded with white men in business suits. "Vodka and tonic!" Hudson yelled over the loud music to the waitress. "What you havin', Marcus?"

"Hennessy, straight. On second thought, make it a double," he said, and the waitress departed to get their drinks. Once she cleared the table, a tall, blond woman with enormous breasts approached the table.

"Hi, Bill! Long time, no see." She kissed him on the cheek. "I was startin' to think you didn't love us no more."

"Just been so damned busy lately. But you know, if I don't love nobody, I love you, honey."

"Would you like me to dance for you?"

"Sure, honey, go ahead." While she started to peel off her clothes, Hudson leaned toward Marcus. "Them titties, fake as shit and hard as a rock. Most disappointing thing in the world."

Hudson was right; sistahs give you a show. All she's doing is playing in her hair and posing. Since Marcus wasn't overly impressed with the entertainment, he turned to the business at hand. "Do you know what happened to Mondrya?"

"I talked to her husband this morning. The police told him that the son of a bitch shot her because she was looking at him. They didn't have to kill her; they could have just taken the money and gone. But these young punks think that shooting women and kids makes them men. Drug dealers with empty souls, all of them."

Marcus looked at Hudson with a bit of contempt. "You're not saying that you think all black people are drug dealers with empty souls, are you?"

"Shit, no! But sons of bitches like that deserve to die a slow, painful death. They oughta bring back firing squads. Line them all up and shoot them. I'd sure volunteer," Hudson went on. "I didn't know that you knew Mondrya."

"We only met last week. I came to talk to—" Marcus started to tell Hudson that he had come last week to talk to him about Frank Collins, but he thought better of it. "To talk to you. I was looking for some investment advice. When they told me that you were not in, Mondrya stepped in."

"Do you have any more questions?"

"No, she was able to answer all my questions. I can't believe she's dead."

"It is hard to believe. I'm having problems dealing with it myself. I haven't even begun to think of what the company is going to do without her. Those are going to be big shoes to fill," Hudson said, draining his glass. "We got lots of shoes to fill now. Last week one of our senior execs, Coleman Wilson, hung himself. I was going to move Mondrya into that spot. But now I have two spots to fill. Investors and stockholders don't take too kindly to this type of shake-up in upper management. But you do what you have to do, Marcus. And as long as everybody keeps making money, no one cares what you do. A man could get away with anything as long as there's enough money floating around." Hudson flagged down a waitress. "How 'bout bringing us two more." He turned to Marcus.

"Hennessy, right? And a vodka and tonic for me, sugar," Hudson said, dismissing her. "Speaking of getting away with anything, congratulations on winning your case. I was sure that son of a bitch Ferguson did it."

"So were a lot of people. A lot of them still think he did it and got away with murder. Which one are you?"

"I'm a numbers man, Marcus. If there is one constant in the world, it's numbers. They always gotta add up. DA's case just didn't add up. Time line wasn't right, and that's where you found your opportunity. Showed us all that they just didn't have the numbers. Kicker was when you marched that good ole boy deputy sheriff in there and he said 'there's no way he coulda drove past me doin' more than forty-five.'"

"'Not on my shift,'" Marcus said in his best good-ole-boy accent. "I thought it was a power move myself."

"Hawkins shoulda seen that coming. Disappointed a lot of influential people. I'm talkin' people with money. And you can't run for office without money." The waitress returned with their drinks. "I wanna settle up, honey. I got to be gettin' back." Hudson paid the check and tipped the waitress handsomely. "You know, Marcus, some of those people, myself included, liked the way you handled yourself during the trial."

"Thank you, Bill. Just doing what a good defense attorney would do."

"Winning the case is important; shit, everyone likes to win. What's more important is the way you handle yourself. Whether people can count on you to do what's right. The public is screaming for somebody they can put their trust in. Or at least gives them a perception of trust; you know what I'm talking about, Marcus?" Hudson took a sip of his drink. "I was wondering if you had any political aspirations."

Marcus laughed. "To be honest with you, Bill, I never gave it any thought."

"Then give it some thought before you answer. But I can assure you that under the right set of circumstances, the money would be there for you." Hudson finished his drink. "I gotta get back, but let's get together in a week or two, and we'll talk about it some more then."

Marcus drove back to his house feeling overwhelmed by the conversation he'd just had with Bill Hudson. *Did he just ask me to run for district attorney?* Once he got past the shock of it and his ego returned to its normal size, Marcus began to question Hudson's motives. Not that he didn't think he was a good enough lawyer. He was indeed capable of doing the job, but why'd he ask? It made Mondrya's message, "I have some things that I'm sure will interest you," make Hudson's sudden offer seem just a little dubious. Did that something involve Hudson? He couldn't be sure. Then he thought maybe his group wanted to capitalize on his name recognition, which was much more likely.

When Marcus came into the house, Carmen was in the kitchen fixing a late lunch for them. He called to her. "Carmen!"

"In the kitchen," she answered. "You're back early. I wasn't expecting you until two. I was making us something to eat."

"I'm gonna get fat hangin' around with you."

"Maybe you should start running with me in the morning. I need to get back to it. I haven't been running since Saturday."

"Whose fault is that?"

"Yours. You're a bad influence on me. Lying up in bed, sleeping till eleven o'clock in the morning."

"If you like, I'll leave you alone tonight."

"What are you trying to say?"

"That I'll forego my usual nocturnal activities and let you

get to sleep early so you can get up at the crack of dawn and run."

"I wasn't sayin' all that, now. Maybe we could just start earlier." Carmen put her arms around Marcus and kissed him. "'Cause at two o'clock in the morning, you're still bringin' it strong and stayin' long."

Marcus looked at his watch and smiled at Carmen. "You wanna get started now?"

"Let's eat first. It will give us energy in the late rounds. Have a seat; the food will be ready soon." She pecked him lightly on the lips. "So, where did you go sneak off to this morning?"

"Nowhere special. Someone just asked me to think about running for district attorney."

"Who?"

"Bill Hudson."

"Hudson Financial, Bill Hudson?"

"One and the same."

"Kinda coincidental that we're investigating somebody at his company and out of the blue he asks you to run for DA."

"I thought so too."

"But maybe he just wants to take advantage of your approval ratings."

"I thought that too."

"When did all this happen?"

"Just a little while ago at Cheetah III."

"What were you doing there?"

"I went to Hudson Financial to have lunch with Mondrya Foster and found out that she was murdered last night in a robbery at a Starbucks. I ended up running into Hudson, and he invited me there to have a drink with him. Like you said, he just came out of the blue with it."

"Who is Mondrya Foster?"

"She was my source at Hudson. She left a message for me

yesterday and said that she had some things that she was sure would interest me. But whatever she had died with her."

"And you were having lunch with her?"

"I wanted to know what she had."

"Is that what you snuck out of bed for? To have lunch with what's-her-name?"

"Carmen, are you jealous?"

"No!" Carmen said quickly and definitely. "Well, maybe just a little," Carmen said, surprised at herself. Her feelings for Marcus were developing faster than she anticipated. Maybe she needed to give herself some space. After all, she had been with Marcus the better part of every day since she'd been in Atlanta. Not to mention all of the last four days.

"Don't be jealous, Carmen," Marcus said, putting his arms around her waist while he kissed her on the back of her neck. She felt his nature press into her backside and let out a low moan.

"On second thought, who needs food." Carmen turned into his arms and kissed his lips. "Let's get started now."

Then the doorbell rang.

TIME TO KILL

Garrett drove slowly down Herndon Parkway on the way back from East Point, a suburb of Atlanta. He turned off the radio. Garrett liked driving in silence; it gave him a chance to think without being bombarded with the musical thoughts, needs, desires, and thug passions of every singer and rapper that came over the airwaves.

Mostly he thought about the past weekend with his children. His first weekend without Paven and his first weekend in years without work. It felt a little funny at first, not rushing out of the house first thing in the morning, but he could get used to it. Garrett picked up the children on Friday night, and they spent the rest of the evening talking. They went to the movies and out to dinner on Saturday and to the park on Sunday. The children told their father that they missed him and wanted to come home. He told them that they had to talk to their mother about that. "She is welcome to come home anytime she wants to."

"Every time I ask her when we're goin' home, she just says she needs time to think," his oldest daughter Aleana said. She was sixteen and reminded Garrett so much of her mother when she was that age.

"I asked her what's there to think about," his son Gary said.

"Your mother and I are havin' some problems right now, and she needs a little time to sort things out for herself."

"I know, she told us all about it. You're never home and she feels trapped," Aleana said. "But why do we have to suffer? I can't live another day with Grandma."

"Why not?"

"She's so picky about everything," Aleana answered with attitude.

"And we always gotta be quiet. We can't have any fun," Monique, his youngest, said. At eight years old, she was the apple of her father's eye. She sat down in his lap. "Daddy, I wanna come home."

"Yeah, Daddy, we all do," Gary said.

"Look, I know your grandmother ain't easy to live with, but give it time. Give your mother and me some time to work this out."

As Garrett drove, he thought about that point, *some time to work this out,* but just how much time was Paven going to need? That, after all these years, he couldn't answer. Their relationship began when they were both in the ninth grade and continued into college. While the two were in their sophomore year at the University of Georgia, Paven got pregnant with Aleana. They were soon married, and Garrett quit school to support his new family. He worked any job he could, until he received an offer to join the Atlanta Police Department. After Aleana was born, Paven went back to college. She was four months pregnant with Gary when she received her degree in chemistry. Now, with two young children, Paven didn't want strangers raising their children. She wanted to stay home for a few years to give them a good foundation. Garrett agreed—*ain't nothin' worse than bad children*—and that's where it began. Garrett took the first of many second jobs. *How could I have let things get this far?*

Garrett loved Paven, almost from the day they met. Sure he had been unfaithful from time to time over the years, but those women never meant anything to him. Although it may have been a contributing factor, that wasn't what this was about. *I took Paven for granted. I was sure she'd always be there.* What he wanted now was his family back.

Since he didn't have to think about going home to be with his family, Garrett did what came natural: Work. So, as promised, he freed up some time from his case to go talk to Porsche Temple. It turned out to be an interesting afternoon. One that he was looking forward to sharing with Marcus. He pulled in the driveway, parked, and approached the house, admiring the gold Mercedes in the driveway. Garrett rang the bell, wondering whose car it was.

"Garrett, come on in," Marcus said, stepping aside to let him in.

"What's up, Marcus. I wanted to tell you about my afternoon with Porsche Temple, but I see you have company."

"No, I want to hear what she had to say."

"I do too," Carmen said, coming out of the kitchen. Garrett shifted his eyes in Carmen's direction.

"Ms. Taylor, I wasn't expecting to see you. You're looking especially radiant today."

"Hello, Garrett. And it's time you started calling me Carmen."

"Okay, Carmen, I see we've upgraded our mode of transportation."

"It was my sister's car."

"Her brother-in-law gave it to her," Marcus said quietly.

"I wish somebody would give me a five-hundred Benz," Garrett threw in, making his way to the living room.

"What did Porsche Temple have to say for herself?" Marcus asked.

Garrett looked at Carmen, somewhat disappointed that, because she was there, he would have to tell the story without all the colorful details. "I rang the bell at Temple's house around three this afternoon. At first nobody answered, but when I rang the bell again, they opened the door . . ."

"Yes?" Simone asked through the barred screen door.

"Good afternoon. My name is Garrett Mason. I'm a private investigator." Garrett held his card up to the door for Simone to see.

"And?" Simone replied, looking and sounding unimpressed.

"I'd like to speak to Porsche Temple. Is she here?" When Simone didn't answer, Garrett said, "Carmen Taylor asked me to speak to her about the murder of Desireé Ferguson."

"Okay," Simone said, with a change of attitude. "You can come in." She put the pistol back in the drawer and unlocked the screen door.

"Thank you."

"I'm sorry," Simone said. "But I didn't know who you were."

"I can understand that. You can't be too careful 'bout who you let in your house. I should have called and let you know I was coming."

"Don't sweat it; you in here now." She smiled. "I'll let Porsche know you're here," Simone said, showing Garrett into the living room. For the next fifteen minutes, he occupied himself watching music videos on BET. He was caught off guard when Misty and Chocolate walked into the room. "Hello, ladies," Garrett said.

"Hi," they both said while Misty unplugged a CD player. Chocolate went out on the deck by the pool and Misty followed behind her. "Porsche said she'll be down in a minute," Misty said as she walked out of the room. So now Garrett entertained himself watching Misty and Chocolate. It wasn't too much longer before Porsche came into the living room. "Mr. Mason?"

"Ms. Temple," Garrett said, rising to his feet.

"It's Porsche. Please, have a seat." Garrett gladly reclaimed his spot while Porsche made herself comfortable on the couch next to him. "Tell me what I can do for you."

"Carmen Taylor asked me to talk to you, and I apologize for just showing up like this. I was telling the young lady who answered the door that I should have called first."

"It's all right. Carmen called me and said she'd asked you to talk to me. So I've been expecting you."

"I'll try not to take up a lot of your time."

"I have all the time you need. How's your investigation going?"

"Well, I'm just getting started and looking for a direction to go in. So, what I'd like to have happen here is for you to tell me"—Garrett paused as he glanced out the sliding glass door—"everything you know about Desireé Ferguson. And if I ask you anything that you don't want to answer, just tell me to back off."

"I've done a lot of things in my life, and I'm not ashamed of any of them. Ask me anything you want. I'm here to help you. If anything I say helps you find who did that shit to her, all the better."

"Let's start with you. What do you do, Porsche?"

"I manage the three girls who live here with me, Mr.

Mason. They're dancers and I'm training them to be professional escorts. I used to be an escort until my habits made me unreliable. But I still have some access to clientele, so I'm putting that information to good use."

"How did you get started?"

"Me and Desireé used to get ourselves invited to all types of parties. Any place we could meet men with money. I met a man at one of those parties named James Martin. He said to call him when I was ready to stop waiting on one of those limp-dick old men to give me money and start making some money on my own. He trained me, just like I'm doing with these girls. I started working for him, escorting, and once a month we'd drive to Miami to pick up two kilos of cocaine."

"Was Desireé involved with James Martin too?"

"No, Desireé never met him. By the time I hooked up with James, Desireé had married Roland and pretty much stopped hangin' out with me. Roland and I never got along."

"Who do you think killed her?"

"Like everybody else, I thought Roland did it."

"Ms. Taylor told me that you hadn't talked to Desireé for a while before she died."

"I used to smoke a lotta cocaine, and those days I was smoking more. But I've been clean for three hundred and eight days. It was Desireé's death that made me wake up."

"How was that?"

"When she died, I lost it. I know I was up in this house smokin' for eight days straight at least. There were different people here smokin' with me and they'd come and go. But somebody was always here smokin' with me the whole time. Shit, I was buyin'. We'd smoke up what we had and call for more. But this time my guy took his time about bringin' it. So while I'm walkin' around frantic, lookin' out the window, I started thinkin' about Desireé and I started crying. Just like that, she was dead. Dead at twenty-seven. And Desireé was so full of life. It made me realize how short life can be. It ain't promised to you. Desireé had everything and now she's dead."

"Did Desireé ever smoke with you?"

"Never. And I never told her that I did. I didn't want her to know. She woulda been so disappointed in me."

"How long did you know Desireé?"

"We met my sophomore year at Spellman. Me and Carmen had a class together my freshman year. She introduced me to Desireé when she came to Spellman that next year. We'd been friends ever since. To be honest with you, I was in love with her then."

"You're a lesbian?"

"No, I'm bisexual. I've always known I was bisexual, but at the time Desireé was strictly dickly, so I didn't approach her with it. I loved her and was happy just to be around her. I was shocked the first time she came on to me—," Porsche started, but Garrett interrupted her.

"You didn't know she was bisexual too?"

"She wasn't. She told me somebody turned her out."

"You know who?"

"I think this is a good time for me to say back off. If who turned Desireé becomes important to you, ask me again and I'll tell you. But now I think I should respect the woman's privacy."

"Fair enough," Garrett said, staring again out the sliding door at what Misty and Chocolate were doing. "You were saying that"—Garrett turned back to Porsche—"you were shocked the first time she came on to you."

"I was shocked because after a while, Roland came in the room and watched us make love."

"He just watched? He didn't join in?"

"Roland is impotent."

"He never heard of Viagra?"

"Desireé said that Roland used to be the Viagra king," Porsche mused. "Until the doctor told him it was bad for his heart. I forget what she called the condition he has, but he had to stop taking it. After that, Desireé started seeing other men."

"You three get together often?"

"Every now and then. Roland preferred watching men having sex with her. Since Desireé was always seeing somebody, anyway, she'd bring one home so Roland could watch."

"Do you know if he ever watched her and Rasheed Damali?"

"Yes."

"Did you know Rasheed Damali?"

"Yes."

"How did they meet?"

"I introduced them," Porsche said quietly.

"How did you know him?"

"He used to work for James Martin sometimes."

"I thought he was on Desireé's card? What was he doin' for Martin?"

"Every once and a while, James would get female clients. Rasheed was his guy."

"Did Desireé know that he was a male escort?"

"I don't know for sure, but I don't think so."

"So the woman you've been in love with for years is involved with Damali. Why didn't you tell her what he was about?"

"I tried to tell Desireé about Rasheed, but she never wanted to hear it. She was too far gone on him. Desireé thought she was in love with him."

"You know where he was from?"

"I don't know where he's originally from, but he came here from Texas."

"That figures. The car he was driving was stolen from there."

"No, it wasn't."

"How do you know that?"

"Because he told me." When Garrett looked strangely at her, she decided not to wait to be asked. Porsche said, "Rasheed was working as an escort while he was in Texas. He burned out there, the same way I did."

"How's that?"

"You start showing up late for appointments or missing them altogether. Or your performance isn't what it used to be, so the clients stop asking for you. Because all you're thinking about is gettin' through with what you gotta do and get paid so you can get high."

"So how'd he get the car?"

"One of his clients gave him that car. But when her husband finally missed it, she told him it was stolen."

"How'd Damali . . . find out?" Garrett asked, staring outside once again at what Misty and Chocolate were doing.

"She called Rasheed and told him," Porsche said, and glanced out the door. "I can ask them to stop if they're distracting you."

"No, that won't be necessary. How do you know all this?"

"Rasheed told me."

"Like you and him were pretty close?"

"We talked."

"Just talked?"

"We started gettin' high together," Porsche said, repositioning herself on the couch. "Rasheed came by here one night looking for Desireé. I was gettin' high. I asked if he wanted a hit. It was on from there."

"Did Desireé know that he got high?"

"No."

"What else did y'all talk about?"

"Just bullshit at first. We didn't do a lot of talking; like I said, I was smokin' pretty heavy those days. But this one particular night, I was in the pool waiting on my guy to bring my package and Rasheed came by. He had just left Desireé's house. He told me how much he hated Roland watching them have sex. He said it was funny at first, watchin' Roland play with that limp dick. But now Roland was getting demanding about it. Tellin' him how he wanted him to fuck her. Like he was directing a porno flick or something." Porsche laughed.

"He ever do you like that?"

"No. He would just sit there quietly and he'd never stay long. Like I said, he preferred watchin' men with her."

"The reason I ask is he may have been filming the whole thing, making his own movies."

"If he was, I didn't know about it and Desireé never mentioned anything like that."

"Maybe she didn't know." Garrett glanced out the door and then back at Porsche. "So now you and Rasheed are gettin' high together."

"We were having sex too. That night he came by, and I was in the pool; he got in with me. We were talking, and one thing led to another."

"I guess Desireé didn't know about that either."

"Not unless he told her."

"Excuse me," Simone said as she came into the living room. "Porsche, do you know if we have any clean towels?"

"Check the linen closet, Simone."

"I already looked there," Simone replied, walking closer to the couch.

"Then what does that tell you?"

"That there are no clean towels," Simone answered quietly as her chin touched her chest.

"Don't ask questions you already know the answer to. And always think before you open your mouth. Knowing what to say and what not to say will make your company more desirable and therefore requested on a regular basis," Porsche instructed. Simone left the room, and Porsche turned her attention to Garrett. "I'm sorry for the interruption."

"Okay, so you and him are gettin' high and havin' sex. Y'all get together often?"

"Not really."

"Once a week, twice a week?"

"Yeah, once a week, sometimes twice. Sometimes not at all."

"You always buy?"

"No, most times when he'd come by, he'd set it out for me."

"Since you were on it pretty hard, he must have come with a lot."

"I'd have to kick in sometimes, but most times he'd come correct."

"Both y'all buy from the same source?"

Porsche looked at Garrett and pressed her lips together, deciding whether it was time to say back off again or not. "No, we didn't," she answered, deciding that finding Desireé's killer was more important than protecting her guy's privacy.

"You know where he got his?"

"James Martin."

"That's right; you did mention that he was a dealer too."

"No, James was a distributor. He'd keep some around for personal consumption."

"How come you didn't get yours from him?"

"I didn't need him knowing how much I was gettin' high. Even though he wasn't callin', I still called myself working for him."

"I guess Rasheed didn't care?"

"No, James would front Rasheed against jobs he did for him."

"I thought you said that Martin didn't get a lot of female clients?"

"He didn't."

"Then how was Rasheed coming so correct?"

"He told me that he owed James a lotta money. He didn't say how much."

"When was this?"

"The week before it happened."

"You know where I can find James Martin?"

"He's dead. About three months ago, he got shot when somebody tried to jack his car. Like I said, Mr. Mason, life is short, and it's not promised to you."

Carmen looked at Garrett and then at Marcus and back to Garrett. "You know what I wanna know?"

"What's that, Carmen?" Garrett asked.

"Why is all this just coming out now?"

"I don't know; Porsche says she never talked to the police," Garrett answered.

"When you were investigating, why didn't you talk to any of these people?"

"Because, Carmen, nobody," Garrett said, pointing at Marcus, "told me to talk to any of these people."

Carmen looked at Marcus, waiting for an answer. Marcus looked at Carmen and then at Garrett. "We're waiting for an answer, Marcus?" Garrett quipped.

"What?" Marcus pleaded.

"Why didn't you tell Garrett to investigate any of this?"

"Carmen, my job was to defend Roland against the prosecution's case. I didn't have to present the jury with alternative theories of how the crime was committed. They had no case."

"He's right, Carmen; the police investigated the crime," Garrett said. "I investigated their case, and this is not their case. All these leads came from you, Carmen. We never heard of any these people until you came along."

"And how would we know about them? Roland sure wasn't gonna tell us about any of this. All this does is gives him a stronger motive for murder," Marcus said passionately.

"No, it doesn't," Garrett said as he stood up.

"What?" Carmen said angrily.

"I don't think this makes his motive any stronger. To me, it dilutes it." Garrett walked to the bar and poured himself a glass of Hennessy.

"How?" Marcus asked. "I'm dyin' to hear this."

"Think about it, Marcus. Ferguson had a young beautiful wife; you'll forgive me for sayin' this, Carmen, but your sister was puttin' on a freak show for his private entertainment. Why would he kill her? He had what most men only dream of. James Martin was the case they should have been pursuing. Rasheed was workin' for Martin doin' God knows what. 'Cause if he was frontin' him dope against work and he didn't get many female clients, that only leaves men. And on top of that, he owed Martin money. That's where this case is leading," Garrett said.

"But he's dead now." Carmen sighed.

"Somebody knows something about him. If he's dead, somebody had to claim the body," Marcus said to Garrett.

"I'm on it," he replied. "This is getting to be a whole lot more interesting than my other case."

"I know somebody who might know something about

him," Carmen said, and both Garrett and Marcus looked at her.

"Who?" Marcus asked.

"A friend of mine."

"What's your friend's name?" Marcus said, sounding a little jealous.

"Denny."

"Denny who?"

"Denny Barnes."

"How would he know about James Martin?"

"Denny rolls in those circles. He's the one who told me where to find Porsche."

"How do you know Denny?"

Carmen smiled. "He was my first boyfriend, Marcus."

"Oh," Marcus said with a silly look on his face.

"Remember, we had dinner with his mother," Carmen said as Garrett looked on like he was watching a tennis match.

"So what's goin' on here, kids?" Garrett asked.

"Nothing," Carmen said, looking at Marcus and smiling.

"Nothing," Marcus said almost at the same time.

"Is there something goin' on here that I don't know about?" Garrett asked.

"No," Marcus and Carmen said in unison with a grin that suggested guilt.

Garrett looked at Carmen sneaking glances at Marcus, and Marcus sneaking glances at her. "Oh, I know what's goin' on here—y'all are fuckin'. I knew there was something different about the way you came bouncin' out that kitchen."

Marcus winked at Carmen, and she smiled her response.

"Well, I'll let you two get back to what y'all was doin'," Garrett said, and got up from the couch. "Marcus, can I see you outside for a minute?"

"Sure. I'll be right back, Carmen."

Marcus followed Garrett outside. "Get in the truck," Garrett instructed. "I just wanted to thank you for sending me out there to see Porsche."

"Yeah, it sounds like it went pretty well."

"Brother, you don't know the half of it."

"What do you mean?"

"I left out the visual details of the conversation."

"Like what?"

"You remember I said the two girls came in the living room, unplugged the box and went outside?"

"And?"

"Have you seen them?"

"No. What do they look like?"

"Misty is brown skin, a little darker than Carmen. By the way, dog, you bangin' Carmen?" Marcus smiled. Garrett gave him five. "The other one, Chocolate, she's a beautiful, jet-black sistah. Both of them fine as hell, long, pretty legs, perfect asses, and enough titties for a muthafuckas. Misty, she's wearing one of her dancer outfits with spike heels."

"What'd the outfit look like?"

"It was purple and lacy. You gonna let me tell the story or not?"

"Yeah, yeah, I'm just trying to get a mental picture. Go ahead."

"Chocolate, she ain't got on nothin' but a thong and platform shoes. They go outside, plugged in the box, and they start dancin'. I ain't talkin' 'bout no side to side night club dancin'. They was shake dancin', dog. I'm talkin' titty-swingin' and ass-spankin' dancin'. Like they were having a contest."

"And you just sittin' there takin' it all in."

"Boy was I. Then Porsche Temple comes in."

"Show's over?"

"No, it's just gettin' started. Have you met her?"

"Who, Porsche? No. She was talking to Carmen at the bar at Goose Bumps. I didn't get a good look at her."

"She's a bad muthafucka too. She comes out in this little silk robe. You know the kind with the oriental pictures and writing and nothing on under it. And she don't have it tied real tight, so every time she moves, I get to see her pretty, dark nipples. Man! So me and her are talkin', and I'm sneakin' looks out the door at them dancin', but now they chasin' each other around the pool. I don't know how they runnin' around in them shoes, but it damn sure was worth watchin'. So Chocolate pushes Misty in the pool. And while she's standin' there laughin', Misty pulls her in. Next time I look at them, they're all up in each other's face, arguing."

"I guess Misty didn't like getting her hair wet."

"You gonna let me tell this or you gonna keep interrupting?"

"Just tryin' to keep my visual goin', man. Go on."

"So I go back to the Porsche show, and she goes Sharon Stone on me. She uncrossed her legs and crossed them again. Beautiful, absolutely beautiful. I look back outside and Chocolate's got a towel and she dryin' Misty off. Next thing I know, she got the towel on the ground, and she's on her knees, eatin' Misty out."

"You bullshittin'?"

"I bullshit you not, Marcus. Chocolate, on her knees, yodeling in the valley."

"And I know they gotta know you're watchin'."

"And I am. But then Porsche calls me on it. She says, 'I could ask them to stop if they're distracting you.' I was like, hell naw!"

"You had a real show."

"Yeah, but they saved the best for last, 'cause that's when Simone came out."

"She's bad. That's who I was looking at while Carmen was talkin' to Porsche."

"Well, she walks in, butt naked and soaking wet, talkin' about 'where are the clean towels.' I tell you what, Marcus."

"What's that?"

"The next time I got some time to kill, I'm gonna make up some questions and go back over there."

WE ARE FAMILY

After Garrett drove off, Marcus went back inside to pick up where he left off with Carmen, only to find her gathering her things together to leave. Carmen looked up as he came through the door. "You're leaving?"

"Yeah, I gotta go."

"Was it something I said?"

"No, Marcus, it wasn't anything you said. But I promised Dominique that we could get together to finish going through Dez's things today."

"You seem to have worked things out with her. That's good."

"We have; it's like she stopped trying to be my mother, and I stopped trying to be her daughter, and now I think we both feel free to be friends. And I found out that she's not bad; actually, she's kinda funny. She used to be so stiff and rigid when we were growing up. So I'm gonna pick her up today so we can get done with it."

"I thought we were goin' to get an early start on our nocturnal activities?"

Carmen saw the disappointed look on his face. "Don't

look like that, Marcus. I'll come back later if you want me to."

"I want you to. I don't want you to go."

"And I don't want to go."

"Then why are you?"

"'Cause I think I need to. To be honest with you, Marcus, I feel like I need to pull back a little. I need to give myself some space."

"I don't want to crowd you, Carmen."

"It's not you. You've been wonderful. It's just that I've been with you the better part of every day since I got here and all of the last four days. And I've enjoyed every minute of it. But I don't want to rush things with us. I know this is a very emotional time for both of us. I just want to be sure that what I'm starting to feel for you is real."

"I understand, Carmen. And if I wanted to be honest with myself," he said, stepping closer to Carmen, close enough to kiss, "I'd have to admit that I've been thinking the same thing. Because I'm starting to have very strong feelings for you too. So you go ahead and do what you gotta do. And maybe, if I'm lucky, I'll see you later."

"You might," Carmen said, stepping closer to Marcus. Her body pressed against his. "I think the chances are good that you will." She touched his face gently and kissed him on the cheek.

"What about the late lunch you made?"

"I forgot all about that."

While Carmen warmed up the food, Marcus went and changed out of his suit into some shorts and a T-shirt. They sat and ate quietly, after which Marcus walked Carmen to the door. She gave him a good-bye kiss on the cheek at the door, which led to another, which led Marcus to kiss Carmen's lips. That kiss led to another, which was a bit more passionate and much longer. And as it always does, one thing led to another and Carmen left an hour and a half later.

Once she was in the car, Carmen called Dominique and told her to be ready when she got there. Roland wasn't at the house when they arrived, but Melissa gladly let them in. When they got to Desireé's room, Dominique picked up where she'd left off. Carmen stood and looked at the computer. "What're you standing there for, Carmen? We still have a lot to do."

"I know, but I want to see if there are more letters to me on her computer."

"What letters? Your sister never wrote a letter in her life."

"I know, but she would start these letters to me and never finish them, much less mail any of them," Carmen divulged as she sat down in front of the computer. "But they read like a journal. She didn't write them every day or anything like that, but when she had something on her mind, she'd write it in the form of a letter to me. I've probably read a hundred of them. They've made me feel closer to her."

"You two were closer than any two people I know."

"Yeah, but there's a lot of things about Dez that I never knew. Some things that you don't know about her."

"You mean about her being bisexual?" Dominique said matter-of-factly.

"She told you?"

"No, Carmen, of course she didn't tell me," Dominique said, noticing the hurt look in her eyes. "I dropped by here unannounced one afternoon. I rang the door, but no one answered, so I got back in my car and was about to leave when Desireé came out with a woman. I got out and was walking toward the house when she kissed her. And I'm not talking about a little peck either."

"Did they see you?"

"No, they didn't. So I walked up like I didn't see anything. They were surprised to see me standing there. Desireé introduced me to her. She was a tall, pretty woman. What was her name? It was some country or something like that. I want to say Paris, but that's not it."

"India."

"India! That's it, India."

"I met her. And she's been calling me all weekend. I hate that I gave her my cell number."

Dominique stopped what she was doing. "Carmen."

"Yes."

"Are you gay too?"

"No, Mother."

"Then why has she been calling you all weekend?"

"She likes me. And she is a nice person, very friendly, and she is so funny. But she's starting to get on my nerves, always talkin' about how I'm making her clit hard." Carmen looked wide-eyed at Dominique and covered her mouth. "I'm sorry. I didn't mean to say that in front of you, Mommy. I'm sorry."

Dominique laughed. "It's all right, Carmen. I've heard talk like that before. In fact, if I'm not mistaken, I had one of those long before you were born."

Carmen laughed. "I am so embarrassed."

"Please don't feel like that, Carmen. I'm just glad that you feel that comfortable around me to say something like that. All I want, Carmen, is for us to be friends. You're all I have now," Dominique expressed on the verge of tears. She turned away from Carmen and picked up one of Desireé's dresses and began to fold it.

"No, I'm not; you still have Daddy," Carmen said as she turned on Desireé's computer. Dominique sucked her teeth but didn't comment.

Once Windows opened, Carmen went into Explorer to search for more letters. As she looked, she thought that there had to be an easier way to find what she was looking for. She clicked on Tools, then Find, then Files or Folders. Carmen typed *.doc in the Name box, chose My Computer from the down box for Look In, and then clicked Find Now. *Searching.* 2471 file(s) found. "There's more than two thousand doc files here." The files were in different directories and none were more than 50 KB. Carmen clicked on Modified to sort the items by date then she scrolled down to the oldest file. The dates went back five years, almost to the day when Desireé married Roland. She knew she would have to at least look at each file. Not only did they make her feel closer to Desireé, but Carmen never could get past the last words from the first letter she read: *I think somebody is.* Carmen was convinced that Desireé knew what was going on, and she would find it in these letters. But there were too many files for her to copy to disk, and she didn't want to spend days at Roland's house reading. She thought about asking Roland to let her borrow the computer, but she didn't want to explain why. In spite of what Marcus and Garrett felt, she still thought that Roland could be responsible for Desireé's death.

From inside the soul of
Desireé Taylor Ferguson

Hi big sis,
There is a bright side to the turmoil that's going on in the life of Desireé Marie Taylor. Guess what, Carm?
I'M IN LOVE!
Now, I know what you are going to say: "But Dez, you're already married." But it's true; I'm in love with a wonderful man. His name is Rasheed Damali. The

*downside is that I know Roland will never let me go. I
signed a prenuptial agreement, and I refuse to leave
with nothing after all I've given of myself to that man.
So for the time being, Rasheed and I will have to keep
playing Roland's game until we can figure a way for
me to get out from under his thumb. Sometimes I hate
the day I met him. He is so controlling. I should have
listened to you and never married him. Rasheed is
good to me, Carmen; he treats me with respect, not
like some object for his entertainment. Porsche keeps
trying to tell me he's no good, but I think she just
wants him for herself, because he is so fine. She's been
getting more and more scandalous since she's been
smokin' that rock. She doesn't know that I know; I may
be naïve but I'm not a fool. And that pain-in-the-ass
India, she just wants to keep me for herself. Sometimes
I wish I had never given her any. She is ridin' hard on
my very last nerve, and if I have to listen to how hard
I'm making her clit one more time, I'm gonna slap the
black off her pretty black ass.*

Carmen had to laugh at what Desireé said about India.
You are right, Dez. India is a pain in the ass. Carmen
tapped the keyboard again while she studied the dates. *It
all began with Suzanne's death.* She looked for documents
dated up to two weeks before Desireé's murder and opened
them.

From inside the soul of
Desireé Taylor Ferguson

Hi big sis,
*Something happened to Suzanne yesterday, and I
just don't know how I'm going to deal with it. Damn, I*

can't even write the words much less say them out loud. But I have to, at some point. I have to stop hiding from reality and face it. But I don't know if I'm strong enough. It made me think about Mercedes. Go ahead and say it: "Not again, Dez." Can't you move on from that? I can and have, but it's what I was thinking. Anyway, what happened to Suzanne has something to do with Frank, her husband. Suzanne told me that he's into something. She didn't tell me what it was, but Frank knows, and he knows what happened to her is his fault. I could see it in his eyes when he told me, so I know it's not what they think. Suzanne doesn't like pain. I wanted so badly to ask him what it was he was doing, but I was too scared. Scared that what happened to her might happen to me.

    I love you, Carmen, and I miss you so much. Come home soon and save me from this life you told me I would hate living.

When Carmen finished reading the letter, she rechecked the dates of the files her search returned. There was a gap of four days where Dez hadn't written anything. Which made sense to Carmen, seeing that she was in denial about Suzanne's death. Her first thought was to call Marcus and tell him what she'd read, but then she remembered that she was giving herself some space, so she decided to read on. Most of the letters were just a line or two about something that had happened to her on that particular day. Then she read a letter that she had to let Dominique read. "Dominique, there's something here that I think you should see."

"What is it, Carmen?"

"I think you should read this for yourself," Carmen said, getting up from the chair to allow Dominique to sit down.

Roy Glenn

From inside the soul of
Desireé Taylor Ferguson

Hi big sis,

Well, it's finally happened; I am officially a mental case. But not to worry, big sis, I'm just seeing someone to talk things out. I've been a little depressed lately, and I even thought about suicide once or twice, so before I get completely off the chain, I thought I should see somebody. Roland doesn't know, and I'm not going to tell our mother either; she is much too judgmental about everything for me to share this chapter of my life with her. Besides, Carm, you know what she'll say: "You are a Taylor, Desireé. You must be stronger than the forces around you. No daughter of mine is crazy." And believe me, Carmen, I'm not crazy, but I just think this is a good thing for me right now. SO DON'T JUDGE ME! _

My shrink's name is Dr. Phyllis Parker; she a nice white woman, in her late thirties I guess. I had my first session two weeks ago; we met last week and again today. We talked for an hour. More like she asks me leading questions and I talk. It's incredible how much I remember about us growing up. To be honest with you, the last time I was really happy was when we were one big happy family. I wish you'd never left. I never told you this and I would never say it to our mother's face, but I think she was dead wrong to leave you locked up the way she did. Anything could have happened to you. And when that woman tried to feel you up in the shower, she could have killed you if you hadn't kicked her ass first and got yourself separated from the rest of those people. I wouldn't have survived that. I would

have let her have my body, as long as she didn't hurt
me.

 Anyway, we spend a lot of time talking about our
mother. I think I know where she's going with all this;
I've always been seeking her love and doing things to
get our mother's attention, but never earning her love
or approval. And since you'd been gone and I wasn't
getting it from her, I sought the love of others. I think
that's why I let the people in my life take advantage of
me sexually. It seems that because of her lack of affec-
tion, I equate love with sex. I give my love freely. But
it's not love that I get in return, so I continue to seek,
but never find love or approval. Damn, Carm, I sure
hope you're not as fucked up in the head as I am. ☺

By the time Dominique finished reading the letter on the
screen, tears were rolling down her cheeks. She looked over
her shoulder; Carmen was crying too. "Is that what you girls
thought of me?"

"Yes, Mother. I can see now what you were trying to do.
But then it seemed like nothing we did was ever good enough
for you."

"I just wanted you girls to always strive for more."

"To never be satisfied, to always want the next rung on the
ladder," Carmen recited the words Dominique had said to
them so many times.

"You remember."

"Of course I do. You'd be surprised how often I hear you
talking to me. I used to hate it, but it's made me stronger,
made me push myself, work harder. But not Dez. I can tell
from reading these letters that I was holding Dez together. I
was her strength."

"Desireé never was as strong as you, Carmen. You two

were so close, and she depended on you too much. That's why I pushed you harder, 'cause I thought Desireé would gain something from your example."

"But the way we saw it, you were making us compete against each other."

Dominique grabbed a tissue from a box on the desk and patted her eyes. "Did you think that I didn't love you, Carmen?"

"I knew you loved me. And I guess Dez knew it too. But I remember us having fun with Daddy. I've had more fun talking to you in the last week than I ever did growing up."

"I did what I thought was right."

"But you were always our mother and never our friend. I'm glad I'm getting to know you as a friend. I was just telling Marcus that you're actually kind of funny." Carmen turned off the computer.

Dominique wiped the tears from her eyes and allowed a smile to peek through. "So when am I going to get to meet Mr. Marcus Douglas?"

"Maybe I'll bring him by the house to meet you and Daddy next time he's around."

"Is there something going on between the two of you?" Carmen smiled the type of smile that answered Dominique's question without words. "I guess the answer would be yes. I haven't seen that many of your teeth since that stupid photographer said you had a cavity."

"I remember that day." Carmen smiled. "You made him show you because you insisted that your daughter did not have cavities."

"I was right, wasn't I? It was just a piece of that black licorice I told you not to eat."

"You were right, but you gotta admit, you were a trip those days."

Dominique smiled. "I was a trip, wasn't I?"

INFUSION

After having dinner at Oscar's in College Park, Carmen and Dominique talked over cocktails. While they sorted out some of the issues between them, they got to know each other more and enjoyed each other's company. They both had to laugh when Dominique asked, "You told Desireé that she would hate her life being married to Roland?"

"I sure did."

"That girl," Dominique said, shaking her head, "she told me that you were all for it."

Carmen's face contorted. "No," she declared. "I told her Roland seemed nice, but he was too old for her. She told me that you absolutely loved Roland and you were all for it."

It was Dominique's turn to twist her face. "No," she declared emphatically. "Now, Carmen, does that sound like me?"

"Well, no, it doesn't."

"Desireé marrying that man went against everything I ever tried to teach you girls about self-reliance." Dominique took a sip of her drink. "But I guess she knew we'd never talk about it, so why not."

* * *

Once she dropped Dominique off at her home, Carmen drove straight to Marcus's house. She thought about calling first. "Nah." She dismissed the thought quickly.

It was after ten when she arrived. Approaching the door, Carmen could hear music playing. As she got closer, Carmen stopped. "No, he ain't bumpin' 2Pac." Carmen smiled. "Quiet as it's kept, I like me some Pac, myself." She rang the doorbell.

When Marcus opened the door, Carmen stepped inside and immediately began to undress. "I didn't think you were the type who would listen to 2Pac."

"Maybe it's the thug in me," Marcus said, and folded his arms across his chest. "But, ah, what are you doing?" he asked as Carmen stepped out of her throng.

"You did say you wanted to get started early on our nocturnal activities?"

"I did say that, didn't I?" Marcus began taking off his clothes too.

In the morning, Carmen told Marcus about the letters she'd read the day before about Desireé believing that Suzanne's death had something to do with Frank. "In this letter, Dez wrote that Suzanne didn't like pain. So the rough sex theory that the police had is out. She was murdered. We need to find out what Frank was into, Marcus."

"I agree with you, Carmen. Do you have any ideas on how we can do that, now that Mondrya is dead?"

"No," Carmen said sadly.

"I doubt if she told anybody what she had found out. Do you know anyone else that knew them?"

"No. I only talked to Suzanne once on the phone."

"We could take another run at Helen Watts, Suzanne's sister-in-law," Marcus said. "But I do have a lead for us to follow up on."

"What's that?"

"Garrett is too busy, so he gave me the address of the woman who claimed James Martin's body."

"What's her name?"

"Patty Morgan."

It wasn't long after that that Marcus got off I-20 at the Boulevard Avenue exit. "Where are you taking me, Marcus?" Carmen inquired as they turned off Memorial Drive, into an area of Atlanta she'd never been before.

"Cabbage Town," Marcus answered as he drove into a part of the city where the poor white people lived.

"Cabbage Town?" Carmen frowned. "Why?"

"This is the address Garrett gave me."

"As long as I lived here, I've never been down here before. I've heard about it. I just never knew where it was, much less had a reason to come down here."

"Neither have I," Marcus said, looking at the directions he'd printed from the Internet.

"Oh gee, something else we can share." Carmen rolled her eyes and looked out her window at the row of small shotgun houses. As they made their way through the narrow streets, little white children stopped to watch. "You think they're staring at us because they've never seen black people before, or is it the BMW?"

"Can't be the BMW, because there goes one right there," Marcus said, and pointed to a red seven series similar to his. "That must be her car, because that's the address we're looking for." They parked the car in front of the house and got out. "I wish some young brothers were out here to watch the car for five dollars."

"You could always ask them," Carmen said, pointing to a group of kids.

"I don't think so."

They knocked on the door, and before too long it opened and they were greeted by an older white woman. "Yeah?" she said, with a look that told them that their sudden appearance was completely unexpected, not to mention out of the ordinary.

"Good afternoon, ma'am. My name is Marcus Douglas. I'm looking for Patty Morgan. Is she here?"

"What you say your name was?"

"Marcus Douglas," he said slower.

"You don't have to say it like that. I'm not stupid, you know, just a little hard of hearing."

"Who is it, Mama?"

"Marcus Douglas!" she shouted.

"The lawyer?"

"Yup," she replied, and turned her attention back to Marcus and Carmen. "Y'all come in."

As they entered the house, a slender woman with long blond hair came into the room. "Are you Patty Morgan?"

"Yes."

"My name is—"

"I know who you are. What do you want?" she asked.

"I'd like to ask you some questions about James Martin and Rasheed Damali."

"What's to ask? They're both dead," she said bitterly.

"I know that. We're investigating the death of Mr. Damali and Desireé Ferguson."

"Yeah, well, like I said, they're both dead. So if you'll excuse me." Patty turned and started back to her room.

"Please, wait," Carmen said. "I'm just trying to find out who killed my sister, that's all. Please."

Patty looked at Carmen. "That was your sister, huh?" Patty's look softened a little. "I'm sorry about your sister." Patty led Marcus and Carmen into the living room and made herself comfortable in the chair while Marcus and Carmen sat on the couch. "Okay, make it quick."

"What was your relationship to James Martin?"

"I used to live with him before he was murdered."

"I thought he was killed in a carjacking?" Carmen asked.

"It wasn't no damn carjackin'. James was murdered and it was set up to look like a carjackin'."

"What makes you so sure?" Marcus asked.

"James was too smart, too careful, to let some nigg—" Patty stopped herself. She looked at Marcus and Carmen.

"Go ahead and say it. We're used to it," Carmen said non-chalantly. "To let some nigger . . ."

"He was too careful to let somebody carjack him. For him to just sit there, it had to be somebody he knew. He would have never just rolled down the window. He always rode with his gun on the front seat next to him. He would have shot 'em or at least driven off."

"Did you tell the police that?"

"Of course I did. But they said he just got careless. Said they had a witness to the whole thing."

"What did the witness say?" Marcus asked.

"He was in the car at the red light next to James. He said there were two guys in an off-white seventy-nine Caddy that was stopped at the light behind him. He saw one guy get out of the car. He walked up to James's car and told him to get out. Next he heard a shot; then he saw him pull James out of the car and get into the driver's seat; then both cars drove off."

"Okay," Marcus said. "You used to live with him before

he was murdered. Did you know Rasheed Damali?" Marcus inquired.

"Yes, he did some work for James sometimes."

"I know that he worked for him sometimes as an escort. But what I'm interested in is the other business Rasheed had with him."

"And what business would that be, Mr. Douglas?"

"Drugs."

"I don't know anything about that. I think you should leave," Patty said as she sprang up from her chair.

Carmen stood up. "Please, Ms. Morgan, we are not the police. We're not here to try and drag you into any drug charge. I just need to know who killed my sister. Nobody's gonna get hurt here."

Once again Patty looked at Carmen with slight compassion, then sat back down. "Look, guys, I know what you trying to do, and I'm sorry about your sister and all, but I'm trying to get my life back together. When James died, it left me in a bad spot. All the money he owed and the people he owed it to—it all came down on me. James owed his people in Miami more than a quarter million dollars. I had to sell our house, the condo in Aruba, all my jewelry, and give them bastards all the money I had saved just to keep them from killing me. I lost everything. Everything but my clothes and that fuckin' car. And shit, that muthafucka ain't even runnin'."

"What's wrong with the car?" Carmen inquired, just to be polite.

"It needs a new fuel injector. And that bitch costs and I ain't got no job."

"I can understand that, Ms. Morgan," Marcus sympathized. "Maybe there's something that we can do to help you out." Marcus reached in his wallet and handed Patty a card. "That's the number of my mechanic; his name is Bradley.

Why don't you give him a call and make an appointment to bring your car in. Tell him to fix everything that's wrong with it and tell him I said to put it on my account. And you can call my secretary tomorrow; she might be able to put you into a job." Patty looked grateful and suspicious at the same time.

"Can I call Bradley right now?"

"Sure."

Patty went and got the cordless phone to call Bradley. He and Patty sorted out all the details before Patty put Marcus on the phone to verify that he would pay for the repairs. Once all that was settled, Patty agreed to talk to them. "So what do you want to know about James and Rasheed?"

"Like I said, tell me about Rasheed and the drugs," Marcus said firmly.

"Whenever James got female clients, Rasheed did them. James knew Rasheed was on the rock, so when he paid him, it was always with money and drugs. Most times Rasheed wanted it all in 'caine." Patty looked at Carmen. "You sure you wanna hear this, honey? 'Cause it ain't no way to sugar coat this stuff."

Carmen nodded her head.

"He said once he met your sister, he didn't need money."

Carmen frowned and dropped her head. "Seemed like a good arrangement; what went wrong?"

"After a while, clients didn't want Rasheed no more. Said he wasn't worth the price. Said he was fine through dinner or whatever, but in the bedroom, he was spendin' too much time in the bathroom gettin' high. And when he would come out, half the time he couldn't get it up. James couldn't have that. He would go along with anything as long as it didn't cost him money. So James flipped the script. He'd let him have some on credit. Told Rasheed it was only because he liked him, but all he was doin' was obligatin' him. Ya see,

James had male clients who wanted to fuck men. He figured Rasheed would do it as long as he could get high. 'Cause, shit, you ain't gotta keep it up to get fucked in the ass. Getting high first would probably make it easier to take and after a while he wouldn't care. But Rasheed couldn't do it. He was *all right* the first time." Patty laughed. "Guy was mad 'cause Rasheed wouldn't blow him, but hey, as long as he paid the bill, James didn't give a fuck. But on the next one, Rasheed made up some excuse about the guy hurtin' him, on ac-counta he was so big and all, and Rasheed left. So the guy didn't pay, and naturally that pissed James off. He went to his apartment and roughed Rasheed up a little bit. Not bad, just enough to let him know that that shit wasn't cool. So James sets him up again—this was a couple of weeks before he was killed—and this time, Rasheed is a no-show. James lost his mind, 'cause by now Rasheed is losin' him business, and he's into James for about ten grand. James went looking for Rasheed, but he couldn't find him anywhere. Then he went lookin' for your sister a few times, but I don't think he found her either."

"Do you know if James ever found Rasheed?" Marcus asked.

"If you're askin' me if I think James killed him, I don't know."

"Could he have done it?" Marcus asked.

"What do you mean?" Patty asked.

"Was Martin capable of killing somebody over money?"

"Sure, James was capable," Patty told them confidently. "He didn't like gettin' fucked over like that. Shit like that is bad for business. Word gets around that your boys can't put out and you're out of business. James wasn't havin' that."

"Do you remember where James was the night of the murder?"

"I don't know where he was. I hadn't seen him for a coupla days, and I remember thinkin' that James did it when I first heard it on the news. But then they arrested Rollie for it."

"Rollie?" Carmen questioned.

"Your brother-in-law," Patty said, looking at Carmen like she was stupid.

"You know Ferguson?" Marcus asked.

"Rollie used to be a good client for years before he married her sister."

"Male or female?" Marcus asked.

"Females only. Rollie was harmless, though; most times he just wanted them to go places with him. Parties, banquets, that type a shit. Half the time he wouldn't even fuck 'em. Just wanted to see 'em naked, watch 'em dance. But like I said, all that stopped when he got married."

"So Roland was a client," Carmen said to Marcus, confirming Desireé's suspicions.

"You'd be surprised at some of the people James had as clients. Some of the richest and most powerful people in this town were clients of his."

"What about Bill Hudson? Was he a client?" Marcus asked.

"Yeah, that shit-eatin' bastard was a client for years." Patty laughed. "One of our best. That boy is a world-class freak." Patty lit a cigarette. "Used to like them two and three at a time. Take them out of town with him on his business trips. That's what cost him his wife." Patty leaned forward in her chair, now seemingly anxious to tell all she knew. "He's out in LA with a couple a girls and his wife shows up at the door with the police and a photographer."

"The police?" Marcus said inquisitively.

"She told the police that he was havin' sex with minors. Which they wasn't. James didn't play that kiddie shit. Anyway, the cops bust in the room and the photographer got Hudson on film doin' both of 'em. She took him for damn near everything he had. He had to fight to keep from selling off his company."

"When was this?" Marcus asked, already knowing the answer.

"Let's see"—Patty took a drag—"had to be in the early nineties. Now I ain't got no proof or nothin', but I think Hudson had two of our girls killed."

"Why do you think that?"

"Because they was the same two girls he always requested for his little freak parties. So when they both turn up dead on the same day, it kinda makes you wonder, don't it?"

"When did this happen?"

"'Bout a month before James was killed."

Marcus tried to piece some things together in his head, then stood to his feet. "Carmen, I think we've taken up enough of Ms. Morgan's time."

"Ms. Morgan, thank you very much for talking to us," Carmen said.

"Please, call me Patty."

"You've been a big help to us, Patty," Marcus said, moving toward the door. "Don't forget to call Janise about a job."

"Don't worry, Mr. Douglas, I'll call her first thing in the morning," Patty exclaimed happily as she opened the door. She watched as Marcus and Carmen walked to their car. "And thank you, you know, for the hook up on the car and everything."

Once they were in the car and away, Marcus looked over at Carmen. She smiled back at him. "Do you think Martin killed them?" Carmen asked.

"I doubt it. If he did find them, why wouldn't he just get the money from Desireé? A guy like that just wants his money. And it wasn't like Desireé couldn't or wouldn't pay him. She was in love with Rasheed." Carmen didn't say anything. She just turned away and looked out the window. "You all right?"

"Yeah, I'm all right. Some of this is hard to stomach, but I'm all right," Carmen said. "I just can't believe that Dez could be in love with somebody like Rasheed and not know what he was doing."

"Maybe she did. Didn't you say that she knew what Porsche was doing, even though Porsche was sure that she didn't know? Give Desireé some credit."

"Maybe you're right."

The light turned red and Marcus looked over at Carmen. "Besides, sometimes you can't help who you fall in love with," he said softly. Carmen looked in Marcus's eyes. She could sense the emotion pouring out of them. *Is he saying that he loves me?* She started to ask him if there was some underlying meaning in his statement, but she decided if there was, and she had a feeling there was, she would wait for him to say, *I love you, Carmen*, in his own time. The light changed and Marcus drove on. "So, let's look at what we got."

Carmen smiled and resettled in her seat. "Okay, let's."

"Desireé's friend Suzanne Collins is found dead in her office under questionable circumstances. Desireé had a feeling that she was murdered because of something Frank was involved in. We know that Frank used to work for Ferguson before he came to Hudson Financial. Then he commits suicide. Mondrya Foster says she found out something that would interest me, but before she can tell me what it is, she gets killed in a robbery. Rasheed owed James Martin money, but we can't ask him anything, because he's dead too."

"It is kind of strange that everybody who's involved in this, who might be able to tell us something, is dead." Carmen laughed. "'Cause dead men tell no tales."

"But there's something else."

"What's that?"

"A common thread that seemed to bind them all together," Marcus said.

"I'm gonna ask you one more time. What's that?"

"Bill Hudson."

COCKTAILS FOR TWO

"I don't know about you, Carmen, but I could use a drink."

"I could use a double myself. But I'm hungry too," Carmen said.

"Okay, so where do you want to go?"

"I saw a little place I wanted to try. It's called Dish, and it's not too far from my condo. We can park there and walk."

Marcus drove back to Carmen's condo and parked the car. He got out and went to open the door for Carmen. He extended his hand, which Carmen accepted with a smile. "Thank you, Marcus. You are such a gentleman."

"Something my daddy always told me was to always treat a lady like a lady. And treat a beautiful lady like a queen."

As they walked, Carmen slid her hand into his. She looked up at him and smiled. Marcus squeezed her hand and gently brought it to his lips and kissed it. They walked hand in hand to dinner at Dish, on the corner of North Highland Avenue and Drewry Street, and were greeted by the maitre d'. She introduced herself as Laura, escorted them to their table, and gave them each a menu. "Your server will be Antuan, and he will be with you shortly," Laura said. "Enjoy your meal."

Carmen and Marcus looked over the menu until Antuan arrived. He took their drink orders and asked if they were ready to order. Carmen told him that she would need another minute to decide what she wanted. "That's fine. I'll get your drinks and be back to take your order."

After they each scanned the menu for a while, Carmen announced, "This sounds good. It's a crispy package of asparagus, sweet peppers, portabella, and fontina."

"That does sound good."

"You see anything you want?" she asked.

"I was thinking about the crispy duck roll with cashew tamarind sauce, but I'm undecided."

"I was looking at that too."

"I'll give you some of mine if you give me some of yours," Marcus bargained.

"Deal." Carmen smiled. "What about an appetizer?"

"I was torn between the steamed mussels and the crispy calamari salad, but I'm already having the crispy duck roll."

"That's right; black people eat too much fried food."

"So, steamed mussels with corn potato and chorizo for me. And for the lady?" Marcus asked.

"I'd like to try the arugula salad and grilled scallops. And I'd like that with toasted hazelnuts and grapefruit vinaigrette."

"Excellent choice," Antuan said as he returned to the table with a touch of flamboyancy. "Have we decided on a main dish?"

"Yes," Carmen proclaimed. "I'll have the grilled swordfish with saffron aioli potatoes and lemon sauce."

"That is excellent; I had it last night. It is absolutely to die for. And for the gentleman?"

"I don't know," Marcus said, glancing at Carmen, remembering how she reacted when he said something was "to die for." She seemed unfazed by it, continuing to study the menu. Marcus thought about all that Carmen had heard about Desireé in the past week. No surprise that she'd developed thick skin.

"Would you like me to give you a few ticks to decide?" Antuan asked.

"Why don't you try the panko crusted skate wing?"

"Nah, I'm just not feelin' that tonight. I was feelin' more like seared Maine diver scallops with baby bok choy and shrimp vermicelli."

"That sounds good too."

"I'll have that, then," Marcus said, picking up the wine list. "And a bottle of Les Macherelles Chassagne."

"You do know your wines, Marcus," Carmen said as Antuan departed the table.

"Not bad for somebody who listens to 2Pac, huh?"

After dinner, Marcus and Carmen sat and talked over cocktails. "Excuse me a minute, Carmen, I think I see somebody I know." Marcus got up from the table and walked over to the bar. Carmen looked on with jealous eyes as Marcus approached a voluptuous redhead. Marcus tapped her on the shoulder; she turned and immediately jumped to her feet to give Marcus a hug that made Carmen's eyes narrow. They talked for a while and then Marcus pointed at Carmen. Marcus grabbed her by the hand and practically dragged her to the table.

"Carmen Taylor, I'd like to introduce you to Joanna Henley, a long-time financial reporter with the *Atlanta Journal*."

"It's a pleasure to meet you, Carmen."

"I asked Joanna to join us for a drink," Marcus said, reclaiming his seat.

"I hope it's all right with you. I told Marcus no and that you seem to be enjoying cocktails for two; I hate being the third wheel."

"Nonsense," Carmen said, cutting her eyes at Marcus. "Please, join us."

"If you're sure; I promise not to stay long," Joanna said as she sat down. "I'm actually waiting for my date." Joanna glanced at her watch. "Who is, by the way, very late."

Marcus signaled for Antuan and ordered another round for Carmen and himself, as well as a glass for Joanna, who opted to try the Macherelles Chassagne. Carmen looked on as Marcus and Joanna laughed and talked like they were the best of friends. To Carmen it felt more like they were the ones having cocktails for two and she was the third wheel.

"Tell me something, Joanna," Marcus said, suddenly turning serious. "Were you working at the finance desk when Roland Ferguson was trying to buy Hudson Financial?"

"That was one of my first assignments. Why do you ask?"

"I was wondering why the deal fell through."

"Nobody really knows why Ferguson walked away from the deal," Joanna said. "We had gotten the press releases and everything, when all of a sudden he walked. It sent the price of the stock into a nosedive."

"That's when the group of private investors came in and bought it."

"Right. But they didn't buy it. Hudson structured the deal so he would maintain control."

"How did he do that?"

"He issued something called *corporate bond debt*." Before Marcus could ask what that meant, Joanna continued. "They are issued by corporations as an alternative to offering equity ownership by issuing stock. Like most municipal bonds and treasuries, most corporate bonds pay semiannual interest and promise to return the principal at maturity. Maturities range from one to thirty years."

"Who was in that group of investors?"

"I don't know, but it shouldn't be that hard to find out,"

Joanna said, and tipped her head to one side. "Funny you should ask about Hudson, 'cause I'm workin' on a story on Hudson. Doin' a little investigative reporting."

Now completely engaged in the conversation, Carmen asked, "Anything you can tell us about?"

"I'm lookin' into the suicide of two people."

"That doesn't sound financial, Joanna," Carmen said.

"It does when one is John Heard, an FTC investigator. He took sleeping pills and vodka. And the other is Coleman Wilson, a senior exec at Hudson Financial. His wife found him hanging in his study."

"That's funny, Joanna, we're—" Marcus kicked Carmen under the table. She looked at him quickly and then back to Joanna. "We were just talking about that."

"You were?" Joanna said curiously.

"About suicide," Marcus said quickly.

"Oh. I was about to ask what you were talkin' about them for," Joanna said, finishing her drink as she saw her dining companion arrive. "There's Mark. What do you think, Carmen, should I play hardball with him for being late?"

"Of course you should."

"That's right, and I'll make him order me a bottle of this wine; it's excellent. Marcus, it was good seeing you again, and it was certainly a pleasure meeting you, Carmen," Joanna said as she rushed off to give Mark a hard time.

"Nice meeting you too." Carmen smiled and waved. As soon as she left, Carmen's facial expression changed. "Why did you kick me? That hurt," she said, and kicked Marcus.

"Ouch! I'm sorry, Carmen. But if you told her that our case had any connection to hers, Mark would have gotten stood up, and you'd be reading it in the paper in the morning. And all that would do is make our killer cover his tracks even more."

"I wasn't thinking. I can see the headlines now: 'Ferguson

Investigation Points to Hudson Financial.' You're right. I'm sorry; sorry I kicked you."

"It really hurt too."

Carmen leaned forward. "Do you want me to kiss it and make it better?" she whispered.

"I thought you wanted to go dancing?"

"First things first."

Carmen led Marcus out of the restaurant and back to her condo to provide sexual healing for his wound. After which she abruptly rolled out of bed and started walking toward the bathroom. Marcus watched her for a while before asking, "Where are you going?"

"I still want to go dancing." Carmen motioned for him to join her in the bathroom, which he gladly did. "I think I'm falling in love with you, Marcus. With everything you say and with everything you do. Every time I look at you, I fall a little further," Carmen said quietly and without looking at him.

"Wow. Where did that come from?"

"It's what I was feeling. So I said it. I'm sorry I said it. I didn't mean to make you uncomfortable."

"It wasn't that; it was the way you said it. I just wasn't expecting it, that's all. Because I'm diggin' everything about you. I don't know if it's love that I'm feeling. All I know is that it feels better than anything I've felt in a lifetime. And I want more, as much you want to give me."

'CAUSE WE'VE ENDED NOW AS LOVERS

"Marcus, Marcus," Carmen said as she shook him gently. "There's somebody at the door."

"Huh?" Marcus mumbled, and rolled into Carmen's arms.

"There's somebody at the door."

"Who is it?"

"I don't know. My psychic powers aren't in tune this early."

"What?"

"Why don't you get up and go see?"

"They'll go away," Marcus said, and eased his body closer to Carmen.

"Get up, Marcus. It might be important." Carmen pushed Marcus away from her body.

"Okay, okay."

Reluctantly, Marcus rolled out of bed and wandered around the room looking for his robe as the doorbell rang again. He walked slowly to the window and looked out. "Randa. The perfect way to start a morning." He turned around and walked back to the bedroom.

"Who is it?"

"Randa," Marcus said, taking off his robe and putting on a shirt and pants.

"What does she want?"

"I don't know." The bell rang again. "But I'm going to find out."

"Do you want me to leave?"

Marcus stopped dressing and sat down on the bed next to Carmen. "No, Carmen, I don't want you to leave. I never want you to leave." He kissed her gently on her lips. "You relax, and I'll go see what my soon-to-be-ex-wife wants at eight-forty-five in the morning."

"Okay," Carmen answered with a kiss. Marcus got up and walked slowly out of the bedroom, closing the door behind him as the bell rang again. As soon as the door closed, Carmen got out of bed and looked around for her clothes. When she remembered that Marcus undressed her in the bathroom, Carmen went in and shut the door.

By the time Marcus reached the door, Randa was leaning on it. He shook his head and opened it. "Good morning, Randa."

"'Bout time," Randa said, standing with her hands on her hips. She was dressed provocatively in a Donna Ricco fly away halter dress.

"What do you want, Randa?" Marcus said, blocking the door.

"To talk to you, Marcus."

"You could try the telephone."

"Why? You never answer it. You haven't returned any of my calls. Marcus, we need to talk."

"Randa, there is nothing to talk about."

"There is a lot for us to talk about," Randa pleaded. "Can I come in?"

I knew she was gonna say that. But this is what you get for letting it come to this. "You can come in, Randa, but . . ."

Marcus uttered, opening the door enough for Randa to ease in.

"But." Randa stopped and sniffed. "You have a woman here. I can smell her perfume. Jean Paul Gauther, if I'm not mistaken." Randa inhaled. "Yes, it is Jean Paul Gauther." Marcus turned away and Randa followed him slowly to the den. He opened the door for her. "It's probably Carmen Taylor," Randa mused as she walked by him.

"Yes, it's Carmen Taylor." *You're fired, Tiffanie.*

"And before you fire Tiffanie, she didn't tell me a thing." Randa sat in one of the chairs in front of the desk. "That girl thinks you walk on water. She won't even say your name around me anymore." Marcus sat in the chair next to her. "You two aren't exactly low-profile, ya know. The high-profile lawyer and the model. The two of you eat in the best restaurants and you go dancing almost every night. People who you don't see, see you, and they're talking about it. They were talking about you the other morning on V103. There's even a rumor that you had this all planned. What really happened was she killed her sister, left the country, and you had Roland step up for it, since you knew he didn't do it."

Marcus ran his hands over his face. "What do you want, Randa?"

"Relax, Marcus. I'm not here to hurt you or to make a scene. This is the only way I can talk to you."

Just then, Carmen tapped lightly on the door and came in. "Hi. I don't mean to interrupt."

Randa rose to her feet. "You're not interrupting," she said, and extended her hand. "I'm Randa Douglas. I've been look-ing forward to meeting you."

"Carmen Taylor." She shook Randa's hand and turned to Marcus. "Can I see you for a minute?"

"I'll be right back, Randa." Marcus stood up and followed Carmen out of the den to the front door. "You're leaving?"

"I was, but after seeing what she's wearing, I'm tempted to change my mind." Carmen smiled. "But I'll give you two a chance to talk. I know you've been putting it off." Carmen laughed a little. "Besides, I couldn't lie in that bed by myself wondering what you two were talking about. It would eat me alive." Marcus opened the door and Carmen stepped out. "Oh yeah, I don't have my car here." Marcus reached in his pocket and handed Carmen the keys to his BMW. "I don't want to strand you here."

"Don't worry, if I need to go somewhere, I have the Durango."

"Thank you, Marcus." Carmen began walking toward the car.

"You don't have to go, you know. This won't take long."

"Maybe not, but if I'm not here, you two can talk things out and be done with it. So take your time. I'll call you later today."

"No." Marcus opened the door for her. "I'll call you."

Carmen kissed him on the cheek, got in the car, and drove away. Marcus went back in the house and turned toward the den. Randa was standing in the hallway. "Now that she's gone, do you think we could talk in the living room?"

Marcus held out his hand and showed Randa to the living room. She made her way to the couch and sat down. "Thank you. I always thought those chairs were *so* uncomfortable."

"What do you want to talk about, Randa?" Marcus asked as he sat down.

"Is this how it's always gonna be between us, Marcus?"

"How do you think it should be, Randa?"

"Come on, Marcus. This is me. I at least thought we could be amiable toward each other."

"I'm not being pleasant?"

"No, Marcus, you're not. You're very stiff and straight-forward."

"I'll try to do better." Marcus put on a fake smile. "How are you, Randa?"

"That's a little better, but I could do without the fake smile. I don't need you to patronize me. But, anyway, I'm fine. I started going to the gym again."

"I can tell; you look good."

"But not like a model, though, right?" Randa asked, and Marcus remained silent. "Okay, Marcus. I'll get to the point. I wanted to know if this thing between you and Carmen was something I had to worry about."

"The only thing you have to worry about, Randa, is signing the divorce papers."

"It wasn't a question, Marcus. It was, but not anymore. I saw the way the two of you looked at each other."

"How did we look at each other?"

"I can tell she's in love with you. That's why she left. She wants to give you a chance to get this over with," Randa said. "Are you in love with her, Marcus?"

"I don't know."

"You do. You just haven't admitted it to yourself yet, but you are."

"Thank you for telling me."

"You see, Marcus, I still love you, and I was still holding out a little hope that you and I could move past what happened and start over. But I know that there is none, at least not now. Maybe there'll be another time for you and I. But now, I just wanna tell you that I'm sorry. Really sorry about what I did to us. Not that it makes any difference now, but he didn't mean anything to me."

"It does make a difference. That's what hurt the most, Randa. That you would jeopardize everything we had for somebody who didn't matter. It'd be different if you were in love with him. But you risked everything we had for nothing."

"I'll probably kick myself for the rest of my life for that. So the only thing to do now is make an appointment with Duck and sign my name," Randa said, rising to her feet. "I want you to know that after it's final, I'll be moving to Los Angeles or maybe Chicago. I can't live here being Marcus Douglas's ex-wife."

Randa walked to the front door.

"If that's what you think is best." Marcus smiled inside.

"Good-bye, Marcus."

"Good-bye, Randa."

"Can you at least give me a hug?" Marcus put his arms around Randa, and she returned the embrace. "I'm sorry, Marcus," she said as a tear rolled down her cheek. "Sorry it came to this."

Marcus freed himself from her arms and opened the door. Randa stepped out slowly. He watched her walk to her car, then quietly closed the door on that part of his life. He thought about calling Carmen and telling her to come back, but he changed his mind. As far as he was concerned, it was still too early. He decided to shower and go back to bed. He would call her when he woke up. Marcus went into the bathroom and turned on the shower. Once it was hot enough, he stepped in. While the water beat down on his body, he thought about Randa. The thoughts quickly faded as thoughts of Carmen entered his mind.

MAKE MONEY

Just as Marcus was about to get back into bed, the phone rang. Hoping it was Carmen calling, Marcus answered quickly. "Hello."

"Good morning, Marcus," Janise said. "I'm sorry to be calling you so early in the morning, but Gloria Giannelli called you this morning."

"Bend-over-and-grab-your-ankles Giannelli? Who's getting sued for sexual harassment?"

"Nobody as far as I know. She said she needed to talk to you about Mondrya Foster."

"Mondrya Foster!"

"Who is Mondrya Foster?" Janise asked.

"She used to work for Hudson Financial. The last message she left me said that she had some information, but she got killed in a robbery at Starbucks before she could tell me. Did she leave a number?"

Marcus wrote down the number Janise gave him and quickly dialed after ending the call from Janise. He had been on hold for more than fifteen minutes before Gloria picked up. "Good morning, Marcus. I'm sorry to keep you holding so long."

"That's all right, Gloria. How have you been?"

"The doctor said I might have some dizziness for a while, but other than a headache, I'm fine."

"What happened to you? Did you have an accident?"

"No. I thought you knew. I got shot in the head. Well the bullet just grazed my head. I was at Starbucks with Mondrya the night she was killed. That's what I wanted to talk to you about. But I'd rather not discuss it over the phone. Can you come to my office today, or could we meet somewhere?"

"Are you still in downtown Decatur?"

"Yes."

Marcus glanced at the clock. "I can be there in about an hour."

"Good. I'll see you then," Gloria said, and hung up the phone.

Marcus dialed Carmen's cell phone, and she answered on the first ring. "That didn't take long. What did she say?"

"Just that she was sorry that she did what she did on a humbug and that she was signing the divorce papers," he said like it was no big deal, but it really was.

"Good," Carmen said to him, seemingly more excited about the information than he was. "I was having a little problem with openly dating a married man."

"Yeah, well, I'll tell you all about that when I see you. But I need you to come and pick me up."

"Where are we going?"

"Hopefully to hear from the dead."

When Carmen returned to pick up Marcus, she was once again driving the Mercedes. Shortly after, they arrived at the law office of Gloria Giannelli. The wait in the reception area took the better part of an hour; then Gloria stepped out of her office. "Marcus," she said with her hand extended. "It's good to see you again." Marcus and Carmen rose to their feet.

"How have you been, Gloria? It's been a long time," Marcus said as he shook her hand. "This is Carmen Taylor."

"Gloria Giannelli."

"Nice to meet you," Carmen said.

"Please, come in." Gloria stepped aside and ushered them in. Once they were seated, Gloria went into her file cabinet to retrieve the priority mail envelope that Mondrya had sent to her office. "Like I told you over the phone, I was with Mondrya the night she was killed. She and I were friends, and she called me wanting to get together to explore the possibility of filing a sexual harassment suit."

"Who was the suit against?" Marcus asked.

"She didn't say, but she did say that she was looking into something for you and that she was planning on using it as an insurance policy to get what she wanted."

"Mondrya left me a message that she had something for me, but she was killed that same day. But I don't know anything about an insurance policy."

"That's why I wanted to see you today. And I thought that we would talk alone."

"Ms. Taylor is"—Marcus glanced at Carmen—"intimately involved in this investigation. You can speak freely in front of her."

"You see, Desireé Ferguson is my sister," Carmen said, looking Gloria in the eye.

"Oh, I see. I didn't know that. I'm terribly sorry." Gloria picked up the envelope and handed it to Marcus. "As I mentioned over the phone, this is my first day back in the office since that night. This arrived here two days after; as you can see, it was addressed to Mondrya, in care of this office. Judging from the postmark, Mondrya must have sent it right before she met me at Starbucks."

Marcus started to open the envelope to examine its contents. "Marcus," Gloria said, and Marcus stopped. "I would prefer that you not open that in my presence."

"Okay, " Marcus said.

"Do you mind if I ask why not?" Carmen asked.

"I am convinced that whatever is in that envelope is the reason I was shot and Mondrya was murdered."

"I thought that it was a random shooting during a robbery. What makes you believe that she was killed because of this envelope?" Marcus asked.

"I had a lot of time to think about what happened. I'm still having nightmares about it. Sometimes what happened plays like a movie. Over and over again in my mind. And then I came into the office and this was waiting for me . . . Now I'm sure."

"Do you mind telling us how it happened?" Carmen asked.

"Yes, Ms. Taylor, I do. But I know that this is important to you." She looked pensive for a moment. "It seemed to me that when they came into Starbucks that evening, they picked us out and shot us. There were three of them: one who went to the register, one who stood by the door, and the other one was the one who shot us. I couldn't help feeling that he walked around until he spotted us."

"Did he say anything to you before he shot you?" Carmen asked.

"I don't think I'll ever forget what he said to me. He said, 'What the fuck you looking at, bitch.' Then he walked up to us and said, 'Oh, so I ain't nothin'! You pretty bitches think y'all better than me. See if you better than this.' Then he shot me."

"Did you tell the police any of this?" Marcus asked.

"No, I didn't, and if you go to them and tell them that I

think Mondrya was murdered over whatever is in that envelope, I'll deny this conversation even took place."

"I thought you said Mondrya was a friend of yours?" Carmen asked.

"She was. But she's dead now."

"And it doesn't matter to you that whoever is responsible for this will get away with it?"

"Like I said, Ms. Taylor, Mondrya is dead, but I'm alive and I plan to stay that way."

Carmen stood up quickly. "Let's go, Marcus." Then she turned to Gloria. "Thank you for calling and turning this over to us. I appreciate it. You didn't have do it; you could have destroyed it as soon as you found out what was in it," Carmen spat sarcastically.

"Carmen," Marcus said, knowing that she was about to get off the chain.

"No, Marcus, it's her kinda attitude, not willing to tell what she knows, that is the reason whoever murdered Dez is walking around free." Carmen opened the door to the office. "I'm glad I don't have friends like you," she said, and slammed the door behind her. Carmen stormed out of the building and headed for the car.

"Sorry about that, Gloria."

Gloria stood up and walked Marcus out. "That's all right, Marcus. To be honest with you, I'm a little ashamed of myself too. But I'm alive and even if I have to leave the city, I plan to stay that way. Good luck with your investigation."

Marcus put the envelope in his briefcase and joined Carmen in the car. She was still on fire when he got there. Other than asking where he wanted to go, Carmen said nothing until she parked the car in front of Marcus's office. "Sorry I lost it back there, Marcus."

"Don't sweat it, Carmen. I like a woman with a little fire," he replied as they both got out of the car and walked inside.

When Janise saw Marcus coming toward her, she immediately started smiling. "Marcus. I wasn't expecting you in the office today."

"I needed to look over some things. I probably won't be here long."

"And how are you, Ms. Taylor?"

"Doing fine, Janise, what about you?"

"Great. In fact, I have some great news for you, Marcus."

"What's that?"

"Your lawyer called and said Randa sauntered into his office this morning, without her lawyer, and signed the divorce papers. He said she didn't even bother to look at them. Just signed her name and left."

"Did she really?" Marcus winked at Carmen. "That is great news, Janise." After exchanging a few more pleasantries with Janise, Marcus and Carmen went into his office and closed the door. Marcus took the envelope out and opened it.

"What's in it?" Carmen asked after only a few seconds.

"Three sheets of paper and a CD. Two of them have a heading that reads 'Frank Collins client list.'" Marcus handed the client lists to Carmen, and he continued reading the other sheet. "And this one says 'notes to Marcus.' It says, 'Observation, FC and CT'—who I assume is Connie Talbert—'appear to be friends'; then next to it she wrote, 'Confirmed.' He continued reading. "According to this, before Frank Collins came to work at Hudson Financial, he used to work as salesman for Atlanta Life, then had a brief stint at Dean Witter in New York. He was fired for, in capital letters, 'GROSS financial mismanagement of his accounts.' When he came to Hudson Financial as an account manager, he was put immediately on the merger audit team, even though he had no audit experience. She remembered a meeting between Frank and Connie, and after that the deal fell through. Then down here at the bottom it says, 'FC, ML HF.' FC we know is Frank Collins and HF is most likely Hudson Financial. But what does ML stand for?"

"I have no clue."

"Then it says 'WONNIEMTEL equals CD.' Any bets on what that means?"

Carmen shrugged her shoulders and shook her head no, and continued looking at the client lists. "Marcus, these are two different lists. But on this one she wrote 'official'," Carmen said, handing the papers back to Marcus. "And on this one the names are obviously fake names. Some of the names are in Spanish, but look at these others—Abe Lincoln, James Madison. They're all dead presidents."

"Not just dead presidents," Marcus said. "Each of them are on some denomination of currency. George Washington is on the one-dollar note, Thomas Jefferson is on the two dollar, Abraham Lincoln is on the five, Alexander Hamilton is on the ten, Andrew Jackson is on the twenty, Ulysses S. Grant is on the fifty, Benjamin Franklin is on the hundred, William McKinley is on the five hundred, Grover Cleveland is on the thousand, James Madison is on the five thousand, and Salmon B. Chase is on the ten thousand. When one series of the hundred-thousand-dollar notes was issued, 1934 Gold Certificates, if I'm not mistaken, Woodrow Wilson was put on them. Even though they're called "dead presidents," three of them—Hamilton, Franklin, and Chase—weren't presidents." Marcus looked and saw how Carmen was looking at him. "Anyway, money, that's the pattern here."

"I've heard of all the rest of them, but who is Chase?"

"Salmon B. Chase was an old abolitionist lawyer and politician from the pre-Republican Liberty Party. As it happened, he was appointed by Abraham Lincoln to be secretary of the treasury and was responsible for the motto 'In God We Trust,' which was introduced on the coinage at that time, but it didn't appear on currency until 1957."

"How do you know all this?"

"I read a lot." Marcus smiled.

"Okay," Carmen said, thinking how far she'd come from Denny Boo. Carmen smiled back at Marcus. "What's on the CD?"

"Let's see." Marcus put the CD in the drive, and it opened up a Windows program that informed them that there was no application associated with it, and asked which program they wished to use. "This is useless to us. It's a safe bet that Mondrya copied it from Hudson Financial's computer system."

"So we need to be at Hudson Financial to find out what's on it."

"Maybe not," Marcus said, and picked up the phone. "Janise, get Garrett on the phone for me, please."

"Hold on, Marcus," Janise said, and before too long she came back to the phone. "I have Garrett on line three."

"Thanks, Janise." Marcus switched to line three and put it on speaker. "Garrett."

"Congratulations, big dog! I hear Randa signed the divorce papers. How does it feel being a free man?"

"I guess it will hit me after a while, but right now"—he smiled at Carmen—"it really hasn't fazed me. What's goin' on with you?"

"You know me, Marcus, work, that's what's goin' on with me. What's up with you? You need me to go question Porsche's freaky crew again? Please say yes."

"Not this time, Garrett. I'm here with Carmen Taylor."

"Hi, Garrett!" Carmen yelled.

"Hey, Carmen. I didn't know y'all had me on speaker.

I'm glad I didn't say anything too off-the-wall. What can I do for you two?"

"I got a CD here that was most likely copied from Hudson Financial's computer system, and I can't do anything with it. So I was wondering if this was something that Jamara could help us with?"

"If it has anything to do with a computer, I imagine that she can."

"When can we get with her?" Marcus asked.

Garrett gave Marcus directions to Jamara's house and told them to meet him there. When Carmen and Marcus arrived at Jamara's house, Garrett opened the door. He introduced to Marcus and Carmen to Jamara.

"Jamara, it is nice to finally meet you. You are as pretty as your name," Marcus said.

Carmen rolled her eyes. "Nice to meet you," she said nonchalantly.

"It is so good to finally meet both of you," Jamara said. "I've heard so much about you, I feel like we're all old friends or whatever."

Marcus and Carmen both looked at Garrett. "Don't look at me. You know I ain't givin' up much of nuthin'," Garrett pleaded in his own defense.

"It wasn't Garrett. If anything, Garrett cleared up a lotta the stuff I've heard about y'all."

"Just exactly what have you been hearin'?" Carmen said, taking on an attitude. "And who have you been hearin' it from?"

"From the radio," Jamara answered.

"The radio!" Carmen said louder than she needed to.

"That's what I was goin' to tell you, Carmen. Randa says we're the topic of discussion on the morning show on V103," Marcus told her.

"Not just on V103," Jamara said. "White folks talkin' about y'all too."

"What about us?"

"Mostly that y'all eat out a lot and y'all go dancin' every night," Garrett said.

"And Randa told me that she was listening when somebody called in and said that you killed Desireé and I made Roland step off for it, because I knew that I could get him off," Marcus said to Carmen.

"I heard that one too," Jamara said excitedly, until she looked at the angry look on Carmen's face. "I'm sorry, Carmen. I don't believe any of that stuff anyway. People with no business got nothing but time to get off into other people's business. They need to get a life." Carmen found a chair and sat down without saying another word. "So, ahh, Garrett said you had something you wanted me to look at," Jamara said, knowing it was time to change the subject.

"Yes," Marcus said, pulling out the CD and handing it to Jamara. "I think that it's from Hudson Financial's computer system. I couldn't open it."

"You're probably right. It is most likely data copied from their system. Unless you are running the application, it's useless."

"So there's nothing you can do?" Marcus said, sounding dejected.

"Maybe," Jamara said. "Maybe not. Do they have a Web site?"

"I'm sure they do."

"Well, let's see what we can do," Jamara said, and invited them to follow her. Marcus and Garrett followed behind her, but Carmen kept her seat.

"You coming?" Marcus asked, looking back at Carmen.

"You all go ahead. I'll be all right."

Jamara led Marcus and Garrett into the den, which she

had converted into a computer room. She logged onto the Internet and went to Hudson Financial's Web site. She created a fake account log-in for herself and proceeded to cruise the site, looking for ways to get into the system. After about an hour of watching Jamara type and mumble, "Hmm," Marcus went back out to the living room where Carmen was still sitting. He sat down next to her and held her hand. The two sat there for the next half hour or so, with neither one saying a word. Then Carmen squeezed his hand. "What's bothering you, Carmen?"

"I really don't like people all up in my business, but I can take that. I know you are now very high profile since you won the case and I understand that. I know that people are going to talk. And I understand that too. But what's really bothering me is that someone could think that I killed my own sister. They don't know me, and they didn't know Dez. It just hurts, that's all."

Marcus was about to say something when Garrett came out of the den. "She's in," he said, and quickly disappeared back in the room. Marcus stood up and held out his hand to Carmen. "What was it that Dominique used to tell you? You're a Taylor. You must be stronger than the forces around you."

Carmen accepted his hand and stood up. "It was hard then. And it's no easier now."

Marcus and Carmen went into the den. Jamara was seated at the computer, and Garrett was standing over her. When the system was accessed, it automatically sent an e-mail:

To: advisory board member <advisory_board@ hudsonfinancial.com >
From: System Administrator <sysadm@hudson-financial.com>
Subject: Unauthorized System Access

This message was automatically generated and sent to the advisory board member distribution list. Please be advised somebody has gained un-authorized access to the system. Recommend corrective action be taken immediately to protect the integrity of the system:

Access Password: SYSTEM ADMINISTRATOR
Access From Terminal Position: Unknown
Position Owner: Unknown

"I'm in," Jamara said, staring at the screen. "But now it's prompting me to enter a password. I don't want to get locked out now."

"I'll be right back," Marcus said, and quickly left the room. When he returned, he had the paper that Mondrya had written her notes on, along with the two client lists.

"What you got there?" Garrett asked.

"These are the notes Mondrya made for me before she was murdered," he said, handing the paper to Garrett. "Take a look at this."

"FC, ML HF. WONNIEMTEL equals CD. What does it mean?" Garrett asked.

"I don't know. But whatever that word is, it equals CD," Marcus answered, pointing at the word.

"Jamara, try typing WONNIEMTEL as the password."

"Okay." Jamara typed the each letter carefully. "It worked; let me see that paper, Garrett." She looked at the paper and smiled. "That's kinda clever."

"What?" Garrett asked. "What does it mean?"

"WONNIEMTEL is 'let me in now' spelled backward."

Marcus smiled at Jamara, and Carmen rolled her eyes again. "That's excellent. Now can you tell us what FC, ML HF means?" he asked Jamara, but she was back in her zone.

Now that she had access to the system, Jamara clicked around to become familiar with how it worked. She went into Explorer and once again tried to access the disk directly. "Since it hasn't asked me to associate it, we at least know we're in the right place."

"Try to access one of the names on this list," Carmen directed, and handed the client list to Jamara. "Try Alexander Hamilton."

Jamara accessed the records of Alexander Hamilton. Everyone leaned in and stared at the screen. *As if they know what they're looking at,* Jamara thought to herself, and smiled. She shook her head and accessed another record, Hegenio Ortiz, and then another. Smiling more with each click of the mouse, it all came together in her mind. "They all seem to be a mix of asset allocation funds and fixed-income securities." Jamara turned around and faced everyone. "I think I know what ML stands for."

"You gonna tell us or make us all take turns guessing?" Garrett demanded.

"Money laundering."

HIGH SPEED

"Money laundering? Are you sure?" Marcus asked.

"No. There's no way I can be one hundred percent sure. But I'm looking at the patterns that are consistent in all the accounts I've gone into."

"What are asset allocation funds and fixed-income securities anyway?" Carmen asked.

"Asset allocation funds are mutual funds that feature a mix of stocks, bonds, and cash equivalents to meet the investment objectives of individual investors. In this case, the mix is mostly cash. Look here, you can see a steady pattern of deposits and payouts. Fixed-income securities are debt securities or IOUs for borrowed money," Jamara explained. "They obligate the borrower to pay the owner interest during the term of the loan and to return the principal or face value when the loan matures. And it's all tax-deferred, so payment of taxes aren't due until some time in the future, which never comes."

"Get as much information on paper as you can, as quickly as you can, and get out," Marcus said as he, Carmen, and

Garrett left the room. They went back into the living room and sat down.

"Money laundering. That's what it's all about," Carmen said.

"Money is the oldest motive for murder, ever since the world began. Other than women, that is," Garrett commented.

"So let's speculate," Marcus said. "See where we are. Frank Collins was using accounts at Hudson Financial to launder money. Suzanne finds out about it and tells Desireé that something is going on."

"But Suzanne is murdered before she can tell her what," Carmen threw in.

Garrett stood up and began pacing as Jamara joined them in the living room. "So now Suzanne is dead, and he's upset about what happened. He's upset because he knows she was killed because of what he was doin'. My guess would be he was goin' to talk and that's why he was killed. Mondrya Foster found out what was going on and they killed her. The question is, who is they?"

"My bet would be Bill Hudson," Marcus offered. "Somehow he knew that Mondrya made a copy of those files and that I might get them."

"What makes you think that?" Garrett asked.

"He didn't tell you?" Carmen said coyly.

"Tell me what?"

"The day after Mondrya was killed, Hudson offers to back me for DA. My guess is that he was counting on me keeping quiet about it in exchange for the position."

"If Hudson knew that your girl copied those files," Jamara said, "it's a safe bet that he knows we accessed the system tonight."

"She's right, big dog," Garrett said, plopping down on the couch next to Jamara. She moved closer to him. Which raised eyebrows on both Marcus and Carmen. "What you gonna do now?"

"Take what we have to the police," Marcus answered.

"Are you sure that's a good idea?" Garrett inquired.

"What do you mean, Garrett?"

"Well, this is just me thinkin' out loud, but the police investigated each of those murders, and you see how that turned out."

"Are you saying the police are involved?" Carmen asked.

"I'm not sayin' anything. But I used to be a cop, and I know how some of them operate," Garrett explained to her. "But, like I said, this is just me thinkin' out loud."

"What do you think we should do, then?" Marcus asked.

"I got a partner who works for the DEA," Garrett announced. "I'll give him a call and try to set up a meeting. Until then, I wouldn't trust nobody. And even then, you should cover yourself."

Jamara stood up and started back to the den. "I'll go and make two copies of everything. One for you, Marcus, and one for you," she said, smiling at Garrett.

"Marcus, do you think Frank told Dez about the money laundering?"

"I don't know. But it would make sense that if he did, that may have been why she was murdered."

"But who did all these killings?" Carmen asked.

"You think it was Hudson?" Garrett asked.

"Have either of you ever met Bill Hudson?" Marcus asked, smiling. "He a scrawny little man; he might weigh a buck fifty soaking wet. He might have done it, but I would think he'd get someone to handle his light work." Jamara returned to the room and handed Marcus the original CD and a copy and gave one to Garrett. "Keep that someplace safe, Garrett. I'm going back to the office to put these in the safe." Carmen got up and started moving toward the door, and Marcus followed behind her. "Give me a call when you set up the meeting with your friend at the DEA. When you do, I'd like you to sit in with us. You, too, Jamara, in case they have questions about how we accessed the information."

"I don't think so." Jamara frowned. "I try to avoid law-enforcement types at all costs. Hangin' around Garrett is enough for me."

"I understand," Marcus said, knowing she was on probation. Garrett walked up to Marcus.

"Here," Garrett said, attempting to hand Marcus a gun. "Take this. You might need it."

"Thanks, but no thanks, Garrett," Marcus replied, pushing the gun away. "I think we'll be all right without it."

"You sure? If we're right about this, at least five people have been killed over this information."

"Really, Garrett, I'll be fine."

Marcus and Carmen walked to the car and got in. "Are you sure we didn't need that gun, Marcus? Garrett is right—a lot of people have gotten killed over this," Carmen said as she drove off.

"We'll be fine, Carmen. Trust me."

"Okay, if you say so. And speaking of Garrett, I think him and Jamara got a thing goin' on."

"I wouldn't be surprised if they did. Jamara's a very pretty woman and besides, he thinks Paven is seeing somebody else."

"What makes him think that?"

"His oldest daughter, Aleana, told him that Paven goes out late every night, and she doesn't come home until early in the morning."

"Sounds like she got a man to me," Carmen said as they approached a red light. Carmen put her foot on the brake, and it went down to the floorboard. She tried again; the brake light on the dash board came on. "There's something wrong with the brakes!"

"What's wrong?"

"They don't work!"

"Look out!" Marcus yelled as they approached the cars already stopped at the light. Carmen was able to maneuver her way around them. Hydroplaning out of control on the wet surface, Carmen sped through the intersection toward an oncoming car whose driver was leaning on his horn. She was almost past him, but he clipped the tail end of her car, causing it to go into a spin. Another car hit them and forced them off the road. The car sailed down a hill headed for a cluster of trees. Carmen pulled up the emergency brake, and the car began to spin again.

"Cut the wheel hard to the left!" Marcus yelled.

Carmen turned the wheel as hard as she could. The back tires burst as the car came out of its spin, continuing to slide down the hill sideways. The car collided with a tree, just behind the rear passenger door, causing the window to shatter. The passenger cabin's multichamber air-bag system deployed from the headliner when the sensors detected the side impact, protecting Marcus from head injury and the broken glass. Carmen fell into Marcus as the front of the car hit another tree and bounced off. They both held each other tight as they jerked in the opposite direction and finally came to a stop.

"Marcus!" Carmen took off her seat belt. "Are you all right?" she said, removing his seat belt.

"Huh?" Marcus muttered.

Carmen was able to climb out of the car; she then attempted to drag Marcus from the passenger seat, as his door had been jarred open. "I'm all right, Carmen," Marcus said, leaning his head on Carmen's shoulder. "I'm just a little dizzy, that's all."

"Really, Marcus? I would have never guessed. You did hit that air bag pretty hard."

"That shit hurt too."

QUINTESSENTIALLY

Before too much time passed, the police had set up barricades at the top of the hill. The area had become crowded with emergency personnel. However, the accident scene was being taken over by two men in suits.

Information had gone out over the emergency channels that Marcus Douglas and Carmen Taylor were the occupants of the vehicle, so the press had begun to gather. Carmen came through the ordeal without a scratch. The paramedics were almost finished checking out Marcus. He had a small cut on the side of his head and some swelling. One of the paramedics bandaged his wound and gave him a cold pack for the swelling, then recommended that they have themselves checked out by their personal physicians at their earliest convenience.

As soon as the paramedics moved away, the two men approached Marcus and Carmen. "Mr. Douglas, Ms. Taylor, I'm Special Agent Lawrence Rietman, FBI," he said, and showed his badge.

"FBI?" Marcus said. "What is the FBI doing at the scene of an accident?"

"Mr. Douglas, I'd be glad to answer all of your questions, but first, are both of you all right?"

"Just a scratch."

"Ms. Taylor?" the agent asked.

"I'm fine. What's going on here?" Carmen asked.

"As I said, I'll be glad to answer all of your questions; however, this is not the time, or place for that discussion. Right now it is important that we get you away from this area. At this time, I'll ask that both of you refrain from making any more statements. Don't answer any questions. Not from me or from any police officers should they approach you. And there is a group of reporters forming at the top of the hill; we'd like to avoid them altogether. So—"

"What is going on here?" Marcus demanded to know.

"Mr. Douglas," the other man said, "I'm John DeBreeze. I believe Garrett Mason mentioned me to you?"

"Yes, he did."

"Please, Mr. Douglas, cooperate with Special Agent Rietman. It is for your safety."

"All right," Marcus said, taking Carmen's hand.

"With your permission, federal agents will take you to a hotel for your protection. I've arranged to have a doctor look the two of you over again at that time. In the morning, you'll be escorted back to the federal building and we will discuss the matter then," Special Agent Rietman said.

Once they were in the car, a female agent joined them. "I'm Agent Azizah Grant. I've been assigned to you for the evening. I'm sure Special Agent Rietman went over with you how things are going to go. I'll be with you at all times until we reach the hotel. At that time, I will enter and sweep the room," Agent Grant said as the car drove off. "Once I've secured the room, you will enter and I will be right outside the door in case you need anything."

"Thanks, Agent Grant. I'm sure we'll be fine," Marcus said.

"Pronounce your name again, please?" Carmen said.

"It's Azizah."

"That's very pretty," Marcus said.

"Ignore him; he thinks everybody's name is pretty. But it is a pretty name and very unique. Does it mean anything?"

"It means mighty and strong."

"That's good to know, but can you shoot?"

Agent Grant smiled her response.

Agent Grant was true to her word. Once she checked the room, she said good night and positioned herself outside the door. Marcus and Carmen began to settle into the room for the evening when there was a knock at the door.

"Who is it?" Marcus answered.

"It's Agent Grant, Mr. Douglas. I have the doctor Agent Rietman discussed with you."

Marcus opened the door and allowed the doctor to enter. After he examined Marcus and redressed his wound, he moved to Carmen. He gave them both a clean bill of health and departed.

"So, what will we do now?" Carmen asked.

"I don't know about you, but I'm hungry. I'm gonna call room service," Marcus said, looking around the room for the phone. "Where's the phone?"

"I don't see it." Carmen joined Marcus looking for the phone. After looking in all the logical places, Carmen opened the door and told Agent Grant, "Excuse me, this may sound stupid, but we can't find the phone."

"It's been removed from the room. Is there something that I can get for you?"

"Yes, some food. We're hungry."

"Okay," Agent Grant said. "Is there a menu in there?"

Marcus quickly looked around the room. "I don't see one anywhere."

"They do mean for us to eat, don't they?" Carmen asked.

"I'm sorry about this, folks. I'll try to get a menu up here soon."

"Thank you," Carmen said, and slammed the door in Agent Grant's face. Then she opened it again. "I'm sorry that I slammed the door. I know none of this is your fault."

"That's all right, Ms. Taylor. I know this can't be easy for you. I promise I'll get a menu up here as soon as I can."

This time Carmen closed the door lightly.

"I'm glad you cleaned that up. The last thing we need is to piss off the person protecting us."

The following morning at nine, Agent Grant knocked on the door to inform Marcus and Carmen that she was ready to escort them back to the federal building. Upon arrival, they were taken to a conference room, where Rietman, DeBreeze, and another man they had never seen before joined them. "Ms. Taylor, Mr. Douglas, this is Special Agent Ward. He is the agent in charge of this investigation," Rietman said.

"And just what investigation is that, Agent Ward?" Marcus asked sarcastically.

Special Agent Ward looked at Marcus and then to Agent Rietman.

"We've been keeping tabs on your investigation since Mr. Mason started asking questions about Frank Collins," Agent DeBreeze said, looking at the other agents. "And to answer your question, Mr. Douglas, we've been investigating Hudson Financial for some time now."

"That's why Frank Collins's file was missing from the police station," Marcus stated.

"That's correct."

"What exactly are you investigating Hudson for?"

"We have reason to believe that Frank Collins was using his position at Hudson Financial to launder money before he was murdered," Agent DeBreeze said. "We had a preliminary discussion with him, and I thought we had a deal for him to implicate Bill Hudson."

"That's when his wife was murdered," Agent Rietman said. "And that's when we entered the investigation. We are proceeding under the presumption that his wife was murdered to keep Collins in line. When that didn't happen, he was murdered too."

"If that's the case, why did the police list his death as a suicide?"

"That's where it gets a little hairy," Rietman said. "We're pretty sure that Hudson has someone in the police department working with him."

Special Agent Ward stood up. "Let's cut this bullshittin' around and get to the point of this. Excuse my language, Ms. Taylor. We know that Hudson is laundering money through those accounts; we know that everyone who gets in his way dies of some 'accidental death.' What I want to know is what your involvement is in this case?"

"We are investigating the murder of Desireé Ferguson. Mrs. Ferguson and Suzanne Collins were friends, and we started out looking for any connection between the two deaths."

"And what have you found out, Mr. Douglas?"

"Mason said you had some information for us," Agent DeBreeze said.

"Yes," Marcus said, going into his briefcase. He handed Agent DeBreeze the CD and copies of the client lists.

Agent DeBreeze looked over the list carefully before passing them on. "Would you mind telling me how you were able to obtain these items, Mr. Douglas?"

"I got the information from Mondrya Foster. She is, or was, EVP of operations at Hudson."

"You said was?" Agent Rietman said.

"Yes, she was murdered recently during a robbery at Starbucks. However, I have information from a source, who wished to remain anonymous, that leads us to conclude that Ms. Foster's death was not a random act but was intended to keep this information from getting to me."

Agent Rietman immediately picked up the phone and requested all information pertaining to the death of Mondrya Foster. As the agents looked over the client lists, Marcus and Carmen sat quietly, exchanging glances. At that moment, Agent Grant came into the room. She smiled at Marcus and Carmen as she walked over and whispered something to Agent Rietman. Whatever it was she told him raised an eyebrow. "We just got back the preliminary report on your car, Ms. Taylor. I see the car you were driving is registered to Roland Ferguson."

"Yes, he's my brother-in-law. The car belonged to my sister."

"Would you mind walking me through the accident, Ms. Taylor?"

"Okay, we had just left." Carmen was about to mention Jamara's name, but remembered her reluctance to be involved with any law enforcement. "I was driving down River Road, and I was trying to stop at the light, but when I stepped on the brake, it didn't work."

"How long have you been driving the car, Ms. Taylor?"

"A little more than a week, I guess."

"Have you had the car serviced during that time?"

"No. Why?" Carmen asked.

Agent Grant sat down next to Carmen, "Ms. Taylor, we checked out the car, and the brakes had been tampered with."

"What did you say?" Marcus asked, not wanting to believe what he'd just heard.

"The brakes on the car were tampered with," Agent Grant repeated.

"How?" Carmen asked.

"The brake line was cut. And it was cut in such a way that it would be very hard to tell when it was done."

"How is that, Agent Grant?" DeBreeze inquired.

"The cut was so small that the brake fluid just leaked out over a period of time. You see, each time you stepped on the brake, a little more fluid sprayed out until there was none left to stop the car."

"Okay," Carmen said slowly. "So what you're saying is that somebody tried to kill me?"

"Yes, Ms. Taylor," Agent Grant confirmed. "That's exactly what I'm saying."

Carmen dropped her head in her hands. Marcus gently placed his hand on her shoulder.

"Mr. Douglas, this is excellent work you've done here. If this disk contains what I think it does," Agent DeBreeze said, and rose to his feet, "we'll be putting Mr. Bill Hudson in jail where he belongs and for a very long time."

"There is one thing that bothers me."

"What's that, Agent Ward?"

"What does any of this have to do with Ms. Taylor's sister being murdered?"

Carmen looked up at Agent Ward. "What do you mean?"

"What I mean is, Hudson and his company are involved in money laundering. And he is probably deeply involved in murder to cover up those activities. For instance, John Heard and Coleman Wilson—you heard of them? Wilson was a senior exec at Hudson." Both Marcus and Carmen nodded their heads, remembering Joanne Henley mentioning their names in connection with the story she was working on. "Heard was an FTC investigator. I received a memo from him stating that Wilson was willing to go on record and tell all he knew about what's goin' on over there. But the very next day, one hangs himself and the other chases sleeping pills with vodka. So we got Suzanne Collins found dead in her office, butt naked. Her husband, Frank, is the only suspect, but he commits suicide, case closed. Now you've made us aware of . . ." Agent Ward circled his hand and looked around the room for help recalling information.

"Mondrya Foster," Agent Grant said as she handed him what information they were able to get.

"Thank you. She gets this information to you, and she is shot in a robbery." He glanced at the report. "No suspects. You folks following me yet? Ms. Taylor, your sister was murdered violently. All of the other murders connected with this case all follow the same pattern. So I'll ask you again— what does any of this have to do with your investigation?"

Marcus looked at Carmen and then at Special Agent Ward. "Nothing."

ARMED AND
EXTREMELY
DANGEROUS

Marcus and Carmen sat quietly in the backseat of Agent Grant's Crown Victoria as she drove them away from the federal building. Agent Grant glanced in the rearview mirror and could see the dejected look on both of their faces as they contemplated Special Agent Ward's final question.

He was right. What did any of the happenings at Hudson Financial have to do with the murder of Desireé Ferguson? Special Agent Ward had made a valid point. Desireé was murdered violently. It was an act of passion. Each of the murders connected to Hudson Financial were committed in such a way that it would minimize police involvement.

Agent Grant turned into Marcus's driveway and turned off the car. Marcus thanked her for the ride and for all she had done. As he got out of the car, Carmen leaned forward and whispered to Agent Grant, "Can you take me somewhere else?"

"I'll take you wherever you need to go. And stay with you for as long as you need me to."

"Good. Can you give me a minute?" Carmen jumped out

of the car and caught up with Marcus. "Marcus, I'm going to have Agent Grant take me home."

"Okay." Marcus turned and started back toward the car. "I'll go with you."

"No, Marcus. I need to be alone for a while."

"Are you gonna be all right?"

"I'll be fine, really. Agent Grant is going to stay with me for as long as I need her to. I'll call you later tonight, okay?" Carmen said, and kissed Marcus on the cheek.

"Okay," Marcus said reluctantly. Marcus opened the car door for her. "If you're sure you'll be all right." He shut the door. "Call me tonight," he mouthed.

"I will," Carmen mouthed back as Agent Grant pulled out of the driveway.

"Where do you want me to take you?" Agent Grant asked as she drove.

"Just drive for now. I need to call somebody," Carmen replied, dialing her phone.

"This Denny."

"What's up, Denny Boo?"

"Waz up, Carm. This your new number?"

"It sure is."

"Hold up, let me save it. Now. Waz up, Carm? I ain't heard from you. I thought you went back across the water and all that was just talk on the radio about you shakin' your groove thang at Bell Bottoms." Denny laughed.

"Nope. Still here. And I'll probably be here for a while. I'm thinking about buying a house."

"No shit. You stayin'? That's cool, Carm; maybe then you'll pencil me into your busy schedule."

"Actually, Denny Boo, that's why I was calling. I need to see you."

"When."

"As soon as you can. I need a favor."

"What you need?" Denny asked.

"I'd rather not say over the phone. I'll tell you when I see you. Can I meet you somewhere?"

"Yeah, why don't you meet me at Grant Park?"

"Grant Park, huh?" Carmen said, and a little smile crept over her face.

"You remember our spot."

"Yeah, I remember. You feelin' a little nostalgic today?"

"Somethin' like that. I'll be there in twenty minutes."

"I'll see you there," Carmen said, and pressed END on the phone. "Agent Grant, would you mind taking me to Grant Park?"

"Not a problem," Agent Grant said as she made her way toward I-20. "Mind if I ask you a question, Ms. Taylor?"

"Sure, go ahead."

"I overheard parts of your conversation. You know, the part about not wantin' to say things over the phone. I know that you were very disappointed by what Agent Ward said. But, please, don't do anything you might regret later."

"Believe me, Agent Grant, I won't do anything stupid. There's just something that I need to get."

When Agent Grant arrived at the park, Denny was there waiting. He was sitting on the trunk of his car enjoying a drink and people-watching. When he saw the black Crown Victoria stop behind him, he got up and started walking away. Carmen jumped out of the car. "Denny Boo!"

"Damn, Carm, you scared the shit outta me."

Carmen stuck her head back in the car. "Thanks for the ride, Agent Grant."

"Do you need me to stay and wait for you?"

"No; I think I'll be safe with him. Safer with him than most places in the world," Carmen said, looking out at Denny. "But I want to thank you for everything."

"All right, Ms. Taylor. But, please, take my card." Grant

handed Carmen her card. "Promise that you'll call me if you need anything."

"Thank you, Agent Grant," Carmen replied happily, and accepted the card. "If I see anything out of the ordinary, you'll be the first person that I call."

"I'll be checking on you," Grant said, and she drove away.

"What's goin' on, Denny Boo?"

"Waz up, Carmen? Who was that? It looked like a cop to me."

"That's because she is a cop. That was Agent Azizah Grant of the FBI."

"FBI! What you doin' with the FBI? Better question, why you bring the FBI anywhere near me?"

"She was assigned to protect me. But I told her that I would be safe with you."

"Why was she assigned to protect you?"

"Somebody tried to kill me."

Denny listened as Carmen explained to him what she and Marcus had been working on and how she came to need the protection services of the FBI. "Marcus, huh? That the stiff you brought to my mom's house?"

"Yes, and he is not a stiff. Marcus is a very nice man."

"Nice man, huh? Bet he ain't nothin' like me?"

"No, Denny Boo, he is nothing like you."

"You probably ain't never got with another thug nigga like me. Have you, Carm?"

"To be honest with you, Boo, there was this one guy I used to date in New York who makes you look like a habitual jaywalker."

"Oh really. Habitual jaywalker, huh? How you run up on him?"

"I met him when I first moved to New York after I left Spellman. You remember Jackie, stayed in the room next to me and Desireé?" Denny nodded. "She didn't go back to school in the fall, so I was staying with her in the Bronx off Jackson Avenue. So me and Jackie were hanging out in the valley one night, and we took the train home. I look up and there he is, standing over me. So he sat down next to me and we start talking. He was wearing a long black coat, and I know he's got a gun in the pocket, 'cause I could feel it bump against my leg every time the train stopped. And he was with this other guy. He was standing by the door, and he's got a gun too. Only his is in his hand, but he's holding his coat over it. So he asks me where I was going and I said to Jackson Avenue."

"I'm gettin' off there too," he said.

"Do you live around there?"

"No. To be honest with you, I'm goin' there to kill somebody."

"Kill somebody! Why?"

"'Cause they tried to kill me. But I don't want to talk about that. I'd much rather talk about you. Is that a Georgia accent I'm hearin'?"

"Yes, I'm from Atlanta."

"Atlanta is a nice city. What brings you to New York?"

"I came here 'cause I needed a change. So I've been hangin' out with my girl here. If I like it, I'll stay. Get back into school, see if I can pick up some work as a model."

"You're a model?"

"I've done some modeling in Atlanta. Some print, some commercials, shows, that type of stuff."

"Freeze," he said, glancing up at him. "Nevermind. Do you have a pen and a piece of paper?"

"What do you want it for?"

"I want to give you the number of somebody who might be able to help you."

"Okay," Carmen said, digging in her purse.

Carmen handed him the pen and paper and he wrote a name and number on it. "Here. This guy's a modeling agent; his name is Calvin. Call him and tell him what you've done and what you're interested in doing and he'll take care of you," he said as the train approached the station.

"Thank you. I'll do that," Carmen said as they got off the train and walked down the platform toward the steps.

When he got to the bottom of the steps, he turned to Carmen. "It was nice talking to you."

"Hey!" Carmen yelled as he started to walk away. "What's your name?"

"My name is Mike Black. Just tell Calvin that I'd consider it a personal favor if he found you something."

As Carmen and Denny walked the paths through the park that they used to all those years ago, she continued, "So I called the guy the next day and that was my first break."

"So he hooked you up, huh?"

"He sure did. And I wanted to thank him, but he never gave me his number," Carmen said. "So I practically had to beg Calvin to tell me some way that I could get in touch with him."

"Why did you have to beg him?" Denny was curious to know.

"'Cause Calvin didn't think Vicious Black was the kind of man I needed to be hangin' around."

"Vicious Black?" Denny asked.

"That's what some people call him, but he doesn't like it."

"Why do they call him that?"

"He told me how he got that name, and I won't bore you with the story, but he runs a gambling and prostitution organization in the Bronx."

"What's so vicious about that?"

"Oh, stop being a playa hater, Denny Boo. I told you when I met him he was on his way to kill somebody. Anyway, we only went out three or four times. He was always busy. But he was my last thug. But, Denny Boo, you'll always be my favorite."

"Yeah, whatever, Carm. So what you need me to do?"

"I need a gun."

"What you need a gun for, Carm?"

"To protect myself. Marcus doesn't think I need one, but too many people are dying over this for me not to protect myself."

"I don't know about this gun shit."

"Why?"

"Carmen, you're a model. You don't need to be carryin' no gun."

"Why, Denny? What? You think I don't remember how to shoot?"

"The thought has occurred to me."

"Well, I'll tell you what; let's go to a shooting range and I'll prove I can shoot," Carmen said confidently. "Will that satisfy you?"

"It'll prove you can shoot, but why can't you just go buy one if you just need it for protection?"

"Because I don't want to wait five days for a background check."

"I know a place where you can get one right now without goin' through all them changes," Denny said. "In fact, that would work out better. I don't want you anywhere near no gun I could get you. Ain't no tellin' who done what with 'em."

Carmen and Denny walked back to his car and then drove to a little gun shop in Jonesboro. An hour later, Carmen walked out of the shop with a new Kel-Tec P-3AT's .380.

One of the easiest-to-conceal handguns of effective caliber that could possibly be found. Denny still wanted Carmen to prove that she could handle the weapon, so he drove her to a gun range.

With her new gun tucked securely in her purse, Carmen had Denny drop her off at the Ritz Carlton in Buckhead. Once he drove off, Carmen got into a cab. It wasn't that she didn't trust Denny, but she didn't want to involve him in the mess she was in. She still wondered who would want to kill her, especially if Desireé's murder had nothing to do with Hudson Financial. But it didn't matter; if anybody came after her, she would be ready.

PICK UP THE PIECES

Marcus wandered around his house like he was looking for something, but he wasn't. He was thinking about what Special Agent Ward told him and Carmen. There was a certain finality in his statement. *What does any of this have to do with the murder of Desireé Ferguson?*

Marcus walked over to the bar and poured a glass of Hennessy. With the bottle still in hand, he drained what he had poured and filled the glass again. He dragged himself to his chair and sat down. He couldn't help but to think about Carmen. When she drove away with Agent Grant, the smile that he had grown to love was gone. Love. Was he really in love with Carmen, or was it just the fact that he had been working so closely with her? He didn't know, and at that moment, he didn't seem to care. Marcus picked up the phone and dialed Carmen's number but hung up just as quickly. "Give her time, Marcus. She said she needed some time." *But suppose she really wanted me to contact her and she just needs a little push?* "Whatever," he said, and finished his drink.

He decided to make constructive use of his time. Marcus

went into his office and got a pad and a pen. He returned to the living room and put Miles Davis in the CD tray, poured himself another shot and began making notes of everything they had learned to this point. He wrote down the conclusion they had drawn from it and where that conclusion led them. In each case, the conclusion led them closer to Hudson Financial. But if those conclusions were incorrect, he would have to consider alternate theories. He picked up the phone and called his office; Janise answered.

"Janise, Tiffanie available?"

"She's not on her line; hold on, Marcus, I'll transfer you."

"Tiffanie Powers."

"Hello, Tiffanie, this is Marcus."

"How you doing, Marcus?"

"I'm fine, Tiffanie; I need your help."

Tiffanie's eyes bucked open and she sat straight up in her chair. Being the ambitious woman that she was, Tiffanie had been looking for an opportunity to step up. "What can I help you with?"

"You know I've been looking into the murder of Desireé Ferguson; well, this morning I ran headfirst into a brick wall."

"What happened?"

"It seems that we backed into an FBI/DEA investigation pointing to money laundering activities at Hudson Financial and several murders that occurred to cover it up. I was sure that those murders were connected in some way to Desireé Ferguson, but now I'm not sure."

"So how can I help?"

"I need a sounding board, Tiffanie."

"Me?"

"Yes, you. You're the best lawyer I know, and there is no one better at speculating on alternate theories of a crime than you."

"I didn't know you thought of me like that, Marcus, thank you. I'll try my best to live up to that," Tiffanie said excitedly.

"Yeah, yeah. Are you working on anything right now?"

"Yes. I was working on the Roberts assault case and I was—"

"Tell Janise to give you all the files related to Desireé Ferguson. Give Janise what you're working on and tell her I said to give it to Smitty."

"The client will be upset."

"Fuck them. You will still be the primary lawyer, and Smitty will report to you. You can still try the case, if it goes to trial, and if necessary you can still act as the primary contact if they object too strongly to the change, but I need you on this now."

"Smitty won't like that."

"Fuck Smitty too; he could stand to gain something from working under you. I've had too many conversations with him about his preparation. He's a good lawyer, but he can stand to tighten up. So, how soon can you be here?"

"Give me an hour," Tiffanie said, straightening up her desk. "Wait a minute. Where is here?"

"My house."

"You want me to come to your house?"

"What's wrong with that?"

"Randa would lose her mind if she knew I was at your house."

"Why is that, Tiffanie?" Marcus asked impatiently.

"You don't know?"

"I don't know what?"

"Randa has always thought I had a thing for you and that something was going on between us."

"Do you?" Marcus asked.

"Do I what?" Tiffanie asked innocently.

"Have a thing for me?"

"I work for you, Marcus. That would compromise our working relationship."

"Good answer. Anyway, I don't think that you have that to worry about. Randa signed the divorce papers."

"I know. Do you think that makes her less dangerous or more?"

"I'll see you in an hour."

Since she did have a thing for Marcus, Tiffanie decided to go home first and change into something more comfortable. Something a bit more provocative so he would notice her as a woman. *But not too provocative in case Carmen Taylor brings her ass over there.* But in good taste so she could maintain her professionalism as a lawyer. An hour and a half later, Tiffanie arrived at Marcus's house, dressed tastefully in a red Austin Reed Andover jacket with pants to match. "What took you so long?"

"I went home to change. I didn't know how long we'd be working, and I wanted to be comfortable," Tiffanie said as she walked by Marcus.

As she passed, Marcus noticed, maybe for the first time, what an attractive woman Tiffanie was. "Well, you do look nice like that."

"Thank you for noticing." Tiffanie smiled as Marcus led the way to the living room.

"Did you give your work to Janise?"

"Yes. And I stopped by and talked to Smitty. I didn't want him to get blindsided or for him to have any ill feelings about reporting to me. We had a little talk about his preparation, and I gave him some gentle suggestions on ways that he can improve. He seemed to take it well."

"Good," Marcus said as he sat down across from Tiffanie. "Thank you for taking the time to talk to him."

"Marcus, do you mind if I ask you a question?"

"Shoot."

"Is there a future in this for me?"

"How do you mean?"

"Whether you intended it to be or not, you have given me supervisory responsibilities. Or one might assume that you have, since the only one who, prior to this, had supervisory responsibilities in the office was you."

"Look, Tiffanie, we are starting to experience some growth, and with the outcome of the Ferguson trial, we will have more. I'm looking for somebody who is willing to step up and assume a greater role. I just told you that I am very impressed with you and the work that you have done for the firm."

"Some people might interpret that as the definition of a partner."

"Damn your ambitiousness, Tiffanie. But that's the thing I liked about you right from the start. Yeah, some people might think that is the definition of a partner. But let's see how this works out before we start talking partner."

"Fair enough. Let's get started."

For the next two hours, Marcus went over all the details of the case. While Tiffanie reviewed the files, Marcus went over in detail all of the information related to the case. Then they began to break it down. "There were no other prints found at the scene?" Tiffanie asked.

"Just the maid, Desireé Ferguson, and Rasheed Damali."

"Anybody check out the maid?"

"Alibi." Marcus flipped through a few papers. "Confirmed."

"No sign of forced entry, correct?"

"Correct."

"So, the perp is let in the cabin; no signs of a struggle at the door?" Tiffanie asked, looking at the crime-scene photos.

"None."

"His body is found"—Tiffanie shuffled through the crime-scene photos—"at the end of this entry hall. That would put him in clear view of Desireé Ferguson in the Jacuzzi."

"That's right."

"Well, if that's the case, I have a question."

"What's that?"

"I'm going to assume that Miss Desireé is in the tub when Mr. Rasheed opened the door."

"That's the accepted assumption."

Tiffanie stood up. "So, Mr. Rasheed opens the door and walks back down the entry hall before the perp starts swinging, and all of this is going on while Miss Desireé is coolin' in the tub. What was she doing while all of this was going on?"

"You know, I asked myself that question too."

"And?"

"At the time it wasn't relevant to Roland Ferguson's defense."

"I'm thinking that they knew whoever it was, or at least Rasheed did."

"To answer the door naked, I'd say he knew him rather well."

"Okay, it at least had to be somebody she felt comfortable enough to be naked in front of."

"The list would be long."

"Excuse me?"

"To put it delicately, Miss Desireé was comfortable naked around a number of people."

"She was fucking everybody, to put it bluntly," Tiffanie said. Marcus nodded and Tiffanie shook her head. "Okay, who are those people?"

"At the time of the murder, two that we know of. She was having sex with Rasheed and a woman named India Carter."

"Woman?"

"Yes, a woman. According to Garrett, Porsche Temple would have to be on that list and another woman who turned her out, but he couldn't get a name on her. There were a couple of men the she was involved with too—Axle Grant, Robert Pettibone, and Ira Stinson."

"At least they're men," Tiffanie mused. "You have anything on them?"

"No. We haven't had time to look at them, with Garrett being tied up in his thing. "

"We'll need to depose each of them. Maybe the perp was somebody Miss Desireé and Mr. Rasheed were having sex with."

"That's a possibility we could and probably should be investigating."

"Anybody else who would have a motive?" Tiffanie asked.

"I can't confirm Desireé's association with him, but James Martin would top the list."

Tiffanie shuffled papers and looked at her notes. "Okay, who is James Martin?"

"Rasheed worked for him as an escort. He owed Martin ten thousand dollars for cocaine he fronted him for escort work he was supposed to do."

"You say 'supposed to' like he didn't do the work."

"That's why Martin was looking for him. It seemed that Rasheed had a problem keeping it up for the ladies, so Martin had him with men."

"Men?"

"Yes, men. But Rasheed couldn't do it."

"Which does give Martin a motive to kill Mr. Rasheed, but not Miss Desireé. Did anybody talk to him?"

"No, he's dead."

"How'd he die?"

"Carjacking."

"All right. Mr. Rasheed owing this Martin money does give him the strongest motive for murder, Marcus."

"We did talk to Martin's girlfriend, Patty Morgan. She couldn't confirm his whereabouts on the night of the murder, but she did say that he was capable and that she thought Martin did it. That was until they arrested Ferguson for it."

"That makes it even stronger."

"But he's dead. Hard to pin a murder on a dead man," Marcus admitted.

They continued on in this manner for hours, with Tiffanie asking questions and offering theories, most of which had already been explored. "I don't know where else to go with this, Marcus. The only two solid suspects are James Martin and Ferguson. One's dead and the other was found not guilty."

"Well, thanks anyway, Tiffanie. Maybe we should just turn over what we have to the police."

"That's what I wanted to ask you!" Tiffanie said, snapping her fingers.

"What's that?"

"You said the FBI guys said that each of the murders that they have connected to Hudson Financial were carried out to minimize police involvement."

"Right. They hinted that there may be someone in the police department working along with them."

"I know it was just this morning, but have you followed up on that?"

"No," Marcus said, reaching for the phone. "But I'll call Garrett and put him on it." The phone rang and Jamara whispered, "Hello."

"Jamara?"

"Yes."

"This is Marcus; Garrett around?"

"Hold on, Marcus. I'll get him." Marcus heard her whisper, "Garrett, wake up, it's Marcus."

Marcus smiled to himself and waited for Garrett to come to the phone. "This Garrett," he said, trying to come out of his nod.

"I need you to look into something, and, no, it's not at Porsche Temple's place. Although I would like to know who the mystery woman is who turned Desireé."

"I'm all over that. What else?"

"FBI hinted that there may be some police involvement in covering up the murders connected to Hudson Financial."

"No shit. Who we talkin' 'bout?"

"Frank and Suzanne Collins, Mondrya Foster, John Heard, and Coleman Wilson."

"Got 'em."

"Add James Martin to that list, and talk to Patty Morgan. Get the names of the two hookers she thinks Hudson killed."

"On it, Big Dog. I'll call you back."

When Marcus got off the phone with Garrett, Tiffanie asked, "What do you want me to do now?"

"Just hang loose for a minute. I want to see what Garrett turns up."

"That's fine," Tiffanie said, sitting in her chair. "Is there anything to eat?"

"No."

"Is there any food in the house at all, 'cause I'd be happy to cook something."

"Nope. No food, Tiffanie. Sorry. Do you like pizza?"

"I love pizza. I love Italian food, period. Sometimes I think I was born Italian and some black people kidnapped me at birth." Tiffanie laughed.

"We could order some pizza."

"What kind? I mean, you aren't one of those people who put weird stuff on it like broccoli or pineapple, are you?"

"No." Marcus laughed. "I'm a sausage, mushroom, and extra cheese man."

"If you add some pepperoni to that, we got an order."

"Sausage, mushroom, pepperoni, and extra cheese it is."

"Where are you going to order from?"

"There's a place nearby, DeVito's 375. If you don't mind staying and answering the phone in case Garrett calls back, I'll run out and pick it up."

"I don't mind, but what if Miss Carmen Taylor calls, or worse, what if Randa calls or just shows up?"

"In both cases, Tiffanie, you are here working," Marcus said, picking up the phone.

"In that case, order some bread sticks too."

"Anything to drink?" Marcus asked.

"Some wine would be nice."

"Anything else?"

"Well, now that you mention it, a little violin and candle-light would create a more suitable atmosphere for the meal." Tiffanie laughed, but she was serious.

While Tiffanie waited by the phone, Marcus went to pick up the pizza. When he got back to the house, Tiffanie was on the phone with Garrett. "I think you'll want to hear this."

Tiffanie handed the phone to Marcus. "What's up, Garrett?"

"I got what you asked for."

"And?"

"Benjamin."

"Benjamin. On which case?"

"On all of them, Big Dog. If he wasn't the lead detective, he was involved in some way."

"Break it down."

"Tiffanie got all that. And what is Tiffanie doin' there, and why is she answering the phone?"

"We're working, Garrett."

"Yeah, right. Well, you two get to work on that pizza and wine." Garrett laughed and hung up the phone.

Marcus turned to Tiffanie, who was already hard at work on her first slice. Marcus shook his head and went to the kitchen to get a cork screw, then returned to the den with two glasses and a bottle of Robert Mondavi 2001 Stags Leap Cabernet Sauvignon. He poured a glass for Tiffanie and handed it to her. "Thank you, Marcus."

"Sorry, they were all out of violins," Marcus said, pouring himself a glass of wine and grabbing a slice of pizza. "I'd be interested in hearing your observations of this latest revelation." Tiffanie swallowed before speaking.

"Well, other than the obvious connection with Benjamin being involved in all of the cases, I was thinking while you were gone that your Agent Ward was wrong."

"How so?"

"The Ferguson murder, even though it was violent, does follow the same pattern as the rest."

"I say again, how so?"

"Because there was only minimal police involvement."

"Right, and now that we know there was a police connection—"

"Hold up, wait a minute!" Tiffanie sprang to her feet. "There's a fuckin' anchovy on my pizza," she said, picking the anchovy off the slice. "I think they are so disgusting!"

"It ain't my fault."

"Anyway, what I was about to say was the FBI has to know about Benjamin. Especially if Garrett could find out in less than an hour. No slight on Garrett's skills, but they have access to all that. So I'm wondering why drop that the way they did?"

"My guess would be that we've been doing a pretty good job investigating this," Marcus said as the phone rang. "Why not drop that on us and see where we go with it. Anything we turn up only makes their case against Hudson stronger," he said as he put the phone on speaker. "Hello."

"Marcus?"

"Yes."

"This is Joanna Henley."

"Hi, Joanna, what's up?"

"I got something for you," Joanna said in a singsongy way. "You're gonna love this."

"Spill it—don't leave me hangin' on a string."

"The private investment group that took over Hudson Financial was headed by Roland Ferguson."

"But I thought they walked away from the deal?"

"That was their plan all along. When they walked out, it drove the stock price into the dirt. Then they came right back and bought it up cheap."

"So Ferguson really owns Hudson Financial?"

"Correctamondo."

"Thanks, Joanna, that's just the link we were looking for. I owe you one."

"Good. Does that mean you'll tell me what you're working on?"

"I'll tell you what, call me tomorrow and I'll give you a front-page story."

IRREFUTABLE

Carmen took the cab to Marcus's house. She got out of the cab and walked slowly toward the door. She had decided not to tell Marcus anything about the gun. She rang the bell and Marcus opened the door. When he saw it was Carmen, his face lit up. "Carmen, I wasn't expecting to see you so soon."

"I know I said I would call first, but I missed you. So I just came. I hope that was all right."

"Of course it's all right."

"I know how some men don't like women to show up unannounced and uninvited," Carmen said, remembering words that Mike Black once told her when she showed up on his doorstep. She went into the living room and sat down on the couch.

"That's true," Marcus agreed as he moved the pile of papers and files that he and Tiffanie had been working on. "Do you want some pizza?" he asked, picking up the box.

"No, I had something earlier. But I will have a piece of this candy," Carmen replied, opening a candy dish. "Peppermint," she said. "Paula M. Dent."

"What did you say?"

"Peppermint."

"No, the name. What was that name?"

"Paula M. Dent."

"Who is that?"

"You remember Peppermint from Pleasers, don't you?" Carmen smiled and Marcus looked confused. "You remember the dancer I sent you?"

"Yeah."

"Well, that is her real name. I told her that Paula M. Dent kinda rhymed with Peppermint. Why?" Now it was Carmen who looked confused. "I mean, you act like it's something important."

"It just may be. After the trial was over, I was with Roland in his study and he was on the phone talking to a Paula Dent."

"So he knows her. He's a world-class freak, like everybody else involved in this mess."

"May be something, may be nothing. But what if I were to tell you that Roland owns Hudson Financial and that the lead detective in all of the murders is our own Detective Benjamin?"

"I'd say that since she knows him, we could at least talk to Peppermint, see what she can tell us."

Marcus and Carmen left the house and drove to Pleasers. They went inside and looked around for Peppermint. Not seeing her anywhere, Marcus asked one of the other dancers if she was there. He was told that Peppermint had just come off stage and was in the dressing room changing.

"I'll get her." Carmen disappeared quickly into the dressing room while Marcus found a table close to the dressing room door. For the next ten minutes, he reluctantly turned away dancer after dancer who came to offer him their table-dancing services. Finally, Carmen emerged from the dressing room with Peppermint. "Peppermint, this is Marcus Douglas. He needs to ask you some questions."

"I thought y'all wanted a dance," Peppermint said. Marcus reached into his pocket, pulled out a fifty, and handed it to her.

"This should cover your time."

Peppermint took the fifty. "Go ahead and ask what you wanna ask." She placed the bill in her already overflowing garter.

"Do you know a man named Roland Ferguson?"

"Not that I can remember. But a lotta men say they know me. And I meet a lotta men up in here. After a while, they're all just faces with money in their pockets," Peppermint said with a smile, and Marcus smiled back.

Carmen dug around in her purse until she found a picture of Roland and Desireé. "Have you even seen this man before?" she asked, and handed Peppermint the picture.

Peppermint looked at the small picture closely in the dim light of the club. "Rollie! That's Rollie."

"So you do know this man," Marcus said, pointing at the picture.

"Yeah, I know him," Peppermint said, handing the picture back to Carmen.

"But you never heard of Roland Ferguson?"

"Why? Should I?"

"Never seen him on television or read anything about him in the papers?" Carmen asked, glancing at Marcus with a smile.

"Honey, I don't have time to sit down and watch television, much less read the paper."

"How do you know Rollie?" Marcus asked.

"I've danced for him a few times."

"Anything else?" Carmen inquired.

"No, honey, nothing else," Peppermint said with a bit of an attitude. "A lotta these hoes up in here sellin' pussy, but I ain't one of them. Besides, that wasn't Rollie's thing. He just liked to watch me dance. Never even tried to touch me. But he damn sure paid good."

"Okay," said a dejected Carmen.

"But I did do him a favor once."

"What was that?" Carmen asked excitedly.

"Rollie called me one night and asked me to meet him at The Underground."

"What did he want?" Marcus asked.

"He asked me to drive his car home."

"Why?" Carmen asked.

"He didn't say, and I really didn't care. He gave me five hundred dollars."

"Just to drive his car?" Carmen said in disbelief.

"No, he wanted me to go in the house, call some number, and play a tape. Oh yeah, he was runnin' on E, so he gave me his credit card to get gas."

"When was this?" Marcus asked.

"About a year ago."

"Were you still in the house when Rollie got there?"

"Nope. After the tape was finished, I left."

"Did anybody see you?"

"I don't think so." Peppermint frowned. "Why y'all wanna know all this about him?"

"'Cause that muthafucka killed my sister that night." Carmen got up from the table and headed for the door.

Marcus stood up. "Carmen, wait!" he yelled.

"Did I hear her right? Rollie killed her sister? I don't believe that."

"Neither did a jury. Thank you for your help, Ms. Dent," Marcus said, and ran out of the club after Carmen.

When Marcus reached the car, Carmen was there waiting for him. "I *knew* he did it. I just knew it, Marcus! He's gonna pay; that muthafucka's gonna pay!"

Marcus unlocked Carmen's door, and she got in, still mumbling, "He's gonna pay." Once he was in the car, Marcus turned to Carmen. "Have you ever heard of double jeopardy?"

"Yes."

"Then you understand that under the law, he can't be tried again for that crime."

"What! You mean he's gonna get away with it?"

"Not really, since he owns Hudson Financial; that makes him a co-conspirator in money laundering and all the murders."

"Yeah, well, suppose he can prove that he had no knowledge of anything about that? What happens then? Suppose he gets another smart lawyer like you? What happens then? He walks away free."

Marcus had no answer. He simply started up the car and backed out of the space.

"What are you gonna do now?" Carmen asked.

"I'll call Agent Ward and DeBreeze in the morning and make them aware of what we've found out."

"Take me to his house," Carmen demanded.

"Why, Carmen?"

"I need to ask him why. For my own peace of mind; I need to look him in the eye and hear him tell me why he killed Dez."

"I don't think confronting Roland is the best idea."

"Fine," Carmen fumed. "Drop me off at the corner. I'll go by myself."

"You're determined to do this, aren't you?"

"Yes, Marcus," Carmen pleaded. "I thought you knew how important this is to me. Especially after I read how Dez was crying out for my help."

"I do."

"I thought since you'd been through this yourself that you would understand why I have to do this."

"I do, Carmen. I'll go with you."

"I have to do this, Marcus. And if you won't go with me, I'll go alone!"

"Carmen!" Marcus said loud enough to get her attention. "I'll go with you."

"Thank you, Marcus," Carmen said softly, and smiled to herself.

Carmen said nothing else during the remainder of the drive to the Ferguson residence. She just stared aimlessly out the window, trying to decide what was she going to do when she saw Roland. Carmen barely felt the weight of the gun in her purse as it rested on her lap. The words *double jeopardy* rang like bells in her mind. Could she, would she, kill him?

Marcus rolled into the driveway and stopped in front of the house. He turned off the lights and looked over at Carmen. "Are you sure you want to do this?"

"I'm sure I have to."

Marcus shut off the engine and got out of the car. He came around to open the door for Carmen, but she was already out of the car and heading for the house. Marcus ran to catch up with her, and they walked hand in hand to the door. Carmen took a deep breath and rang the doorbell. Some time passed before Melissa opened the door. She led Marcus and Carmen to the study and told them to go on in. Roland looked up when the door to his study opened and an angry-looking Carmen walked in with Marcus close behind.

Carmen now knew what she was going to do.

When Roland saw who it was, he smiled. "Carmen! And Marcus! Come in, come in. I was just about to have a drink. Won't you join me?"

"Thank you, Roland," Marcus said, and Carmen cut her fiery eyes at him. "We'd be glad to."

Roland stepped to his bar. "Bacardi, isn't it, Carmen? And Hennessy for the gentlemen," he said gladly as he poured their drinks. Carmen sat down in one of the chairs in front of Roland's desk and opened her purse. She slowly and carefully moved her gun to the top. Marcus handed Carmen a glass handed to him by Roland and sat down in the chair next to her. Once Roland finished pouring his own drink, he sat down behind the desk. "So, what brings you two out tonight?"

"You—" Carmen started, but Marcus cut her off quickly.

"You know that we've been investigating your wife's murder and we've found out some disturbing information. And before we went any further, I felt it necessary to ask you about it."

Carmen rolled her eyes.

"Disturbing? I don't like the sound of that." Roland chuckled. "By all means, Marcus, go ahead."

"Our investigation has led us to several other murders."

"Other murders?"

"Yes, Frank and Suzanne Collins, two executives at Hudson Financial, and an FTC investigator."

"What could any of that possibly have to do with Desireé's murder?"

"We have documented evidence of money laundering at Hudson Financial, and those murdered seem to be associated with them. My sources tell me that you head the investment group that owns Hudson Financial."

"Yes, that's true. But my group are merely investors. We have no involvement in the operation of the company. Bill Hudson handles all that. But I'm glad you made me aware of these things before it became public knowledge. That will drive the stock holders crazy."

Carmen glared at Marcus. "This is getting nowhere!"

"Carmen," Marcus pleaded.

"No, Marcus. I told you he would do this." Carmen took her gun out of her purse and pointed it at Roland. "We know you did it."

"Put the gun down, Carmen," Marcus said, holding his hand out. "We don't need to do this."

"It's all right, Marcus," Roland said calmly. "You know I did what, Carmen?"

"I know you killed Desireé."

"What are you talking about, Carmen? I couldn't have—"

"We talked to Paula Dent," Marcus said. "We know she was driving your car. We know that she was the one at your house that night."

Roland looked coolly at Marcus, then at Carmen. Then back to Marcus. "I always knew you were a good lawyer. Smart. Had integrity. That's why I chose you. Somebody that judge, jury, and the press would believe when you said I wasn't guilty," Roland said as he glanced at Carmen. "There's no need for the gun now, Carmen. I won't give you any trouble."

"Why'd you kill her?" Carmen demanded. "I read her letters. She wanted a divorce. Was it money?" she spit out. "Did you kill her for money?"

"Nothing so crude. I loved Desireé. I would have given her anything. Yes, Desireé wanted a divorce. We talked about it the night before . . ." Roland was unable to say, *I killed her.* "I told her that I didn't want a divorce. I told her that we could work it out. That I would stop"—he paused and looked away—"stop making her do those things for me. It wasn't a problem for her. Not at first anyway. She seemed to enjoy it. Until she met that low-life Rasheed. She thought she loved him." Roland paused for a moment and looked at Carmen. "That night she told me again that she wanted a divorce, but this time she said that if I didn't give her a divorce, that she would see me in jail. She said she had talked to Frank Collins. He told her that Bill Hudson had Suzanne killed. She knew that my group controlled Hudson Financial."

"So, you decided to kill her," Carmen spat out.

"No. I was going to give her what she wanted. I had just told her that when Melissa came into the room. She told me that somebody was at the door, and she thought that I might want to see him alone. She always was very protective of Desireé, ever since they . . ."

"Melissa and Dez were . . . ?" Carmen asked, eyes wide open.

Roland nodded his head. "Melissa used to bathe Desireé and give her hot-oil massages afterward. That's where it began; she was Desireé's first."

"Who was at the door?" Marcus asked, trying to keep the conversation on task.

"It was James Martin. I'm sure by now you know who he is," Roland said, and Marcus nodded. "Martin told Desireé and I that Rasheed Damali worked for him and what and whom he was doing it with. He said Damali owed him money for cocaine, and he wanted Desireé to tell him where to find him. Naturally Desireé was very upset when she found out the truth about what Damali was doing. Having relations with men and such," Roland said nonchalantly. "Martin believed her when she told him that she had no idea where he was. So after I gave him the money he was owed, he left quietly, but Desireé was still fit to be tied. She felt, quite naturally, that he should have told her what he was doing. So much potential for AIDS. So as you can imagine, Desireé was furious. I told her that I would handle it. She wanted to know what I was going to do, but I told her not to worry. That I would take care of everything."

"So you got Paula Dent to drive your car, get gas with your credit card, and call Connie Talbert from your house to establish your alibi," Marcus said.

"Yes."

"Why did you kill Desireé?" Carmen asked angrily, her hand weary from the weight of the gun.

"I asked Desireé when she was going to see Damali again. She told me they planned to meet that next night. I told her to arrange to meet him at Laurel Mountain. After I met Paula, I drove my other car out there. When I got there, Damali opened the door. I came in carrying the club, but he didn't notice. He was naked; he didn't even bother to cover himself. And why should he? I'd seen him that way before. He assumed I was there to watch. Desireé was just getting in the Jacuzzi. She began shouting at Damali, saying that he lied to her, used her. She screamed that he put her life in jeopardy. 'Fuckin' men for money. Fuckin' men! How could you do that to me?' By that time, Damali saw the club in my hand. He started to back away from me, reaching for his pants, but it was too late for that. I raised the club and swung it at him. I hit him with it over and over. The whole time I was watching Desireé. Seeing the look in her eyes. Seeing how she was enjoying watching me beat a man to death for her. I looked at her knowing that I had to kill her too. She already knew I was involved in everything going on at Hudson Financial. She already swore to see me in jail for it. Knowing that I killed Damali would have given her too much power, too much control over me. I couldn't allow that to happen."

Marcus looked at Carmen, her hand shaking as she pointed the gun at Roland. Tears flowed from her eyes.

"What happens now, Marcus?" Roland asked resolutely.

Marcus started to speak, "You'll have to—" but was startled by the sound of a gun firing three times.

Marcus looked quickly at Carmen and just as quickly at Roland. He had been hit three times in the chest. His now-lifeless body slumped in the chair.

"Now, you just hand me the piece, pretty lady," a voice came from behind them.

Marcus and Carmen whipped around to look in the direction of the voice. Bill Hudson stood behind them. He pointed his still-smoking gun at Marcus, pressing the barrel against his temple. "I said, hand me that piece. I ain't gonna ask you again."

Carmen slowly placed her gun into Hudson's outstretched hand.

"That's a smart girl." Hudson looked at Roland. "Fool! You always were a fool, Roland," he said as he came around the desk. He looked at Marcus and Carmen, shaking his head. "And you, Marcus. You know the DEA and the FBI are camped outside my house? Probably in there right now, tearing it apart. Then I come over here and find this fool spilling his guts." He glanced over at Roland again. "Now look at you, Roland. Dead. Dead because you're a fool! Real shame, too, Marcus, 'cause Roland Ferguson was the smartest man I ever met. But he was a fool. A fool for these women. That's why we're here. Men being fools for these women."

Keeping his gun trained on both Marcus and Carmen, Hudson jerked the chair and Roland's body fell to the floor. He sat down in the chair. "Fools. Gotdamn fools. Weak for these women. So now, what am I going to do with you two? And shit, you, Marcus, gotdamn it. Why couldn't you just let things lie where they were? You coulda been well on your way to being the next DA in this town. But, no! You had to push it, had to involve Mondrya in this shit. She was a pretty young thing when she came to work for me. I watched her grow into a fine woman, smart as a whip too. Now she's dead because of you. Why? Shit, I know why. 'Cause you're a fool for her!" Hudson shouted, and pointed at Carmen. Then he laughed a little. "But, shit, pretty as she is, I mighta had to be her fool too. Frank Collins was a fool. Let that whore Suzanne bluff him into tellin' her where the money came from in those off-shore accounts."

"So you killed Suzanne," Marcus said. "Raped and beat her to death."

"That's where you'd be wrong. I didn't have to rape Suzanne; the slut wanted it. But what does good ole Frank do? Instead of fallin' back in line like a good boy, he starts playin' footsy with the DEA. Then he fucks around and tells Desireé everything. That set Roland off. I tried to tell Roland not to worry, that I would handle it. But what does the fool do? He goes off and beats her and that limp-dick dope fiend to death. When all he had to do was wait a day or two and his problem would have taken care of itself."

"You punctured the brake line on Desireé's car," Marcus said.

"Who did it isn't as important as the fact that it was done and that woulda finished it. But since the brakes didn't finish you two, you have to be dealt with," Hudson said, picking up the phone. He dialed a number. "Let me speak to Benjamin."

"Detective Benjamin is currently unavailable. Who's calling?"

Hudson quickly hung up the phone. "Shit!"

"I guess you can't count on Benjamin to handle your light work," Marcus said smugly.

"Guess I can't."

"How'd you get your hooks into Benjamin?" Marcus asked.

"That was Roland's doin'. About fifteen years ago, Benjamin had a fire at his house, and that fire claimed the life of his wife; that fire with his wife being trapped inside was no accident. But you see, Roland, being the smart man that he was, found out from the investigator that it was arson. So when Benjamin filed a claim, Roland paid it but let him know that he knew that he set the fire to cover the murder and tucked Benjamin away neatly in his back pocket. So now Roland had him a cop, and me, I had me a prosecutor."

"Izella Hawkins."

Hudson nodded. "So when Benjamin came to Roland with this money-laundering thing, we were all set. All the pieces were put in place. We had us a good ten-year run. Until these grown men started getting foolish over these women. Cause of trouble since the world began. I always thought that Roland was smarter than that." Hudson shook his head, glancing down at Roland. "So now what am I gonna do with you two?"

"You don't have to kill us," Carmen said quietly.

"Yes, I do, pretty lady; and I'll tell you why. That got-damn disk you gave to the fuckin' FBI."

Hudson sat quietly, thinking about what he was going to do with Marcus and Carmen. Then he smiled at them and started to laugh out loud.

"What's so funny?" Marcus asked.

"Well, here's how this is gonna play out. The police are gonna find Roland dead. It seems pretty lady here found out that he really did kill her sister and came over here to kill him. Then you two love birds are going to disappear."

"Any reason why the police won't think that you killed him?" Marcus had to ask.

"'Cause I'm in Puerto Rico, as we speak. I'll let the Puerto Rican police arrest me tomorrow and extradite me back here where I'll swear that I had no knowledge of what Roland was doing. Collins was his boy and so was Benjamin. I never had any direct contact with Benjamin; he always thought he was getting his orders from Roland. So you see, I'll get me a smart lawyer like Marcus here and I'll be out on bail by lunch-time. And cleared of any charges in no time." Hudson stood up. "Now if you don't mind, let's all go quietly to your car."

Carmen and Marcus walked slowly out of the study with Hudson close behind. As they walked down the hall, Carmen gasped when she saw Melissa lying on the floor. "Don't worry, she's not dead. She has to find Roland's body and tell the police that you two were here." Hudson laughed.

As Hudson stepped over Melissa's body, she grabbed him by the leg. He fell to the floor, which caused the gun to fall from his hand and slide across the floor. Marcus quickly turned around and kicked Hudson in the face. Melissa crawled on top of Hudson and began hitting him as hard as she could about his back, head, and shoulders.

Carmen went after the gun. "Hold it!" she yelled, moving closer to Hudson and pointing the gun.

Melissa got off Hudson's back and stepped away, but not before she got in one good kick. Marcus recovered Carmen's gun from Hudson's pocket. Carmen took a step closer to Hudson, now aiming the gun at his head.

"Ease off, Carmen," Marcus spoke softly. "Ease off and give me the gun."

"He's the reason my sister is dead," Carmen said quietly. She began to cry.

"I know, Carmen, but your killing him won't change that. So please, Carmen, give me the gun."

Carmen took a step closer to Hudson, aiming point blank at his head.

"I love you, Carmen," Marcus said, and moved closer to her. "I don't want to lose you over a piece of shit like him."

"I love you, too, Marcus, but if it's all the same to you, I'll just hold on to the gun until the police get here."

"I'll call 911," Melissa said, and went off to dial.

"Hold it, Melissa," Carmen said, reaching into her pocket. She retrieved Agent Grant's card. "Call her. Let her be the one to take him in. A fool brought in by a woman."